***Vampires.* Now that he recognized them for what they were, Oz realized that he could smell them. Their scent was cold and visceral, like raw beef.**

The two stood behind Oz, blocking his way to the pier and beginning to snicker. The one standing next to the human guy muttered something in French. Oz figured he didn't have a heck of a lot of time to spend trying to translate. The only thing he had going for him was that thc guy in charge—the human—didn't want him dead. At least not yet.

Not yet. But why not? Who the hell was this guy and what did he and his vampire lackeys want with Oz? The answer came to him almost immediately. The basic physical description matched the only person in the world who had ever tried to hunt Oz before—Gib Cain. Which meant the reason Cain didn't want him dead yet was because he was waiting for the full moon.

So he could skin Oz alive.

Buffy the Vampire Slayer™

Buffy the Vampire Slayer
(movie tie-in)
The Harvest
Halloween Rain
Coyote Moon
Night of the Living Rerun
Blooded
Visitors
Unnatural Selection
The Power of Persuasion
Deep Water
Here Be Monsters
Ghoul Trouble
Doomsday Deck
Sweet Sixteen
The Angel Chronicles, Vol. 1
The Angel Chronicles, Vol. 2
The Angel Chronicles, Vol. 3
The Xander Years, Vol. 1
The Xander Years, Vol. 2
The Willow Files, Vol. 1
The Willow Files, Vol. 2
How I Survived My Summer Vacation,
Vol. 1
The Faith Trials, Vol. 1
Tales of the Slayer, Vol. 1
The Journals of Rupert Giles, Vol. 1

The Lost Slayer serial novel
Part 1: Prophecies
Part 2: Dark Times
Part 3: King of the Dead
Part 4: Original Sins

Available from SIMON PULSE

Child of the Hunt
Return to Chaos
The Gatekeeper Trilogy
Book 1: Out of the Madhouse
Book 2: Ghost Roads
Book 3: Sons of Entropy
Obsidian Fate
Immortal
Sins of the Father
Resurrecting Ravana
Prime Evil
The Evil That Men Do
Paleo
Spike and Dru: Pretty Maids
All in a Row
Revenant
The Book of Fours
The Unseen Trilogy (Buffy/Angel)
Book 1: The Burning
Book 2: Door to Alternity
Book 3: Long Way Home
Tempted Champions
Oz: Into the Wild

The Watcher's Guide, Vol. 1: The Official Companion to the Hit Show
The Watcher's Guide, Vol. 2: The Official Companion to the Hit Show
The Postcards
The Essential Angel
The Sunnydale High Yearbook
Pop Quiz: Buffy the Vampire Slayer
The Monster Book
The Script Book, Season One, Vol. 1
The Script Book, Season One, Vol. 2
The Script Book, Season Two, Vol. 1
The Script Book, Season Two, Vol. 2

Available from POCKET BOOKS

Oz: Into the Wild

Christopher Golden

An original novel based on the hit television series
by Joss Whedon

SIMON PULSE
NEW YORK LONDON TORONTO SYDNEY SINGAPORE

First Simon Pulse edition May 2002

SIMON PULSE
An imprint of Simon & Schuster
Children's Publishing Division
1230 Avenue of the Americas
New York, NY 10020

The text of this book was set in Times.
Printed in the United States of America.
2 4 6 8 10 9 7 5 3 1
The Library of Congress Control Number: 2002101788
ISBN: 0-7434-0038-0

In memory of Paige Farley Hackel:
Adventurer

Acknowledgments

Thanks are due, as always, to Lisa Clancy and Micol Ostow at Pocket Books; to Caroline Kallas and Debbie Olshan; to my wife, Connie, and our sons, Nicholas and Daniel; and this time around to Scott Allie at Dark Horse Comics, Logan Lubera, and John Totleben, who helped bring a very different version of this story into the world.

Prologue

Every time he closed his eyes he could feel her flesh tearing in his jaws and smell the copper scent of her hot blood as it soaked the fur of his snout. He could taste it. All of which was impossible, of course, for though Daniel Osbourne was a werewolf, on those mornings when he awoke after a night beneath the full moon he could remember almost nothing.

Except in his dreams.

Often in his dreams, Oz touched the beast within, saw through the eyes of the wolf. To his great relief, like most dreams, these images usually faded not long after waking.

Usually.

But not always.

When they did not . . . well, he kept them to himself.

Lycanthropy was his disease, and a unique one at that. It was not debilitating, really, nor was it painful save for during the change itself. Three times each month—on the night of the full moon and the nights immediately before and after—the coming of dusk wrought a terrible change upon his body, forging from the man a monster. It would not kill him, this disease, this beast that lay dormant like some benign tumor the rest of the month. But if he should be allowed to run free when the beast rose to the surface, it might kill others.

His flesh was a cage. Three nights a month, the wolf broke out.

Last night, it had killed.

It was just after nine o'clock on a cool November morning in Sunnydale, California. Oz sat on a freshly painted bench in Hammersmith Park, unshaven, unshowered, his mind more than a little numb. The sun felt good on his skin more for the simple fact that it was day than because of its warmth. Beside him sat his aunt Maureen. Out of the corner of his eye he could see the stylish cut of her red-blond hair as it fell across her face, and the pixieish little point to her nose. But she wasn't looking at him.

Worry lines creased Aunt Maureen's forehead as she stared out across the green lawns and winding paths of the park. Mothers and nannies shepherded small children in play groups. Joggers and bladers moved swiftly along the paved trails, weaving among the trees.

But she wasn't looking at any of that. Aunt Maureen was watching Uncle Ken and their son, Jordy, playing with a bright orange and yellow Nerf football. Jordy was just a little guy, struggling with the playground politics of elementary school . . . and with lycanthropy. In truth, it had been a simple bite on the finger from his little cousin that had turned Oz into a werewolf.

Hard to imagine right now, watching the kid laughing as he tried to tackle his dad, and Uncle Ken going down hard like Jordy was the meanest defensive end in the game. Jordy snatched up the Nerf and ran for some trees, where he spiked the ball and did a stumbling little rhythmless dance of victory.

Oz smiled watching them, just for a moment, before images of torn flesh crashed through his mind again. He ran his tongue along his teeth, trying to tell himself that the taste of blood was gone. With a deep breath he focused on Uncle Ken and Jordy, hoping that watching them could make him forget again, just for a few more seconds, but knowing that it wasn't going to happen.

"So, Daniel . . . ," Aunt Maureen began.

He glanced at her, then away.

"This Veruca. She was like you?"

A shudder went through him at her use of that phrase—*like you*—and at the tiny catch in her voice as she said it. Most people would have missed it entirely, but Oz had spent a great deal of time with his aunt and uncle, and their son. Aunt Maureen had always been a formidable woman, but she had been forced to become even stronger since her discovery that Jordy was a werewolf. All it had taken for him to infect Oz was that little nip of the teeth while roughhousing, but as far as they knew, Jordy had not bitten anyone else. For an elementary school kid, that was nothing short of a miracle, and Oz chalked it up to Aunt Maureen and Uncle Ken's steely resolve to protect their son even as they were forced to protect others from him.

But she had said *like you* instead of *like you and Jordy.* No matter how much fortitude she evinced in her day-to-day dealings with her son's condition, that was sheer practicality. It still broke her heart every day.

"Yeah," Oz confirmed. "Veruca was a werewolf."

"The things she said . . . you don't believe that?"

He ran a hand over the red-gold stubble on his chin, his eyes still on Jordy and Uncle Ken. The Nerf ball forgotten, the kid had tackled his father, and now the two were wrestling on the grass, Jordy lunging at his father, leaping on his back, only to have Uncle Ken drop him to the ground or let him tumble away. There was not a moment's hesitation in Uncle Ken, though the risk of accidental infection was high. Nobody knew that better than Oz.

"Daniel?" his aunt pressed.

He turned to look at her. Aunt Maureen's eyes searched his, and he knew that she needed answers to these questions as much for herself and for her family as she did because she cared about him.

But there were no easy answers.

Veruca had told him he was living a lie. Oz treated lycanthropy like the condition it was. Three nights a month the wolf escaped his flesh and bone cage, so he had his girlfriend, Willow Rosenberg, and their friends put him in one made of concrete and steel. When it was over, he was just Oz again.

But, according to Veruca, he hadn't been "just Oz" since the day Jordy bit him. She insisted that being a werewolf was a more fundamental change than that. He wasn't a human being sometimes and a wolf other times—hell, if he were to believe her, he wasn't even human at all anymore. No, Veruca had believed that their kind were little more than animals with two faces, that a werewolf was a beast twenty-four/seven, but just a little wilder on those three nights of the full moon. And that werewolves were far superior to humans. She had wanted Oz to be her mate. They belonged together, or so she'd said.

Oz hadn't bought any of it, not the full-time beast part or the mate part. He had a girlfriend already, thanks.

Veruca had gotten pretty insistent. When the full moon came around, she started killing. Then, just last night, she had tried to kill Willow. Oz didn't remember much. He, of course, had also been a wolf. But he had dreamt this morning of the night before, of gnashing jaws and the ripple of muscles under his fur, of the terror in Willow's eyes.

Oz had killed Veruca. He had saved the girl he loved from that beast.

But the one thing that he could not shake from his dream, the one thing that stayed with him and probably always would, was the terror in Willow's eyes. It was there when Veruca tried to kill her, of course, but it was also there when she had looked at *him*. Worse than that, he understood her fear. Much as it hurt him to confess, even to himself, Oz was now convinced that Willow had a reason to be afraid. She would never admit it, of course. Things would go back to normal if he simply kept quiet and allowed that to happen. The problem was, he just could not do that.

Veruca was wrong. He was not a monster. Not a beast. The beast was something inside of him. But there was no denying that he was a danger not only to Willow but to all those around him. He was going to have to find a way to tame the beast within him, to control it, to master the dark, primal urges that churned in his hidden heart. For the sake of all those he cared about, and for his own sake as well, it was time to take drastic measures.

Oz watched Jordy chasing his father, and then he turned to Aunt Maureen. "Nah. She just wanted an excuse to let the beast out. But there has to be a way to get control of it, really rein it in."

There was a sudden gleam of pride and affection in her eyes, but lines of concern creased her forehead. "You're leaving, aren't you?"

"I'm going to try to get some answers, yeah. For me, and for Jordy, too."

Aunt Maureen smiled and reached over to twine her fingers in his. Oz took a long breath, his decision made. Then he heard Jordy calling his name and looked up to see his little cousin running full tilt toward him across the park. He nearly lost his footing when he reached the paved path, but somehow he managed to keep from falling.

"Daniel," the boy said breathlessly, a broad grin on his face, his smile jagged and uneven where baby teeth sat side by side with larger, adult teeth. "Come on! Wrestle with me! Dad's been destroyed and he needs reinforcements."

Oz saw that Jordy was right. Uncle Ken lay stretched out on the grass in a silly mockery of exhaustion.

"All right," he said. "But just for a little while. I have to go soon."

Jordy's face lit up as he grabbed Oz's hand and pulled him off the bench as though the boy were towing him.

"You're leaving today?" Aunt Maureen asked. "You're not going to say good-bye to Willow?"

Though the sun was warm and bright above, Oz felt a chill run through him. He turned to face his aunt, still moving but forcing Jordy to work that much harder to drag him off. "I saw her before I came over here. My stuff's already in the van."

His aunt was a beautiful woman, and when she bit her lip as she did now, sadness in her eyes, it hurt him to see it.

"It's all happening so fast, Daniel."

Oz stopped. Jordy tugged on him, crying out in protest, demanding that he come along and wrestle.

"The clock's ticking, Aunt Maureen," Oz said. "The full moon's never very far away."

With that, he turned and ran across the park with

Jordy. When the boy tackled him, Oz went down hard on the grass, exaggerating the fall. Jordy loved his father, of course, but there was a freedom to the boy's laughter when he played with Oz. He was so very small, but he knew that when he was roughhousing with his cousin Daniel, he did not have to worry about being careful, about biting.

They were two of a kind.

Aside from Willow, Oz knew he was going to miss Jordy the most.

Chapter One

Twenty-seven Nights Until the Full Moon

Oz sat on a stool at the bar in Cueball's and watched the daylight dim behind the frosted-glass windows as dusk came to Santa Monica, California. He was not yet twenty-one, but he had been drinking water since coming into the joint more than an hour earlier, so no one bothered to ask him for I.D. Not that Cueball's was the sort of place he expected to get much of a hard time if he decided he did want a beer. It was a combination billiards hall and bar, but with a kind of hip, edgy atmosphere that somehow made it attractive to a clientele more accustomed to dance clubs. Women in spaghetti-strap tops and guys with goatees shot pool with hip-hop thumping out of ceiling-high speaker stacks.

Only in California.

The guy behind the bar was a former Marine, if the tattoo on his left bicep was to be believed, and his bald pate gleamed under the multicolored lights of the bar. Oz figured he had to be Cueball.

A pair of girls in belly tees and jeans that looked crisp and new sat at a table near the front of the place and from time to time when he glanced at the door he caught them watching him. The blonde looked away every time, but this time the other, a brunette with exotic Mediterranean features, only smiled. Oz raised an eyebrow as she rose from her chair and walked toward him with a strut that made him guess she was a model instead of the actress he had presumed her to be.

She had to have at least four inches on him in height, even without the low heels on her stylish shoes.

"Hi," she said brightly, openly appraising him, one hand resting upon her hip.

Oz nodded. "Hey."

Her mouth was beautiful: thick lips painted pouty red, but not in that collagen-about-to-explode way. It was even prettier when she smiled.

"I don't know what it is, but there's something about you."

"I'm gonna say thanks, even though I'm not sure if that's a good thing," he told her.

"Neither am I," she replied, thrusting out a hand. "I'm Brandy. Do you want to buy me a drink or play a round of pool or something?"

Oz glanced across the floor at the blonde who had been sitting with Brandy. She was surrounded by a trio of guys who had swept in on her the moment she was alone; the vultures had descended. He looked back up at Brandy. "Pool's not my game."

Her smile was sly now. "Well, then, what is?"

"Hell, kid, at least buy her a drink." Oz turned to see Cueball standing behind the bar, bulging arms crossed in front of him. *Add a pipe and a little white hat and he's*

Popeye, Oz thought. "You've been taking up a stool forever and haven't spent a dime."

"Sorry. Waiting for someone."

"Someone who ain't gonna show, you ask me."

Turned toward the bartender, Oz did not notice that he had lost Brandy's attention until he heard her whisper.

"Oh, my."

Brandy was staring toward the front door of Cueball's. Up near the front, her blonde friend was now completely ignoring the guys hovering around her and instead was staring intently at the figure that swept in off the street.

"Wow," Brandy whispered.

"He gets a lot of that," Oz said. "Stage presence."

Caesar Torres was all about stage presence. He played lead guitar for a local L.A. band called Feo who was just starting to get a little national exposure. Oz had seen a small article on them in *Spin* that described the group as a cross between Santana and Barenaked Ladies, which was about the dumbest and most inaccurate thing he had ever heard. But he supposed what was important was that they'd gotten the coverage in the first place. Of course in the band photo, Caesar had been right out in front posing like he thought he was Antonio Banderas in *Desperado.*

All attitude, that was Caesar Torres. But he carried the burden of that image without any strain at all. While there certainly were women who sniffed at his charms and thought him a pompous idiot, in Oz's experience with Caesar, Brandy's reaction was far more common.

"That's who you're waiting for?"

"Yep."

Caesar strode across the hardwood floor. There was a lull between songs on the sound system and his heavy footfalls echoed through the place. He slipped around Cueball's customers as though they were moving in slow motion and came to a halt only a few feet away from Oz, completely oblivious to Brandy, who stared at him hungrily.

"Hey," Caesar said.

Oz nodded. "Hey."

Brandy tossed her hair back, eyes sparkling. "Hi. I'm Brandy."

Caesar smiled at her, reached out, and shook her hand. "It's a pleasure. I don't wanna be rude, Brandy, but I've gotta talk to *m'hijo* here a minute, okay?"

He was giving her the brush-off, but Brandy did not seem to notice.

"All right. But when you're done, I'm sitting right over there with my friend and we'd love to buy you guys a drink."

With that she turned and strutted back across Cueball's toward where she had left her friend. Oz noticed that though Caesar had barely given her a glance before, he took the time now to watch her move across the room. Just before Brandy turned around, Caesar faced Oz again.

"She's into you," Caesar said.

"It's my animal magnetism."

Caesar laughed and slid onto the stool beside him. "Hey, before I forget, we were hopin' you guys could open for us at a couple of gigs next week."

Oz played guitar as well. His band, Dingoes Ate My Baby, was out of Sunnydale but had played up and down the West Coast. They had never quite gotten the buzz that Feo had going at the moment, but there was still time. Time, at least, for the rest of them. The band was yet another thing Oz was leaving behind. And he hadn't said a word to any of them.

"Not me," he told Caesar. "Going AWOL for a while. Call Devon, though. I'm sure the Dingoes'll be able to get someone to sub for me."

Now Caesar frowned, apparently catching something in Oz's deadpan delivery that struck him as odd. "Where are you headed?"

Oz lifted his water glass from the bar. Condensation had formed on it, making it slippery and leaving a damp ring on the wooden surface. He rolled the ice around a little and took a single, short swig of water. Then he changed the subject.

"You still going out with Desiree?"

Slowly Caesar nodded. His gaze had gone cold, and he studied Oz closely. "Yeah, man. Me an' Dizzy are still hanging. What do you want with her?"

"I need to take a trip I can't afford to make by plane."

There was a long silence after that as Caesar rolled the vague words around in his head. Oz could see the curiosity in his friend's eyes, but he ignored it. The things he wanted to know required some travel, and he was bound to run into people on the way—the world was full of them, no getting around it. But the more alone he was, the less of a trail he left behind, the better. Desiree—he had no idea what her last name was—worked for the Los Angeles Port Authority, checking over shipping manifests and ports of call for merchant vessels and freighters.

"I guess you ain't goin' on vacation," Caesar said.

Oz sipped from his water glass, ice clinking. Cueball had been down the bar serving customers beer from the tap and margaritas—no wine drinkers in this crowd—but now he walked back toward them and glared unapologetically. They were taking up space and not putting any money in the till. Oz stood up from the stool.

"We should go."

For a long, last moment Caesar regarded him, then he, too, stood. "All right. We'll go see Dizzy. She's at work now, anyway. But you need anything, *m'hijo,* you know you can ask, right?"

"Yeah. I do. Thanks for that," he said. But this was a trip he had to take by himself, a journey only he could make.

As they walked out of Cueball's, Oz spotted Brandy and her blond friend engaged in a game of pool and some serious flirtation with a group of guys who had out-of-town written all over them. The girls had entertained a momentary fascination with Caesar, but they had moved on.

Which was exactly what Oz had to do now. The problem was, no matter how far he traveled, no matter where his journey took him, until he found a way to protect the people he loved from the savagery inside of him, there would be no moving on. Just moving. Staying alive. Hunting for peace instead of prey.

Nearly an hour later, Oz pulled the van into a parking lot surrounded by twelve-foot chain-link fencing. The gates were open, but it was obvious that that wasn't always the case. On the far side of the lot was a featureless six-story building that might have held the offices for just about anything from computer software companies to the FBI. This was the rear of the building—the front entrance wasn't quite as plain—but even from the lot, Oz could see past the building to the ships in port. They varied in size along those piers, the creaking, rusted freighters alongside more modern merchant ships, and a fat-bellied, impossibly huge cruise vessel kept at a distance from the others, as though it found their company distasteful. Or, at least, its passengers did.

The Los Angeles Port Authority building was far from the only structure that loomed above the piers. The waterfront was crowded with gray, aging structures on land as well as at sea. But the Port Authority had a bigger parking lot. Not that it mattered, but Oz took notice. It said something about their control over the area that they could squander such valuable land instead of just building a garage under their offices.

Caesar lived in Santa Monica, and they had left his car where he had parked it on Pico, not far from Cueball's. On the drive over they had talked music, some of the bands that were new to L.A.'s musical landscape and just tearing up the place. It had been only a couple of months since Oz was last in the city, but already it seemed he had been gone too long. That was the way the club scene was, though, changing every day.

Oz pulled into an empty spot near the rear entrance of the building and killed the engine. He wondered if it was common for Caesar to visit Desiree at work, and if her employers minded. But he said nothing. It wasn't his business.

The two guitarists slid out of the van and slammed the doors in unison. As they walked across the poorly lit parking lot Oz could hear a distant buoy and the low shushing noise of the surf against the pilings on the piers down below. It was a kind of ambient noise, very subtle, and he wondered if he would cease to hear it if he stayed there long enough. Wondered if the people who worked there even noticed the ocean anymore.

There was a security camera above the door, and Oz let his gaze linger on its lens a moment, giving it a good look. He always figured if you tried to hide your face you'd look suspicious. Beyond the glass door a fiftyish guy with dark skin and gray hair stood up and walked toward them even as Caesar pressed a buzzer. The security guard was in uniform and armed, and the palm of his right hand rested upon the leather flap that was snapped down over his sidearm. From the guy's face it was clear that he meant business—that he *always* meant business. This was serious security, but these days, one could never be too careful.

The guard pushed open the door, glaring at them balefully. Oz couldn't blame the guy. Caesar was dressed all in black, and Oz himself needed a shave and had on a bowling shirt and pants with a tear in the left knee.

"What can I do for you?" the man asked.

Caesar flashed him an amiable smile. "We're here to see Desiree Adams. She's in the traffic manager's office on the third floor."

"I know who she is. Who are you?" the guard asked gruffly.

"Her boyfriend," Caesar replied.

For a long moment the man hesitated. Then he rolled his eyes and stepped aside, letting them slip through the open door before pulling it shut behind them.

"She'll have to come down for you. You can't be in the building unescorted at this hour." The guard made his way back to his desk and picked up the phone with a huff, making it very clear what he thought of Port Authority employees receiving social visits from their boyfriends. He mumbled something they could not hear into the phone and then set it back on its cradle before slumping back into his chair. The guard did not even bother to look up at them or suggest they have a seat, but it was clear they were meant to wait.

Apparently the patented Caesar Torres charm didn't work on grumpy middle-aged security guards.

"You made a new friend," Oz told him.

Caesar made an obscene gesture. The two of them stood there for several minutes in silence after that until there came a soft *ping* from the bank of elevators and the doors of the one nearest them slid open. Desiree—*Adams,* Oz thought, *gotta remember that*—was just as attractive as he'd remembered her. Not beautiful in any conventional sense, she had a pride and confidence that lent her a sultry grace, and her ebony skin had an uncommon luster.

A deep frown creased her forehead as she stepped out into the foyer, probably either worried about what would bring Caesar down here or pissed off that he had. But her eyes lit up when she saw that her boyfriend had not come alone.

"Oz!" Desiree said. The frown disappeared as she hugged him tightly and kissed his cheek. "How you been? And what are you doing down here with this sad excuse for a boyfriend?"

"Good to see you, Desiree."

She pulled back, held him by the shoulders, and stared at him. "You know, you are the only person who calls me that. I kinda like it."

"Then I'll make sure I keep doing it," he replied.

"Dizzy," Caesar interrupted, his voice serious. He glanced over warily at the security guard. "Oz needs help."

All the brightness went out of her then. She took his hand. "All you had to do was say," she told him. "Let's go upstairs."

Desiree shared an office with three other people, but at the moment she was the only one around. Someone in the traffic manager's department had to be around at all times, so their hours were staggered. There was track lighting in the ceiling and a lamp on her desk, but the broad picture window that it faced had only the night sky and the dark of the ocean beyond it, and the room seemed dim because of it. Her computer was on, brightly colored windows overlapping one another. A red light blinked on her phone, indicating messages, but Desiree ignored it as she sat on the edge of her desk and turned to him, arms crossed.

"How can we help?" she asked, including Caesar without even glancing at him. Despite her jabs at her man, it was obvious that they were very much a couple.

Oz hesitated, but only for a second. He had come this far. No turning back now. And until he'd found what he was looking for, there was no *going* back, either.

"I need to get to Fiji."

A smile spread across Desiree's features, and Caesar actually chuckled.

"Fiji," Desiree repeated dryly. "You *need* to get to Fiji?"

"Dude, I thought you said this wasn't a vacation," Caesar teased.

Oz kept his eyes on Desiree. "It isn't."

Immediately her good humor dissipated. "You're serious."

He nodded. "Some of these cruise ships must stop there. South Pacific, that kind of thing. Not thinking a stowaway kind of deal. More along the lines of getting a job. I can cook, if that helps. A travel agent in Santa Monica told me it takes about three weeks. I need to go within the next few days."

For a long moment the three of them just stood there in the dim light of the office, the red light on Desiree's phone blinking as though it were angry.

"When you need a favor, you don't mess around," Caesar began. He moved closer to Desiree as if to present a united front. "I mean, there's gotta be protocol for this kind of thing. No one's gonna just hire you off the street. Not to cook or steward or swab the decks. These cruise lines pay pretty nice. Lots of people want jobs like that, and they have résumés, man. And it ain't like you're gonna get booked on a cruise to entertain, just you and a guitar. I've heard you sing."

Oz glanced at him, acknowledging his comments with nothing more than a raised eyebrow before turning back to Desiree. She wasn't looking at him, though; she was staring at the floor and she had her right hand up to her mouth, one finger across her lips.

Then her eyebrows went up. "Caesar's right," she said, raising her eyes. "No way you're going to get a gig on a cruise ship, especially not overnight like that. But there might be another way."

In total command of her space, Desiree spun her chair and sat down in it before turning to her computer. She punched a few keys, dragged the mouse and clicked a window, then began entering information into a form that had popped up.

Oz moved up beside her, and Caesar appeared behind him, but both of them remained silent as lists of words and numbers and codes came up on the screen. Desiree grunted softly and, when he looked down at her, Oz saw that she had a smile on her face. She picked up the phone, dialed, and when someone answered on the other end she put on her most official voice.

"Mr. Ostergaard, this is Desiree Adams in at L.A. Port Authority. How are you tonight? Good, good. Fine, thank you. Listen, I've got a strange request for you. I have a friend who's looking to get his feet wet, so to speak. I'm guessing you have a full complement, but he'd be willing to work a run or two just for the experience and to have it on his résumé."

She glanced up at Oz, who nodded his encouragement.

"Right. No pay. You'd just have to feed him. I thought it couldn't hurt to have an extra utility man around, especially for free. He's green, but I can vouch for his work ethic."

A broad smile blossomed on her face. "Wonderful. Thank you. He'll be there."

Desiree hung up the phone and turned around in her chair. She raised her right hand and blew on her fingertips. "You have to admit, that was pretty spectacular."

"What just happened?" Oz asked.

She stood up and went to Caesar, relishing the moment. Her boyfriend gazed at her in wonder and slipped an arm around her. Laughing softly, she turned to Oz again. "You're going to Fiji."

"Cool."

That frown creased her forehead again. "Don't you want to know the rest?"

"Do tell."

"Guy I just talked to is the steward on a ship called *Sargasso Drifter.* It's moored out there right now. A merchant ship, but what the captain's been doing for the last year or so is container transport."

"In English," Oz prompted her.

Desiree chuckled. "Let's say you want to move to Europe or freakin' Antarctica or something. You pack up your house, put all your belongings in a big rented metal container that looks like the trailer that goes on the back of a Mack truck. A crane puts it on the ship, they sail it to your destination, and another crane takes it off. A hell of a lot cheaper than trying to fly a house full of furniture and stuff overseas."

"I'll try to remember that," Oz noted. "Assuming one day I'll own stuff."

"So this boat does nothing but carry these containers around the world?" Caesar asked, obviously just as uninformed about such things as Oz was, even though he spent all his free time with Desiree.

She pointed to him. "That's it. *Sargasso Drifter* ships out at dusk tomorrow night for Sydney, Australia. I checked the manifest. They've got a single container going to Fiji." Her gaze ticked back toward Oz. "He said he'd meet with you for lunch tomorrow. You heard the story I gave him. Utility personnel are the grunts on a ship like that. You'll be cleaning bathrooms and changing bedsheets for the officers, and all you'll get for your trouble is three squares a day, but you'll get to Fiji."

Oz gazed at her steadily, gears turning in his head, calendar dates shuffling. "Does the manifest say how long they expect to be at sea before they reach Fiji?"

Frustrated by his lack of excitement, Desiree sighed as she went back to her computer. She tapped the mouse, and the information appeared on-screen again. For a moment she concentrated, apparently working out the dates in her head.

"The first stop is actually in Hawaii, according to the manifest. They have a couple of containers to drop there, probably some to pick up as well. Twenty days to Fiji, with stops. Twenty-four to Sydney."

"Plenty of time," Oz said quietly, mostly to himself. If he continued on to Sydney, that would be cutting it close. But if he stayed on Fiji until after the next full moon, he figured he would be able to confine himself.

"Dizzy, you are unbelievable!" Caesar told her.

But Desiree was staring expectantly at Oz. He offered her the merest trace of a sheepish grin, went over, and gave her a quick, light hug.

"True," Oz said. "You have no idea how much I owe you."

She waved a hand at him. "Just get the job first. Then we'll talk about payback. Bring me some seashells from Fiji."

"Done," he promised, though he knew it might be a lie.

There was no way for him to know if he was ever coming back.

Shortly after midnight, Gib Cain crouched among the trees on a ridge in Miller's Woods and watched the Slayer dig a grave. It seemed appropriate to him, for what better time than the witching hour for such dark business? The girl was not alone, either. The bespectacled Englishman who served as her Watcher took a turn with the shovel as well, while that punk Harris kid and the Rosenberg girl stood watch.

They were doing a bang-up job of sentry duty, considering that Cain had a clear view of the group and their nocturnal activities down through the tree line and they hadn't noticed him. He stayed well downwind, though. The Rosenberg girl's boyfriend—the werewolf, Osbourne—was nowhere in sight, but if he was around he'd pick up Cain's scent for sure. Hell, for that matter, the Slayer might catch a whiff of him as well. He didn't have enough experience with Slayers to know whether or not their enhanced abilities included increased acuity of the senses.

Cain heard their mutterings to one another, but at this distance could not make out the words. With his night vision lenses on, however, he saw their faces with perfect clarity, and therefore could not have missed the anguish on the Rosenberg girl's face. It made him wonder if her werewolf boyfriend was the one wrapped up in the painter's tarp on the forest floor at their feet.

The Slayer was down in the grave now, carving the earthen walls with her shovel. They had picked the perfect spot for a grave, in amongst the thick roots of encroaching trees but somehow not hitting any of those obstructions. The girl—Summers was her name, and not one Cain was likely ever to forget—climbed out of the hole and brushed dirt from the knees of her blue jeans. As she did so, she glanced around. It was an idle glance, probably more a matter of general concern than any real awareness that they were observed, but still Cain stiffened.

The last time he had been in Sunnydale he had tried to kill the Osbourne kid. Oz, they called him, like a monster ought to have a precious little nickname like that. *Oz. What a name for a werewolf.* But Buffy Summers had made it clear that the beast was under her protection, and threatened Cain if he should ever try to hunt the monster in Sunnydale again. The truth of the matter was, he had been hesitant even to come back to this happy, shiny, rotten-to-the-core little Southern California burg.

But here he was, hunting in her territory again.

Not hunting Oz, though. Cain wasn't stupid.

The woods around him formed a kind of windbreak, a little valley in the midst of the forest where the trees did not grow quite so close together and where beer cans stood testament to past visits from local teens looking for a place to party or grope each other or both. At the moment, though, there was no one in this area of the woods except for the Slayer's little troop of self-styled monster fighters. It was a school night, after all.

As Cain watched, Summers and her Watcher dumped the corpse into the fresh grave and began to fill in the earth. When the task was completed, they covered it with brush and twigs from the forest floor, even moving a few large rocks and pounding them in deep so it would appear that they had always been there. There was very little talking amongst them during all of this, and when they were through, Summers went over and gave Rosenberg a quick hug and the four of them trudged out of Miller's Woods, past the old, dilapidated cabin on the far side of that small valley.

But they paused there to stash the shovels inside the cabin, a sure sign that they intended to return, or suspected that they might need to.

For long minutes Cain did not move. At length, however, he rose and went down into that valley with as much stealth as his decades as a hunter had earned him. As he crossed the forest floor, he paused and glanced curiously down at his feet. With a heavy boot he pressed at the earth between two thick roots and found it soft. Too soft. With the toe of his boot he dug a divot in the dirt.

Another grave. It occurred to him that though Buffy Summers was a vampire Slayer by job description, there were a lot of other monsters out there in the dark, most of which didn't disintegrate when you killed them. Looked like some of those dead horrors ended up here, in the Slayer's own personal cemetery. He wondered what else he might unearth if he took the time to look—but that was time he did not have. And he had come here looking for one monster in particular.

Cain went to the cabin and retrieved one of the shovels, certain to keep an eye out for anyone returning. It took him nearly two hours to excavate that hole in the ground and drag the body up from it, wrapped in that tarp. When he was through, Cain took only a moment's rest, leaning upon the shovel, before bending to unwrap the corpse.

When he saw the color of the fur, and then the face of the wolf, he swore under his breath.

"Damn it."

Veruca, he thought. The female werewolf had not been difficult to track, traveling as she did with a rock band for which she sang. Cain had been hunting her for two weeks, waiting for the perfect moment, when her trail led him to Sunnydale. At first he had been hesitant to reenter the town, fearing the Slayer's wrath. Eventually he figured that the Summers girl wasn't likely to be protecting all werewolves, certainly not savages like Veruca.

He crouched and inspected the corpse more closely, narrowing his gaze. In the darkness of the forest it looked as though Veruca's throat had been ripped out. *That* sure as hell wasn't the work of the Slayer.

Oz, Cain realized. *Had to be Oz.*

The one that got away. Now that beast had cost him. If he didn't take a werewolf's pelt immediately upon its death—or, even better, while it was still alive—the fur did not have the same shine to it, or the same suppleness. He'd be lucky to get a third of the fee he otherwise would have been able to ask for Veruca's pelt.

Furious but resigned, Cain slipped a bowie knife from its sheath. He pushed the fingers of his left hand into the wound in the she-wolf's throat and held tight while he inserted the knife with his right hand and began to slice. All the while, his mind kept going back to Oz.

And that look on the Rosenberg girl's face: because her barbaric boyfriend had killed? No, why care that he had killed another werewolf? Cain figured there was only one explanation, once he put the pieces together.

Oz had left town.

As he skinned Veruca's corpse, a thin, cruel smile crept across Cain's features. For if Oz was on the road—on the run—then he was out of the Slayer's territory. And as far as he was concerned, that made the beast fair game.

The hunt was on.

Chapter Two

Twenty-six Nights Until the Full Moon

How a Swede named Karl Ostergaard had gotten a job as ship's steward on a merchant vessel sailing under the Panamanian flag was about as big a mystery as anything Oz had ever run across. But he figured it was better not to ask. Particularly since the man in question was large and grumpy and gave every indication that the latter condition was just as permanent as the former. He had hair that had once been blond and was now not quite white, thinning on top, and a mustache that made him look very much like a walrus. He wore round wire-rimmed glasses that were too small for his face.

They sat in a spectacularly average little restaurant a few blocks from the Port Authority called Burger Meister's. It had surprised Oz somewhat that a seafaring man like Ostergaard—particularly one who wasn't American—would be gung ho about hamburgers when there were so many seafood restaurants around. On second thought, though, he figured the guy had had more than his share of fish in his fifty-odd years, so who could begrudge him a burger now and then?

"You are a friend of Desiree's?"

Oz nodded.

Ostergaard's bushy eyebrows knitted. "She is a good friend to have."

"Have you known her long?" Oz asked.

"We have never met," the steward replied gruffly. Then a beatific smile spread across his features. "But she has a lovely voice, don't you think?"

"It's one of her many fine qualities."

For a moment the big man frowned and studied him as though attempting to determine if he was being facetious or not. Oz regarded him coolly.

"You are fortunate, you know. Not merely to have Desiree as a friend, but because hiring is usually done by my staff rather than myself directly. Merchant ships do not carry as large a crew as we once did. Even more fortunate because we are an independent freighter. If we were part of a fleet you would have had to go through the fleet office, and it is highly unlikely anyone there would even take the time to speak with you, never mind giving you a job. Even if you really *are* willing to work for nothing."

Oz raised his eyebrows. "Would Desiree lie to you?"

Ostergaard smiled slightly, and now he seemed to look at Oz anew. It was as though he saw something he had not noticed before. "No. I don't think she would."

"So why did you agree to meet me?" Oz asked. "Aside from Desiree's melodious voice, I mean."

A pretty Latina waitress with cocoa skin interrupted them then. She had a pencil jutting out from above her left ear, and Oz thought it was sexy. Her name tag identified her as Patty, but that seemed much too plain and normal for the woman, and he determined to think of her as Aurora instead.

"What can I get for you gentlemen?" Aurora asked.

While Ostergaard ordered, Oz watched him. He knew he ought to have been more forthcoming with the man, but he was simply not very good at that. Nor was he certain what exactly he should say to secure his place on the *Sargasso Drifter*'s crew. He had already arranged for Caesar to take care of the van while he was gone, but that was assuming a lot. Desiree had seemed pretty sure Ostergaard would take him on, and there was a certain logic to that—who was going to turn down free labor? But there were no guarantees.

The waitress turned toward Oz. "And you, sir?"

Sir. That was pretty funny. Anyone calling him sir. Rupert Giles was about the only person he could imagine people calling sir, and that probably had more to do with him being British and kind of uptight rather than his age.

Though he was pretty sure Ostergaard was used to being called sir. In fact, on shipboard, chances were Oz would be calling everybody sir. He'd have to get used to that.

"Cajun burger, rare, chili fries, and a cream soda, please."

Aurora hurried away with their orders.

"Now, where were we . . . Daniel, is it?" Ostergaard said, stroking his walrus mustache.

"Yes, sir," he said, trying the word on, finding he could manage it. "But everyone calls me Oz."

Ostergaard didn't flinch. Oz figured nicknames were pretty common in his business, though he doubted the burly steward had one unless it was *walrus*. He had asked the man why he had agreed to meet with him if his underlings usually did that sort of thing. Now he wasn't sure that had been a wise question, and he thought he ought to just get on with it.

But Ostergaard remembered. "Ah, right. You wanted to know why we're having lunch today." A smile appeared on his face, half-hidden beneath his mustache. "I confess I was intrigued. You want a job on a tramp freighter to get some experience aboard ship. You're willing to drop everything and go this very night. You must realize, Oz, the days when young men ran away to the ocean to see the world and find adventure disappeared with Jack London a very, very long time ago."

Oz understood, then, what had prompted Karl Ostergaard to meet with him.

"But that's what you did, isn't it, sir?" he asked.

"Perhaps," Ostergaard replied, eyeing him carefully. "You realize that you won't be learning the skills of a seamen on this journey? You'll be little more than a particularly scruffy chambermaid."

"I understand that."

The waitress brought their drinks and set them down before buzzing off again. Ostergaard took a gulp of steaming hot coffee, but his eyes never left Oz.

"We'll strike a deal. You'll serve on the *Drifter* for the duration of the Sydney run. If the captain and I are satisfied with your work by the time we arrive there, we'll pay you a little something, and then we'll talk about where we're headed next. I assume you have a passport?"

"Yes."

Ostergaard set his cup down and stuck out his hand. "Excellent."

Oz took his hand and shook. "Thank you, sir."

"Pier seven, eight o'clock sharp."

"I'll be there."

Twenty-five Nights Until the Full Moon

Gib Cain was two kinds of hunter. On the one hand he went after the big game, and he had a necklace of werewolf fangs to prove his skill. But tracking the beasts under the full moon across damp moorlands and urban jungles alike was only part of the job. Most of the time, werewolves wore human faces and lived human lives, and that required that he be another sort of hunter altogether. Thus Cain had mastered many of the tracking skills used by private investigators. Most of them were simple enough, though if asked he might be forced to admit that locating Daniel Osbourne had not been as easy as he had expected.

The kid didn't use credit cards.

In the twenty-first century, if you had access to the right records, credit cards were almost as good as a global positioning system in tracking. Cain was no hacker himself, of course. He had basic computer skills, but most of his investigative technique involved a few phone calls, some easy research, or intimidation. Despite how glamorous Hollywood made it seem, most investigation work was comprised of those things, though where he used intimidation, many substituted sweet talk and charisma. Cain, sadly, was incapable of the onc and sorcly lacking the other.

Fortunately his line of work had brought him into contact with numerous less-than-savory individuals who could provide him with all sorts of services, not the least of which were unregistered weapons and computer hacking. Osbourne wasn't using credit cards, but no matter where the kid was headed he had to have money. An illegal look at bank records indicated he had pulled a few hundred dollars out of his account the day he'd left

Sunnydale. Then, yesterday afternoon, he'd gone into a branch in Los Angeles and drawn nearly all his savings out, a little more than a thousand dollars.

Los Angeles. That was a start.

But he had to find out what the kid was doing down there in L.A. If he needed that kind of money, chances were he planned to be gone awhile. Cain considered posing as an associate dean from U.C. Sunnydale and talking to the werewolf's relatives, but that was too close to home. The Rosenberg girl and the Slayer knew what he looked like, and Cain did not want to risk drawing attention in town if he could avoid it. Instead, he set his sights on the other members of the band Oz was in. Devon and the other guys in the Dingoes were more than mildly annoyed to discover Oz had skipped town without so much as a heads up to them. Thanks mainly to their pique, Cain was able to compile a list of Osbourne's known associates in and around L.A. within a few hours of discovering that was where his prey had fled.

All of which brought him late that afternoon—after an exhaustive series of stops at bars and low-rent apartments—to Grayburn Avenue, a backstreet in Sherman Oaks. The only parking was in the lot behind a convenience store where weeds shot up through cracked pavement. A sign announced that the parking was for customers only and that violators would be towed. Cain went inside and bought a Slim Jim, then gnawed on the salty, rubbery jerky as he walked across the narrow street toward a long, squat stucco building with bars on the first-floor windows.

On the main road that intersected with Grayburn a block away cars sped past, trying to beat the yellow light. None of them turned down Grayburn. It was nearly five o'clock, and Cain knew people would begin returning home from work soon, but he did not plan to be here very long. Even so, he had been at pains to be as inconspicuous as possible. He wore blue jeans and a button-down blue shirt rolled up at the cuffs. In his right hand he carried an unassuming, charmingly battered leather briefcase. His brown hair was cut military short, and though dark sunglasses hid his eyes, he knew that wouldn't draw attention. This was L.A., after all. Everyone wore sunglasses.

When he had first stepped out of his truck, Cain had not heard anything out of the ordinary. Now, though, as he strode purposefully across the street, he heard an amplified shriek that could only have been a pick sliding along the strings of an electric guitar. It came from beyond the stucco building in what he realized had to be a courtyard.

Good, he thought. But now there was no time for hesitation. He had to get in and out quickly, with the information he required.

Cain glanced once more up and down Grayburn Avenue and then set the briefcase on the ground. He clicked it open and raised the lid. Inside was a set of locksmith's equipment as well as a big, badass drill. In the courtyard beyond the building at number 87 Grayburn, a drumroll tore through the air sending birds fleeing across the sky, and a driving bass and guitar rhythm followed it. They practiced in the afternoon, Cain had been told, to avoid pissing off the neighbors. By 5:30 they'd have quit for the day.

The raucous music was loud enough to cover the drill. He pulled it out, clicked off the locking mechanism, and pulled the trigger. It whined and spun, tip almost invisible to the eye, and he cored out the lock on the front gate of the building in eight seconds. He bent, returned the drill to the case, then closed and locked it. When he stood upright again, briefcase in hand, he glanced around casually. As far as he could tell he had not been observed, but there was no way to guarantee that. Time was of the essence.

With thick, strong fingers he grasped the gate and gave it a hard shove. The lock rattled and then fell in pieces to the concrete walkway. He pushed his way in and let it clack shut behind him on its spring. Cain did not even glance at any of the windows but instead walked through a breezeway that led through into the courtyard.

The square of yellowing grass in the center of the stucco apartment building was nothing special, but given that the building itself seemed more like a barracks or a prison hospital than a home, he had not expected much. On the far side of the small lawn a cement patio had been transformed into a makeshift stage for a quartet of musicians, extension cables snaking back into an apartment through an open sliding-glass door. Children's tricycles and toys, and barbecue grills decorated the other patios, but this one, belonging to Noel Hanford, had nothing in common with those. One or two of the other patios actually had small gardens. Cain thought it was a wonder that the music of Hanford's band—the Numbskulls—hadn't killed the flowers ages ago.

A thirtyish woman too large for the bikini she was wearing sunned herself on one of the patios with a Corona beer and a cigarette for company. She seemed not to notice the Numbskulls rehearsing, but Cain was certain she more than noticed. Across from that apartment, two boys, perhaps ten and twelve, sat just outside the door to their home and alternated between staring at the band and at the bikini-clad woman.

Cain gritted his teeth. Witnesses. But it could not be avoided now. If no one had seen his unorthodox entry, he could still get in and out and his generic appearance be only vaguely recalled by any of them.

He went directly across the courtyard to Hanford's patio and waved lightly, amiably, until the drummer noticed him and faltered in his pummeling rhythm. The bass player—all tattoos and shaven head—swore at him and turned to glare, not noticing Cain. The Numbskulls had two guitarists—long, greasy-haired Gary Roth, and Hanford, whose blond, bespectacled, clean-cut good looks would have been bizarrely out of place with his band mates if Cain hadn't seen him playing a blazing lick on his Stratocaster a moment before.

Roth was the first one to notice him. He frowned and put a hand against the guitar strings to muffle the sound. Hanford looked at him and then glanced up, caught sight of Cain, and did likewise. Then they were all looking at him.

"Ah, hell, Gary," said the drummer, whose name Cain hadn't gotten, "don't tell me you broke parole again."

In the blissful silence, Cain smiled good-naturedly, not even glancing at the sunbather or at the two boys, though he knew that they would all be watching him now.

"Not a parole officer, guys." Cain held up both hands as if in surrender. "Sorry to interrupt your rehearsal. You guys were smoking just now. Gotta get myself down to the Litter Box to see you."

This was Hanford's apartment, but he was also both the driving force behind the Numbskulls and the smartest among them. That much was plain just from looking at him. He stared at Cain with narrowed eyes.

"What can we do for you, Mister . . . ?"

He wanted a name. Cain didn't give him one. Instead, he looked a bit surprised, sheepishly amused by his own lack of decorum. He shook his head and laughed.

"Oh, sorry. I'm with Gibson Management. We've got a new act showcasing at the Litter Box next week, and they just lost their second guitar. Jeff, that's the guy on vocals, he jammed once with Dingoes Ate My Baby and wanted to track down a guitarist from that group. Daniel Osbourne. Max down at the club said you guys know him?"

An expression of confusion swept across Hanford's features. Then understanding dawned. "Oz. You mean Oz. Dude, nobody calls him 'Daniel.' I don't think I even knew that was his name. But listen, the Dingoes are out of Sunnydale, that's a couple hours' north. Why don't you try them?"

Cain put on an exasperated expression and threw up his hands. "Don't think I haven't tried. Apparently he's on a road trip down this way, and none of those guys know how to reach him. But I need to track him down right away. No offense to you guys, but Jeff wants Oz."

Hanford shrugged. "Nah. Oz is a good guy. Not the best player around, but not the worst, either. If he gets lucky, good for him. But we can't help you finding him. I mean, I haven't heard from him." He turned to the others. "You guys seen him around lately?"

They all shook their heads. Cain was cursing inwardly when the bass player scratched at his bald head and looked as though he was thinking—and that it was an effort that pained him.

"Know who he's tight with, though? Caesar Torres."

The drummer had been fumbling lightly on his snare with his sticks, setting up a low rasp in the background of the conversation, but now he looked up. "What?" he asked, almost irritated. "That pretty boy from Feo? What the hell's Oz doing hanging with that guy?"

The bass player shrugged. "They're buds, I guess."

A spark went through Cain, a thrill he got on every hunt. For a moment he had thought he might be losing his prey's trail, but now he had it back again. So far, nobody had bothered to ask him how he'd gotten back there in the first place. More than likely they assumed a resident had let him in. But he did not want to be around when someone discovered the break-in. And he was getting frustrated. Every hour that passed, the trail got colder. Osbourne could be a long way from L.A. by now. With all these witnesses, he was having to play it nice, but Cain was losing his patience.

"Anyone know where this Torres lives?"

Hanford nodded. "Santa Monica. Off of Pico somewhere. Pretty sure he's listed."

Caesar's building backed up to the rear of a Thai restaurant whose odors always made him hungry at one in the morning. The two structures shared a parking lot, so it was next to impossible to get a space if you came in between six P.M. and one A.M. When he spotted the empty spot next to the Dumpster, Caesar figured he had lucked out.

He hefted a small bag of groceries against his body with his left arm and maneuvered out of the van, sliding the keys into his right pocket. He clicked the lock and then banged the door shut with his knee. It occurred to him as he turned toward his building that the lot was unusually dark. An upward glance revealed that someone had shattered a couple of the lights that normally illuminated the area.

Caesar scowled. "Freakin' punks."

Aware that the bag of groceries cut into the man-in-black cool of his carefully contrived image, he wanted to get the stuff inside and put away quickly. But as he walked alongside the van, he was brought up short by the appearance of a dark figure that stepped out from behind the Dumpster, blocking his path. Behind him was the Thai restaurant. The van on one side, the Dumpster on the other. Caesar knew he was looking at some trouble.

"Help you with something?"

"Yeah," replied the shape. "You can, actually."

The guy was wearing a baseball cap. He could see that now, despite the dark. Beyond that, though, he was not much more than a shape and a grin. A big guy, too. Caesar saw that now. At first glance he did not seem quite so large, but appearances were deceiving. He began to wonder again about the possibility of retreating.

But it was too late for that.

Caesar was fast—he had played baseball in high school and been damn good at it—but when this guy came at him, he might as well have been standing still. With a jab of his left hand the guy faked Caesar out, then swung with the right. The blow struck his temple, and the guy followed it up, not giving Caesar a second to breathe or think. He grabbed a fistful of Caesar's hair and slammed his head against the Dumpster. There was a dull thud with no echo.

In the darkness, between the two immovable objects, Caesar looked up and saw that the remaining lights of the parking lot gleamed upon the stranger's cruel eyes. He was up close now, hot breath on Caesar's face, inhaling the same air, sharing that little space. His eyes were not the only things that shone. A glint of silver revealed the arc of a ridged hunting knife only inches from Caesar's cheek.

"I'm looking for Oz. I think you know where to find him. The clock is ticking, and I am running out of patience."

All his life Caesar Torres had exuded an easy confidence that won him friends and lent him an air of intelligence as well. The truth of it was that Caesar could not have pulled this off without actually being reasonably smart. At the moment, though, he had nothing intelligent to say. He let his mouth droop open stupidly and stared, unable to utter a sound.

"Caesar," whispered the man whose eyes would be the only thing he could later remember about his description. That and the baseball cap. "Where's Oz?"

Finally thoughts started tumbling together in his mind. Oz had been hell-bent on getting out of Sunnydale, yeah, but not just Sunnydale. He'd wanted to go to Fiji of all places. They were friends, so Caesar didn't ask too many questions. He had figured Oz was looking for a vacation or actually knew someone in Fiji—hard as that was to imagine—and needed to get to them for some reason.

It was pretty clear now that Caesar had been wrong. Oz wasn't running *to* anything. He was running away.

This wasn't the first time he had had a knife held on him. Caesar hadn't liked it much the first time, either, but he had managed to walk away from it without losing a drop of blood or gaining any scars. He swallowed hard and stared into those gleaming eyes, ignoring the blade.

"I haven't seen him in we—"

He had started to say weeks, when the blade disappeared beside his head and pain blazed in his ear. Caesar swore loudly and bit his lip. The stranger had sliced the upper curve of his left ear, and blood trickled down inside it, dripping from the lobe.

All the denials he wanted to utter froze in his throat. He had no idea who this freak was or what else he might do. So Caesar said nothing.

"You are driving his van, you idiot," the stranger grunted.

Crap, Caesar thought. Hate and humiliation coursed through him like poison, dragging fear along behind them.

"All right," he said. "Don't matter, anyway. He's gone. Got a job on a freighter headed to Australia. He owes you money or something, you're gonna have a long wait, I think."

The gleaming eyes narrowed, and the silver blade—tip darkened with Caesar's own blood—waved in front of him.

"Why Australia?"

Though he could feel the hot trickle of his blood on his neck now, Caesar began to shrug, about to tell the guy he had no idea. Then the stranger pressed the flat of the blade against Caesar's lips, and he tasted the copper tang of his own blood and he knew without a doubt that this was not fooling around. This was the genuine article psychopath right here. And if he didn't get what he wanted from Caesar, he'd keep looking, and the search might eventually take him to Desiree, and he couldn't have that. Couldn't stand even the thought of it.

"He wasn't going there. He was headed for Fiji. He didn't say what for. Probably won't even make it to Sydney. And I swear to God that's all I know."

"The name of the ship?"

In a panic, Caesar realized he couldn't remember. It would have been the simplest thing for the guy to find out—just find a freighter headed for Sydney the day before. Probably only one. How hard could that be? But no, he wanted an answer now. He wanted Caesar to remember.

And eventually, Caesar did.

It would prove to be a painful memory.

After his first full day as part of the crew of the *Sargasso Drifter,* Oz was sorely tempted to jump overboard. He had never imagined that cleaning bathrooms and floors could be so strenuous, but now the muscles in his back and shoulders ached deeply. The night before, he had slept fitfully, tossing and turning, agitated by the sway of the ship and the rumble of her engines. Tonight, however, he knew that the combination of his exhaustion and the sea air was going to have him sleeping like a baby.

His shift over, his belly full of what the guys down in the galley ambitiously called dinner, he stood now on the deck and gazed out at the open ocean. The sea rolled beneath them, sublimely powerful, unknowably deep. His skin felt brackish, and he knew that if he touched his hair it would be brittle from the salt air.

When he closed his eyes, he saw Willow. In his mind she was not smiling that extraordinary, precious smile of hers but staring at him with a gaze lost and empty. It was the look she had given him when he told her he was leaving. And Oz could not blame her. Of everything he had left behind, he knew that Willow was the reason for the pain in his heart. Not merely that he had abandoned her, but that she could never truly understand his reason for doing so. She knew, certainly, that he had to find out the truth about what he was, about the beast caged inside him, that he could no longer be around people he cared about without bearing horrible guilt for putting them in danger. Danger from himself.

Yet as much as she knew that, he had seen in her eyes that she did not really understand it. Had he asked her, she would have come along. Oz was certain of that, and it was proof that she truly did not get it. It was because he loved her that he had to go alone, had to face the beast within.

Brow furrowed in contemplation, he opened his eyes. As he gazed at the ocean again, he began to relax, to breathe deep. Hard as it was to leave Willow behind, there was a thrill to all of this as well. Not merely the setting off on his own but the newness of everything, the vast unknown that stretched out before him. Every day was a journey, his Uncle Ken was fond of saying. But this was a journey unlike any Oz had undertaken in his life.

The wind shifted, and he caught a pair of scents on the air. Curious, Oz turned to find that two of the steward's men were approaching him from the hatch that led below. One was a tall guy with caramel-colored skin and thinning hair; Oz thought his name was Albert. The other—Robideau—was stout and deeply tanned, maybe five foot five but broad-shouldered and a bit heavy around the middle.

"'Ey," Robideau said amicably. "How'd yer first day go?"

"Still here," Oz replied.

The taller one held out his hand. "Don't think we were properly introduced. Alfred Canfield."

Alfred, not Albert, Oz thought.

"Oz," he replied.

"We play a little poker in the mess. Makes the trip shorter," Robideau said.

"And your pockets lighter," Alfred added.

Robideau grinned good-naturedly. "Want to join us?"

For a moment their generous camaraderie nearly won him over. He was on his own, away from home, all his friends left behind, and it would have been easy to go along with them. But a firm voice spoke up in the back of his mind, then. *Friends are what you're running away from.* Inwardly, he winced at the idea that he was running away from anything, but there was truth to it that he could not deny. He was looking for a way to go back home without fearing for their safety. But for now he *was* running from his friends. *For now.*

"Sorry," Oz replied, hoping they could sense his genuine regret. "I don't think I'd be very good company."

Robideau seemed surprised, but Alfred smiled and nodded.

"All right, my friend. But it's an open invitation. Like Robideau said, it makes the trip pass by faster."

"Thanks," Oz told them. "I look forward to losing my shirt to you guys another night."

But that was a lie, too.

It was going to be a very long journey.

Across the street from the pier, in the shadow of the Port Authority building, Cain sat in his truck and stared at the place where the *Sargasso Drifter* had been moored before it had sailed the night before.

Fiji, he thought for perhaps the hundredth time that night. *What the hell is in Fiji?*

He ought to just let the kid go. Whether Oz was in her territory or not, Cain knew that the Slayer was going to think of him as under her protection. Never mind that he didn't relish the idea of traveling halfway around the world to get the beast's pelt.

On the other hand, he had been forced to walk away without skinning Osbourne once already. And the buyer he had in place for Veruca's fur had been willing to pay top dollar. Werewolf pelts were about the most valuable commodity of their type on the black market. Elephant tusks were worthless in comparison. Cain didn't want to let that money get away.

But more than that, being scared off from killing Oz the first time around still stuck in his craw or he wouldn't have gone to the trouble he'd already gone through to get at him.

With an ironic smile, he picked up the cell phone from the seat beside him and punched in a seemingly endless stream of numbers. Halfway around the world, in a dusty little town in the Australian outback that Cain hoped never to see again, a phone began to ring.

On the fifth ring, a sleepy voice answered in a harsh rasp that barely sounded human.

"It's Cain," he told that nightmarish voice.

"I need you to meet me in Fiji."

Chapter Three

Nineteen Nights Until the Full Moon

Oz stood in Mr. Ostergaard's cabin and glanced around at his handiwork. He had learned quickly from Gavin, the other utility man onboard, that it was a good idea to give the officers' quarters special attention. But Oz would have done that for Ostergaard, anyway. He had no particular love of being a shipboard chambermaid, but if he was going to be doing the work, he figured it wouldn't hurt to do it well. Ostergaard was a good man and had given him a break. The least Oz could do to repay him was not rush when it came time to straighten the man's things and make his bed.

The floor had been vacuumed, and the head cleaned to sparkling. Oz went to his cart and picked up a rag and a can of spray polish. He was at the bureau when the door clicked and swung open. Mr. Ostergaard noticed him immediately but seemed startled to find him there.

"Oz?" the man said. Then a smile blossomed on his face, his cheeks reddening with good humor as he looked around his quarters. "I'm sorry. I must have the wrong room. I know I left mine a pigsty."

"That's one way to describe it," Oz agreed. Then he gestured to the bureau. "I just need to dust and I'm finished here."

"It's not very considerate of me, is it?" the chief steward remarked. "I suppose I ought to pay more attention to the mess I leave behind."

Oz raised an eyebrow and regarded him seriously. "We all have our jobs. As long as you all keep the ship on top of the water and pointed in the right direction, not gonna be any complaints from me about cleaning up."

Ostergaard shut the door and ventured farther into the room. He leaned against the far wall and watched Oz at work for a minute or so before clearing his throat.

"I am surprised to find you here, my friend," the man said, stroking his walrus mustache. "The captain gave the whole crew shore leave in shifts. Isn't it time you saw some of Honolulu?"

Oz finished dusting off the bureau and went to the window. The officers' quarters nearly all had portholes, but the captain's and Mr. Ostergaard's both were high enough to have actual windows. Through the glass he could see the pier and beyond that the lights of the city of Honolulu. He had always wanted to see Hawaii, but not like this, crammed into a few hours of solo adventuring.

"I'm thinking next time," he said, turning back to the steward. He gestured around the room. "Couldn't let you come back to that pigsty."

But Ostergaard was staring at him now, and Oz could read a surprising emotion in the man's face: disappointment. Again, he stroked his thick mustache and for a long moment he said nothing. Oz only regarded him patiently, curious though he knew his expression would not reveal it. At length, the steward shook his head.

"Maybe I was wrong about you?"

"How do you mean?"

Ostergaard took a long breath and blew it out. "I made a judgment call when I brought you onboard. It was obvious you were running away from something as much as you were running to the sea. But you were eager, and I figured you would work hard because of it."

With a frown, Oz glanced around the cabin, feeling defensive but uncertain how to phrase a response to that.

"No, no, that's not what I was wrong about," Ostergaard reassured him, not unkindly. "You work as hard as any utility staff I've hired. As hard as some of the able-bodied seamen I've got. I doubt I've ever met anyone as easygoing as you are, though, and that's where I was wrong. I thought you'd fit in here, thought you'd get along with the crew. Despite your reticent nature, you have a certain charm."

Oz nodded once. "Taking that as a compliment."

"It ought to be," Ostergaard said, very serious now. The man shook his head and strode away from the wall, back to Oz. "But it isn't. Something is troubling you, my friend. Whatever it is, whatever this ghost is that's haunting you, it's keeping you from really being a part of this crew. You do your share and more. You're holding up your end of the bargain, without a doubt. But if you truly are considering a life at sea, you must learn to engage your shipmates. I have heard some of them talking. Your solitude makes them distrust you, makes them grow calloused toward you.

"That is not healthy for the crew or for the vessel you serve upon. In an emergency, we must all be comrades, regardless of station. They don't have to like you, but at least they have to be able to make that decision, to know you enough to decide. You haven't given them the chance."

The freighter rolled gently on the ocean, its motion in port barely noticeable to Oz after a week at sea. The *Sargasso Drifter* creaked. Somewhere off in the bowels of the ship a hatch slammed with a clang. But the innards of that vessel were uncharacteristically quiet. Oz had been looking forward to that time aboard the ship. What free hours he had were spent reading, and his contact with other members of the crew had been limited to mealtimes and his own requests to borrow books from those who had them.

A hard knot of reluctance in his chest began to unwind. He let out an inaudible sigh and met Ostergaard's steady gaze before going over to his cart and arranging his cleaning equipment. Casually he rolled the cart toward the door, where he turned and gazed back at the Steward.

"I think I might look good in one of those grass skirts. Can I get you one?"

That walrus mustache bristled with the Steward's broad grin. "I've got a dozen in my closet, or hadn't you noticed?"

"Snooping isn't my thing."

Ostergaard chuckled. "Well, that sets you apart from most of the utility crew I've known. Enjoy Honolulu."

Oz gave him a look that indicated it wasn't out of the realm of possibility, then lifted the cart over the small lip at the bottom of the door.

It took him twenty minutes to get his gear stowed and to change his clothes. The crimson shirt emblazoned with the name of his favorite Chinese restaurant—Dragon Inn—was old and a little ragged now, but it was comfortable and clean. He bunked with Gavin, the other utility man, who was a few years older and had eyed Oz with suspicion from the moment he came onboard. Gavin had turned out to be an ideal cabin mate, considering he was almost never in his quarters, and when he was, he was usually asleep. This was the first time Oz had returned to his quarters and been disappointed not to find Gavin there.

Probably ashore, he thought.

Oz headed aft to where Robideau bunked with Alfred. From the corridor he caught the scents of both men. They hadn't gone ashore yet, though he knew that their leave was about to begin. He hesitated a moment before rapping his knuckles on the door.

"Yeah?" Robideau called from within.

"It's Oz."

There was a momentary pause during which Oz imagined the two men inside had glanced at each other curiously, and then Robideau called for him to come in. Alfred was buttoning up a clean white shirt that looked silk—nicer than anything Oz had with him on this trip. Robideau wore khaki pants, and a black T-shirt with the Harley-Davidson logo on the breast. The shirt was a size too small for him, but the man was blissfully unaware.

"What brings you down our way?" Robideau asked.

"Hey," Oz replied. His gaze ticked over to Alfred and back to Robideau. These were the same guys who had been so friendly to him after his first full day at sea, but now there was a kind of curtain that hung between them, a distance that separated them from him. Oz knew he had put it there, and though none of his reasons for doing so had changed, for the first time he felt some regret about that.

"Shore leave?" he asked.

Alfred paused at the second button from the top and turned to look at him, both eyebrows raised.

"You goin' ashore, Oz?"

"Thought I might. You guys know anywhere to get a decent meal?"

Robideau laughed. "Anything that wasn't prepared onboard this ship'll taste like the food of the gods."

But Alfred did not laugh. Instead, he watched Oz cautiously. "Robideau hasn't been here before, but Honolulu's coming home for me. I lived here for seven years." As he said this he studied Oz and then he hesitated, as though deciding upon something. After a moment he abandoned any plans to do the last few buttons on his shirt, and crossed his arms.

"You want a good meal, come along with us. Like nothing you ever had," Alfred promised.

"Is it a *luau*? 'Cause 'stuff yourself at a *luau*?' Pretty high on my list of things to do during my high seas adventure."

Finally Alfred's serious expression wavered, the edges of his mouth turning up into a smile. "Not a luau, man. That's for the tourists."

"What are we, then?" Robideau asked.

Alfred punched him lightly on the arm. "We're sailors, man. Tourists, pfft." He waved a hand in the air, then looked at Oz again. "Come on, Oz. You never had pasta like this."

Oz's usual stoic reserve nearly cracked. He raised both eyebrows. "Italian food. Not that I'm especially prejudiced, but . . . Hawaii? Italian food?"

"Trust me," Alfred said earnestly.

Honolulu was not as exotic as Oz had imagined it would be. As he walked the streets with his shipmates he glanced around at the hotels and office buildings, at the traffic and businesspeople on the sidewalks, and it occurred to him that many of the residents of this city had lost all sense of the paradise that this was supposed to be. It reminded him of a story Devon had told him about a trip he'd taken with his family to Italy. They'd been walking through Rome and crested a hill only to find themselves looking down upon the Coliseum. Majestic despite its age and its crumbling walls, Devon had said the ancient structure looked out of place to him. "Like someone had just plunked it down right there in the middle of the city, and then nobody noticed." At the time Oz had pointed out that when one saw something every day, it lost some of what made it special. There was an air of that about Honolulu as well, no matter how many palm trees and tropical birds he might see.

When he said as much to his companions, Alfred nodded in agreement. "Not everyone's like that, but no question, Honolulu's a city now. But it's just one place. All those pictures you've got in your head about what paradise is supposed to be? That's Hawaii. It's all here. You just have to come back when you've got time to explore."

Robideau was between them, and the stout little man clapped them each on the back. "I'm gonna do just that. Come back here and spend some time discovering paradise. But first I have to find a honey to do it with."

Alfred laughed politely, but Oz remained silent.

"You have a honey back home?" Robideau asked him.

Oz thought about it a moment. "Sort of."

Alfred nudged Robideau, but the little man didn't seem to notice. "'Sort of.' What's that mean? You either do or you don't."

"She was when I left. But I couldn't exactly say when I'd be back. Or if."

They walked along a sidewalk and then crossed a broad street with brightly lit tourist-trap restaurants beckoning to them. The trio ignored those and kept on toward the next block.

"Oz, you don't have to talk about what's personal to you," Alfred assured him. "Robideau, he's nosy, but he'll mind his business if you tell him."

"Don't talk about me like I'm not here," Robideau protested.

Alfred ignored him. "It's one of the oldest rules for sailors. A man doesn't want to talk about where he's been, that's his business."

Though he was reluctant to continue the conversation, he was mindful of what Ostergaard had said earlier, so Oz shook his head. "It's okay."

But he could see from Robideau's wide, questioning gaze and the look on Alfred's dark features that neither one of them believed him. For several moments they kept walking, and then Alfred glanced over at him. "What's her name?"

"Willow."

"That's nice."

"Yeah."

For all his bluster, it was a sincere, almost sentimental Robideau who turned to him then. "Don't worry, pal. The tides will carry you home eventually. They always do."

None of them spoke again until they had reached Il Bacio, the Italian restaurant Alfred had bragged about. There were some tourists there, but mostly locals. Oz was pleasantly surprised to find that it was everything Alfred had said it was.

Fifteen Nights Until the Full Moon

The village was called Lingka, though few outsiders knew it even had a name and it would not be found on any map. It was nestled in a valley in the mountains of Tibet, some hundred miles northwest of the city of Lhasa. Once upon a time this valley had been inhabited only by the nomads who herded yak through here on the way from one place to another. The nomads grew accustomed to stopping here to rest themselves and their herds. There was a river nearby where they could drink, and the divine architecture of the mountains in that range was such that the cold wind off their peaks rarely dipped too far into the valley.

In time, a nomad called Jin decided it would be helpful to have a permanent dwelling there. When he grew old and did not want to wander anymore, Jin came one day to his home in the valley and did not leave again. Within a handful of years, barely an eye blink compared with the time that stretches between then and now, the village of Lingka was born.

The evil that lurked in the mountains had yet to show itself.

The people of Lingka farmed most of what they needed and traded grains and vegetables with the nomads for meat. It was a pleasant balance, made the more so because both the wanderers and the villagers sprang from the same ancestors. The stream gave them water, and the sun and the mountains their life. It was not very warm there in the valley, but none of the villagers had ever lived anywhere else and so they did not know the difference. Even through the long winters the villagers lived a quiet, peaceful, simple life. In many ways, for those who had no interest in the outside world, it could have been paradise.

Yet it was not.

For the mountains around Lingka cast long shadows, and often times things lurked within those shadows, prowled there. Hunted there. Upon the snow-covered peaks and inside the darkest caves were horrors that the elders in the village only whispered about. Demons, it was said. The nomads spoke openly of the terrible mutilations visited upon their herd, the snatching away of yaks . . . and sometimes of others of their tribe who had wandered off too far alone.

On the face of the snowcapped mountain that rose to the west was an ancient monastery, older than the village itself. From time to time the villagers had sought solace from the monks there, and some of the homes in the valley had been visited by those holy men, who placed charms and wards against evil upon them. Thanks to the ministrations of the monks, it was believed that the people of Lingka were safe as long as they did not stray from the village alone. Sometimes, however, children are too stubborn to believe the warnings of their parents, too determined to prove their elders nothing but superstitious old fools.

Sometimes children set off from Lingka and did not return.

There were those in the village who believed that perhaps all of that fear was merely superstition after all, that the young ones were right. After all, children who wandered off might well have managed the trek to another village; the older ones might even have made it as far as Lhasa, where they could have found work. If no one in the village was willing to make the journey, they would never know the truth. But even those who suggested such possibilities knew the truth in their hearts.

The demon of the eastern mountain had taken them. Of this horrid creature they knew nothing but the name that had been told in whispered legends for generations—Muztag—and that a menagerie of nightmarish creatures served him, dwelling in a fortress built into the side of the mountain, so high above that most days it was invisible from the village, lost in the clouds or the glare of the sun. At times a trick of the light allowed it to be seen, though at that distance it was little more than a scar on the face of the eastern ridge.

Late this very afternoon, Kangri had paused in the process of putting up the frame for the house in which he would live after his marriage to Shisha. Hammer in hand, he had used the back of his sleeve to wipe beads of sweat from his forehead. It was cool, but the sun was very warm and the work was strenuous. As he glanced upward and eastward he had seen it there, the gray blemish on the snowy white mountainside, and he had shivered.

His mother had told him that it was nothing, the ruins of an ancient temple, cursed centuries ago and abandoned. Kangri's father believed in the demon of the eastern mountain, however. But the only way to ascertain the truth would be for someone to go up there, and whichever story was true, no one dared. Kangri was an intelligent man, and his bride-to-be a formidable woman. They hoped to have many children, but there was trepidation in his heart at the idea of bringing them up in the shadow of such evil.

Yet though the sight of the ruined temple near the mountain's peak made him pause in his work, made his stomach twist with dread, after a moment he set back to work on the house in which he hoped to raise those children. It had always been that way in Lingka, the specter of the demon of the eastern mountain hanging over the village like a harbinger of death, and thus would it ever be.

By the time the people of Lingka had come to accept that Muztag might be more than a myth, they had been here in the shadows of the mountains for generations. It was their home, and they would not allow fear to drive them away. Kangri had wondered many times if they were a courageous village, or simply too stubborn for their own good.

Kangri worked all that long afternoon, and when the sky had grown so dark that he could no longer see to align pieces of the frame for his home, he at last climbed down and put his tools away. His shoulders and back ached and throbbed as they always did on days when he had the time to work on the small dwelling, but he smiled at the knowledge that he had made progress. The wedding would take place soon after he finished work on the home.

The wind was cold, but not unusually so. Though he had all but forgotten the feelings he had had earlier upon seeing the ruins upon the mountain, a sense of unease lingered in him, and he shook it off as best he could. Kangri had promised Shisha that he would take his evening meal with her family tonight, and he knew he had little time before he was expected there. He glanced at the horizon, where the last glimmer of day quickly disappeared over the western mountain range.

Quietly, he cursed. Time had gotten away from him, as it so often did. If Shisha had one complaint about the man she was soon to marry, that would have been it.

Kangri pushed his fingers through his raggedly cut hair, straightening it as best he could. The dwelling he was building was situated not far from his parents' home, and he walked briskly through the village, where houses of varied sizes were arranged in a series of concentric circles rather than any sort of grid, as though by building their homes to face one another they might protect themselves from whatever lurked out in the dark crags and hillocks of the valley.

He walked through the center of the village, brushing at his clothes with his hands. Though the sun had only just fallen, Kangri saw very few people outside. Wu Han, who was withered and bent with age, walked slowly through the village with a bottle in one hand and a walking stick in the other. A pair of older boys, not quite men, had built a fire and sat on either side of it talking quietly, as if they wanted to brave the night but secretly hoped that it would not notice them.

Kangri felt better that he was not alone, out there after dark.

The older boys waved to him and called out a muted greeting as he trudged past them. Kangri waved back but kept silent. He was a young man himself and small of stature, and the boys seemed to like him because of it. Now he picked up his pace, easily passing Wu Han. Though in the darkness he could not see it yet, he could hear the stream that passed through the village at its northern end.

Then, intertwining with the rippling sound of the stream, he heard a rustling in the air above him, like the wings of a vulture scouring the valley for dead things. Kangri glanced up, narrowed his gaze, but saw nothing out of the ordinary. There was a thin, broken layer of clouds above, but he could not see the stars.

He began to walk a bit faster, and in a few moments his steps took him to the edge of the stream. In the dark the water looked black, save for the places where it poured over stones. There the broken water gleamed silver. Kangri knelt and placed his small, calloused hands in the cold water and rubbed them together vigorously. He enjoyed the clean feeling of the stream passing over his grimy skin and pushed up his sleeves so that he could plunge his forearms in. After a moment he bent lower and splashed water on his face, ran wet hands through his hair. He cupped his hands and dipped them into the stream, drinking the fresh mountain water, then repeated the process several times before splashing his face again.

A cry of pain and anguish carried across the night air to him, and Kangri froze there on his knees at the stream's edge. For a moment he could not move, and then, as if suddenly recognizing that he might be in danger, he scrambled backward from the water and climbed to his feet.

The night was silent. No other shouts or cries seemed forthcoming. He spun around there at the northern edge of the village and tried to determine where the cry had come from. Wu Han was out of sight now, having retired to his own abode. The fire where the boys sat together flickered distantly now, but he could see their silhouettes in the illumination from that small blaze. They had not moved.

His gaze swept to the north, to the half dozen or so homes on the other side of the stream where most of the village elders lived. Lingka was too old and too small to have any real government, but the elders were there to settle quarrels and mete out punishments when necessary. The small structure nearest the stream on the opposite side belonged to Shache, the most respected of the elders. The home was no larger than the one Kangri was building, but respect in Lingka was not earned by the size of one's dwelling place.

Kangri began to glance away from Shache's house when something shimmered in the darkness, black and silver like the flowing water of the stream. It was there just inside the front door for a moment, and it seemed to float like mist out into the night. When he blinked it had gone, either a figment of his imagination or a spirit so swift as to have slipped away into the dark too fast for his eye to see.

But the open door was not a figment of his imagination. It creaked as the wind made it swing back and forth slightly, as if moved by some invisible hand.

Without meaning to, or knowing he was going to do so, Kangri turned and glanced up through the night sky at the mountain ridge to the east. It was shrouded in clouds and darkness, but he could feel it looming there, its monolithic presence unnerving him again.

When he looked back at Shache's home, the door

still hung open. Kangri felt a terrible anxiety sweep through him, prickling his flesh like an army of insects moving under his skin. He glanced over his shoulder toward the home of Shisha's parents and the urge to flee, to run back to them with this tale of phantasms roaming the village, but he dared not seem a coward in the eyes of his future wife or her parents. What was worse, Shache had a young wife whom he had wed after his first wife had died, and she and Shisha were close.

Kangri drew the back of his hand across his mouth, trying to decide what to do. His skin was cold.

He stared at the open door to Shache's house and decided that it was nothing. It might have been an animal or merely a passing cloud across the stars—though there was no starlight to speak of—and the wind could have blown the door open.

Hurriedly, so as to rob himself of the time to change his mind, he strode along the stream to the small footbridge. With a last glance back into the village at the flickering fire and the dark silhouettes of the boys around it, he took courage from their presence and walked quickly to the open door of Shache's house.

Kangri stepped close to the open door that creaked in the breeze and he called out to Shache or anyone inside who might hear him. When there came no response, he grew suddenly aware of the speed of his heart thumping against his chest as though it had suddenly swollen near to bursting. He tried to swallow, but it pained him to do so.

Even as he reached out his right hand and rested his fingers on the wooden door, muscles tensed to shove it open, the wind shifted direction. There must have been an open window in the house, for the sudden change in the breeze pushed the door as if to shut it, and carried the odor from within to him.

He had prepared enough animals for cooking in his life to know the smell of blood. But it was too late for Kangri to back away now. He had already given the door a shove and he was rooted to the threshold as it swung quickly open.

Inside that small dwelling, the floors were strewn with what little remained of Shache and his young wife and their two small children. The walls were spattered with blood, and the stench of it made his stomach convulse and forced him to stagger several steps backward, away from that scene.

Quietly, Kangri prayed to the gods of his village.

He turned to flee, to run to Shisha's home, to rouse the entire village in hopes that no one else would fall prey to the evil that had committed this atrocity. As he did, his gaze rose again, not to the east this time, but to the west, where he could barely make out the dark shape of the monastery against the backdrop of the snowy peaks.

In the midst of his horror, a flicker of anger went through Kangri. The monks had blessed Lingka, had promised that the fiendish things that roamed the mountains and lurked in the shadows of its caves would not come into the village. They were supposed to protect the people of the village, to make certain that as long as they kept together and stayed near Lingka, they would be safe.

But none of them were safe now. The evil had come into the village and struck at its very heart.

Kangri ran with eyes wide toward Shisha's house and suddenly realized that he was screaming, crying out with despair the news of the slaughter. Even as he did so, a horrible certainty filled him.

The demon of the eastern mountain had grown stronger. The darkness was no longer afraid of the light.

Chapter Four

Five Nights Until the Full Moon

Though it was dark outside, the moon fat and gibbous once more, Oz could not see it from the depths of the *Sargasso Drifter,* and perhaps that was best. He sat on the frayed carpet on the floor of the cabin Robideau and Alfred shared and sipped at a lukewarm bottle of Corona while Alf dealt the cards.

The ocean was rough this night, but he had almost ceased noticing it at all. The ship pitched and swayed, but Oz only took another swig of beer, leaned back against the cabin wall, and watched the intent expression on Robideau's face while Alfred finished the deal. In the week since he had first joined their game, Oz had lost $1,314 to Alfred. Which might have disturbed him if not for the nearly three quarters of a million dollars Robideau owed the man.

The game was eternal. The rules stated that any debts would be paid, if possible, out of future lottery winnings or through a last will and testament.

Oz reached out and picked up his cards. Deuce of clubs. Nine of diamonds. Jack of hearts. Jack of spades. Ace of diamonds. Aces and deuces were wild. He raised an eyebrow as he regarded the best hand of poker he had gotten over the course of what had to amount to ten or fifteen hours playing cards the last seven days.

With a crisp snap, he plucked the nine of diamonds from his hand and laid it facedown. "Just one."

Robideau narrowed his gaze, face flushed red from too much whiskey. "What're you holding?"

"Cards," Oz told him.

Alfred smiled and studied Oz curiously as he slid a single card across the carpet. The man was sitting cross-legged, a position that seemed effortless for him. Robideau, on the other hand, had his stumpy legs jutting out in front of him. Oz found this card-playing Robideau fascinating. So amiable any other time, during a round of poker he was charmingly irascible.

"I'll take three," the stout, three-quarter-million-in-debt seaman grumbled.

"I don't know why you even try," Alfred said, a look halfway between pity and mockery on his face as he dealt a card to Oz and three to his cabin mate.

"Only to humor you," Robideau replied. "Give you something to do so you won't whine like a baby."

Oz picked up his card and turned it over. Seven of clubs. He felt only a twinge of disappointment, however. Four jacks ought to be good enough to trump his opponents. Robideau scowled as he looked at his own cards, and Alfred shook his head in silent amusement. For himself, he had kept all five of his cards, not asking to draw new ones from the deck. It was cocky of him, but Oz could muster a certain amount of admiration for that. And, after all, the guy nearly always won, and at fifty bucks per player per hand, always added up pretty fast.

"All right, show 'em," Alfred said.

There was a staccato knock on the cabin door, and then it was opened without any response from those inside. A flash of annoyance crossed Alfred's features as they all glanced over to see Jim Vargas, one of the stewards under Ostergaard, poke his head in.

"Gentlemen," Vargas announced almost formally. "Thought you'd like to know we'll be in Fiji by dawn. There's no setup for container removal at the wharf in Fiji, so they're going to have to use an all-purpose crane. That means we have to wait for them to get around to us, so we're going to be here longer than we'd hoped. All three of you are at liberty until eighteen hundred hours tomorrow night."

Vargas the steward smiled. "You might want to get some sleep. The clock's already ticking on your day in paradise. Trust me, you won't want to waste a minute."

Without waiting for a response, Vargas pulled the door shut and continued along to the next cabin. The sound of him rapping on another door could be heard momentarily. Robideau had a triumphant smile on his face.

"You know, I used to hate that guy," he said.

"All right," Alfred said, returning his attention to the cards. "This is the last hand, then."

Oz laid down his cards. The two men glared at them a moment and then threw their own to the carpet in a disgusted scatter. After a moment in which he mentally subtracted one hundred dollars from his overall debt in the game, Oz rose to his feet.

"Beauty rest," he said, by way of explanation, and he headed for the door.

Despite their loss, his friends' frustration evaporated in seconds, and they were now in good spirits. They were very much looking forward to the next day, and part of their excitement was passed to Oz. His own anticipation, however, was considerably tainted by the knowledge that though he would be getting off the ship with them in the morning, he would not be coming back.

Four Nights Until the Full Moon

In the early hours of the morning, the *Sargasso Drifter* navigated the many small islands in the Koro Sea that made up the southeast of Fiji and sailed to the south of the largest island, Viti Levu. Shortly after sunrise the ship put into port at Sigatoka.

Oz was on deck when the *Sargasso Drifter* moored in Fiji, and though he had prepared for the natural beauty of the place, he found himself overwhelmed by it. As the ship had moved along the southern coast of Viti Levu he had marveled at the white sand beach and the tropical vegetation, the calls of birds that fluttered in the branches of bamboo and coconut trees. He could only imagine the snakes and lizards that slithered in among the mangroves.

Even now, as his view of the natural treasures of the island was interrupted by the mundane industrial presence of the docks and their accompanying ships, he could see the hardwood trees and the mountains rising up in the distance.

Kong, he thought. *I'm on Skull Island.*

A small flicker of a smile twitched at one corner of his mouth and then was gone. Just as he had in Hawaii, he felt as though he were committing a terrible sin visiting paradise without Willow at his side. The view was a consolation, the sheer pleasure of his surroundings, in spite of the sweltering heat. As was the knowledge that his purpose here was far from pleasurable, and that he would be forced to leave some of his belongings behind.

Down in his cabin, Gavin was still sleeping. On Oz's bed, his backpack was already stuffed with what clothes he could carry, his shaving kit and toothbrush, shampoo and soap, and all the money he'd brought with him. He wanted to travel light, but he also did not want Mr. Ostergaard or the captain to realize he planned to abandon them here in Fiji. At least not until he was already gone. Oz wasn't a coward and cringed at the thought of sneaking off like one, but he hoped to avoid a confrontation. On top of that, there was always the possibility that he would not be able to find the person he had come to see, and would continue on to Sydney after all.

If that happened, things were going to become very difficult for him in a few days. Alone in Sydney under the full moon . . . but he did not want to think about that now.

Some two hours later, after a large breakfast, he went ashore with Robideau and Alfred. Though they were adversaries at cards, they were never less than boon companions at all other times. Oz had a number of guys he thought of as his friends—the Dingoes, Caesar, Xander Harris—but he'd never had one who acted as his sidekick the way these two men did for each other. That closeness between the two made him even more grateful that they had befriended him, and even more sorry that he was now going to ditch them without a word.

Fiji was all that he had envisioned it to be from the outside. The village had modern conveniences—telephones, restaurants, and shops—but it was the farthest thing imaginable from Honolulu. The three sailors strolled along the streets for a time, noting small stores they wanted to come back to later to buy trinkets for those to whom they would eventually return, and locating a restaurant that seemed suitable for an early dinner. Alfred suggested that they find the nearest populated bit of beachfront and do nothing but watch Fijian women walk by and swim, until their brains would melt from too much relaxation. Robideau agreed, as long as they could come into possession of a cooler filled with beer and ice.

Oz thought it was early in the day for beer—on ice or not—but he made no objection when his friends found a place to purchase it. In fact, he chipped in his share.

As they wound their way through Sigatoka back toward the shore, Oz let his friends get a bit ahead of him. They became involved in a debate about the cinematic merits of Gerard Depardieu, and though he had a few opinions on the subject himself, he lagged farther behind and, in a moment when he was certain they were entrenched in conversation about *Green Card,* he ducked into a narrow alley between a Polynesian restaurant and a shop that seemed to sell only hats and fans.

Oz was well aware that most people saw him as laid-back, even blasé. He might even allow that there was some truth to that. But when he wanted to be, he was nearly as swift and silent as the beast that huddled beneath his skin. He ran fleetly down the alley and into a grassy area behind the restaurant, where a stand of hardwood trees grew by themselves, looking as out of place as he felt. Though he knew it was only his imagination, it seemed to him that the wolf inside him was agitated, that it sensed the quickening of his pulse and the imminent arrival of the full moon, only four days, four nights away.

Thoughts of the *Sargasso Drifter,* of Alf and Robideau, and of Mr. Ostergaard flickered through his mind frequently all through that morning. But he did his best to push them aside as he moved through the village. Twenty minutes after he slipped down that alley he had located a gas station where he could rent a car for the day. No Avis or Budget here, this was an island operation, with island rules. The insurance he had on his van wasn't going to cover an accident on Fiji, and they weren't going to sell him any. If something happened to his rental, he'd be paying for it.

Fortunately, when they led him to the battle-scarred green Jeep, he realized there was little he could do to it that anyone would notice.

Once he had paid for the day up front and let them copy his passport, Oz climbed into the Jeep and dropped his backpack into the passenger seat. The Buddha-like man at the rental agency had provided him—for a small fee—with a fairly well-detailed map of the island. With it spread across the dashboard, it took Oz only a minute to locate Mount Tomaniivi, the highest peak on all of Fiji. According to his information, the village of Toka Vatu was on the south side of the mountain, about halfway up.

Toka Vatu was not on the map. But Oz had not expected it to be.

He took a moment to study the map and he glanced around, working out exactly where he was at the moment. Inside the glorified gas station he had bought himself a couple of bottles of water. Now he screwed the cap off one and took a small sip before closing the bottle again and laying it on the seat. He left the map spread out beside him and ran both hands through his hair, grown thick and bushy over the weeks he'd been at sea. Early that morning he'd looked in the mirror and considered shaving the meager beard that had begun to grow on his face. In the end he'd left it. When he got a haircut, he'd worry about shaving.

Oz started up the Jeep and pulled it out onto the rutted main road of Sigatoka, engine purring. The big Buddha at the rental place obviously didn't care what the vehicle looked like, but someone had been taking good care of what was under its hood.

Slowly at first, consulting the map every few minutes, he drove north out of Sigatoka. Though tempted, he did not even glance in the rearview mirror. The *Sargasso Drifter* was behind him now.

So intent had he been upon his abandonment of his shipmates that he had noticed the heat and humidity but not really been burdened by it. Now that he was enclosed in the Jeep, the air felt close and sticky around him. There was no air-conditioning in the Jeep, but Oz opened all the windows and turned on the vent. The outside air rushing in was warm, but at least it was in motion.

As he drove north out of Sigatoka, the landscape around him became even more tropical. Lush greenery was populated by what seemed dozens of different species of colorful birds. The view of the mountains rising up before him reminded him again of Skull Island from the movie *King Kong*. Not the 1970s remake, either, but the original from the thirties.

He drove through several other villages and past vast fields of sugarcane, but soon the land began to rise and the hardwood and sandalwood trees to outnumber the coconut and bamboo. From what Alfred had told him during their journey, he knew that the Fiji Islands had been created by undersea volcanoes, which meant the mountain he was headed for had been the biggest and nastiest of those volcanic eruptions. There was something vaguely unsettling about that. It did not help that he'd also overheard Ostergaard and a crewman named Jim Armstrong discussing the fact that it was hurricane season in the South Pacific.

Volcanoes and hurricanes.

Still, he considered the threat a small price to pay for paradise, and for the answers that he hoped to find here.

The sun moved across the sky until it was high

above; morning had turned to noon, and the streets had given way to narrow, unpaved roads. Even when he reached what the map identified as the Highland Road, which would take him up the southeasterly face of the mountain, he found that it was little more than a cart path, with stones and roots and potholes large enough to lose a child in.

The Highland Road was a series of switchbacks crisscrossing the face of the mountain, and Oz came several times to rivers flowing down toward the ocean. He paused only briefly each time before forging across in the Jeep, water rushing past the tires. It was the rainy season in Fiji, which explained all those rivers washing down the mountain. Fortunately the sun had been shining that morning, but the farther upward he drove the more cloud cover gathered above. Several times he stopped at small villages and asked about his destination. Always the locals merely ushered him on, pointing upward.

The Highland Road had barely earned the name to begin with, but as the minutes ticked by it became less a road and more a vague trail. It wound upward, and suddenly the landscape on both sides dropped away into a pair of deep ravines, the road a kind of aqueduct. Oz was grateful for the Jeep's four-wheel drive as the tires clung precariously to the path. So close was the edge that had he stopped to appreciate the view he could hardly have gotten out of the Jeep without falling over the ridge. It became so steep that the engine growled in protest.

When the forest sprang up again on either side of him, Oz slowed and took a deep breath, only now aware of how anxious he had been. From the brush came the noises of various birds and animals moving through the branches and in the undergrowth. A hissing sound seemed to fill the air, and a shudder went through him as he wondered how many snakes it would take to make a sound that loud. He took a few long draughts of water and then put the Jeep in gear again to continue on his journey.

Once more he came to a river, falling in a tumult across his path and down the side of the mountain. It was breathtakingly beautiful, sparkling in the sunlight that broke through the thin cloud cover in spotlight rays. It was also fast and deep.

But Toka Vatu was somewhere on the other side, and he'd come too far not to keep going. Trying to force images of the Jeep sliding down the river to fall off into some bottomless ravine, he put it in gear and surged forward. At first it seemed no deeper than the others, but halfway across the water came up over the tires and washed across the floor of the Jeep right under his feet. Oz felt the entire vehicle begin to slide sideways in the water.

Heart thumping loudly in his ears, he cursed and gunned the engine. The tires spun a moment without touching anything and then at last found traction at the bottom of the river. The Jeep lurched forward, shedding water as it went and then he was on land again.

It had been nearly three hours since he had begun his trip into the mountains. Now as he rounded a bend he noticed an even narrower trail that went straight ahead. Tree branches hung in a canopy across the path and they brushed the roof as Oz pulled under them. He killed the engine and stepped out, staring up at the mountain's peak still high above. From his pack he took an apple and banana he had brought with him from the ship that morning and ate them slowly. When he was through he climbed back in and continued carefully down the narrow path. Twice he had to get out and haul fallen trees from his path and often he reached points where it seemed the path was about to disappear, only to have it widen again. Even in those spots where his trail seemed clear, Oz worried what would happen if he never reached a place where he might turn around. Backing all the way out of there seemed like a treacherous prospect.

At last the Jeep rolled into a clearing, and he saw a meager village around him made up of houses with woven-mat walls and thatched roofs. Children played in the midst of the village, but beyond it Oz could see that the clearing continued to an open field where sugarcane and rice grew. There were people working in the field, and others crushing some sort of plant in large wooden bowls in front of a house nearby.

He shut off the engine but did not move. Activity in the village had come to a halt, with everyone save a handful of the smallest children pausing to stare at him. Children, those strange little children with their bright orange jack-o'-lantern skin, narrow features, and hair like porcupine quills. On their parents, the effect was even more startling.

Demons.

So he had found Toka Vatu after all.

Oz swallowed and found his throat dry, but when he reached over for his water he realized that one of the bottles was already empty. He could probably fill it up from one of the many rivers, but decided to save the second one for the trip back down. Whenever that might be. Without hesitation, he stepped out of the Jeep and pocketed the keys. These villagers were hardly the strangest things he had ever seen, and they seemed harmless enough.

Still, he walked cautiously as he began to approach the nearest home, where a woman—a female demon—was standing inside the door with a child cradled in her arms. He forced an awkward smile onto his face and kept his hands down and open, palms out to show he was unarmed.

"Hi. How's it going?" he began, the faux smile disappearing. "Hoping you can help me. Do you know Sarah Atwill?"

The female narrowed her gaze and studied him. Oz was not certain, but he thought the expression on her face might have been amusement. He heard children laughing behind him and turned to see them scattering, running toward the field. Where they had been playing there now stood a fortyish human woman with hair so blond, it was almost white. She was thin but looked strong, radiating with a healthiness that made her beautiful.

"I'm Sarah Atwill," she said, brows knitted. "Who the hell are you?"

Something seemed to give way inside Oz, and he let out a sigh of relief that turned into a low chuckle. All through his insane journey he had feared that he would reach this place, this retreat where the Litoka demon tribe had made its home, and find that they had gone, or at least that Sarah Atwill was no longer here.

He stared at her, the raised chin and suspicious gaze, the crossed arms, and all he could think of was some harsh English schoolmistress who belonged more on some BBC series than in the wild mountain forests of Fiji.

"Am I meant to know you, then?" she asked in her crisp, clipped English accent. "Because otherwise I'm growing impatient. We don't get a lot of visitors here, you see."

"I guess you don't," he observed. "Pretty presumptuous, I know, but I wondered if you could help me. Or at least Giles said if anyone could, it would be you."

It was as though the sun had suddenly shone through the cloud of her severe expression. Sarah Atwill smiled.

"You don't mean Rupert Giles?"

"I don't? Pretty sure I do."

Then the smile went away again, and Sarah stepped toward him, gazing into his eyes. "You're a lycanthrope."

Oz raised his eyebrows. "That obvious, huh? Not usually something people can tell just by looking."

"It's the only reason Rupert would have sent you to me. What's your name?"

"They call me Oz."

"Oz," she repeated dubiously, a hint of disapproval in her voice. "Not what your mother calls you, though."

"I've been called a lot of things," he replied, uncomfortable with the personal turn the conversation had taken.

Abruptly, Sarah's expression softened. She thrust out her hand as though it had been a long time since custom had required her to greet someone with a handshake. Oz could understand how her social skills might get rusty living up here. He glanced around, noted with some surprise that the demons were all but ignoring them now, and he took her hand.

As they shook, Sarah spoke in a voice barely above a whisper, words heavy with sorrow. "You shouldn't have come all this way, Oz. Rupert knows there isn't a cure."

Oz scratched idly at the thick stubble on his chin. "So do I. I'm not looking for a cure. Just some control."

Her expression was grave. "What did he tell you about me?"

Giles had actually told him a great many things about Sarah Atwill. According to him, no one in the world had spent more time studying werewolves. The Watchers Council looked to Sarah whenever the subject came up. His own research had not uncovered any way for Oz to control the beast inside him, but Giles had suggested that might be because most werewolves were like Veruca . . . they gave in to the beast willingly.

"He told me if anyone could help me figure out how to fight it, you could."

Sarah reached out to him again, this time to glide her hand gently along his arm. She met his gaze unwaveringly, and before she spoke, he knew what she was going to say.

"I'm afraid you've come a very long way for nothing."

For a moment, Oz was paralyzed. He swallowed hard and then, when he felt he could move again, he turned away from her and stared back the way he'd come, through the long, dark forest tunnel that led to this peaceful retreat, where a tribe of demons could hide away from the world. The sky pulled at him as if daring him to look up, to search for the ghost of the moon on the horizon. A handful of days until it was full. And there was nowhere for him to hide.

He did not even look back at her.

"I should go," he said. "It isn't safe for you if I stay."

Oz started back toward the Jeep, mind numb, unable or unwilling to begin trying to figure out where he might trap himself to stop the beast from taking lives. Here she was, after all, the one woman in the world Giles thought might be able to help. He'd found her, and that in itself was incredible. Yet it was all for nothing.

"Oz," Sarah said as he reached for the door of the Jeep, "Rupert Giles doesn't know everything."

Unable to breathe, he turned hopefully toward her. Sarah seemed hesitant, but after a moment she went on.

"There's a . . . well, a monastery, I suppose it is, though it's more a sort of sanctuary. Nothing religious about it, unless you think faith in oneself is a kind of religion. I've never met the master there, Shantou, but I knew a lycanthrope once that had near complete control over his condition. He claimed Master Shantou had taught that to him."

Oz stared at her impatiently. At length he inclined his head just a bit. "Hoping you're gonna tell me where this place is."

A flutter of a smile moved across her face like birds taking flight, then it was gone and Sarah Atwill was all seriousness again. "I can see why Rupert likes you. No nonsense. Right, then. The monastery's on a mountain in Tibet, or at least it's meant to be. I'm sure I've got a map in my house that will help."

Another wave of defeat threatened to wash over Oz, but he was having none of it. "Tibet it is," he said dryly.

Now a shadow seemed to pass over the woman's features and it was not nearly so fleeting as her smile. She frowned and glanced at the sky, seemed to pause to do a bit of mental calculation.

"Yeah," Oz noted. "Four days."

"Maybe we can find a cave to keep you in, somewhere very remote," she suggested.

He shook his head. "No thanks. I want to keep moving. But if you know anyone in Sydney, I'll be there the day after tomorrow."

"I'm sorry, but I don't. You might call Rupert, though. Obviously he has a great many connections. The Watchers' Council—"

"Not his biggest fans about now," Oz interrupted. He didn't bother to mention that he was reluctant to have contact with anyone back in Sunnydale, even Giles. He wanted to keep out of Willow's life, let her get on with things without him, until he could face her again with the beast under his control.

"I see," Sarah replied. "Well, when you speak to him, please give him my love."

Oz shot her a sidelong glance. "Verbally, right? 'Cause Giles, not really the most huggable guy."

She laughed at that. "Yes, verbally." Sarah Atwill beamed. "You're a fascinating young man, Oz. I hope you find what you're looking for, and I hope we meet again."

"Me too," he replied, reaching out to shake her hand again. He was surprised to find that, despite his disappointment, he meant it. Sarah Atwill seemed a genuinely decent person, not to mention interesting, given that she'd chosen to live her life up on a mountain in the middle of nowhere with a bunch of demons.

After Sarah had retrieved the map from her hut and pointed out the location of the monastery on it, Oz said good-bye. He climbed back into the Jeep, turned it around, and began the trek back down the mountain. But any good feeling Sarah had brought out in him dissipated almost immediately. Though the sun still shone through breaks in the clouds, a light rain began to fall. There were still many hours left before dark, yet he could feel the moon waiting just at the edge of the day, like a secret lover who knew that though he ought not come to her, he would not be able to stay away.

Chapter Five

Four Nights Until the Full Moon

"Sarah sends her love."

Oz stood in a tucked away little corner in the lobby of the Outrigger Reef in Sigatoka. He had his back to the elegant island paradise that had been re-created in the hotel's huge foyer, the phone pressed to his ear. On the other end of the line, thousands of miles away, Giles hesitated.

"Really?" the Watcher asked. "That's . . . kind of her. We knew each other only briefly, from a Council retreat at Innsbruck. I wouldn't have thought, well . . ."

"Guess you made an impression," Oz told him. "Anyway, Tibet?"

"Ah, of course," the Englishman said.

Oz could almost picture Giles standing in the narrow little galley that passed for a kitchen in his apartment, sipping at a hot cup of tea. Probably half asleep despite his claim that he'd been doing research when the phone rang.

"Once upon a time it might have been even more difficult," Giles began. "Fortunately, now that China has taken possession of Hong Kong once more, there is a vulnerable spot. It happens that I have an old acquaintance there that may be able to help you, or at least point you in the right direction. After that, I'm afraid you're on your own."

"I'll manage," Oz told him. "I appreciate what you've done already. No chance you have a friend in Sydney willing to keep me in a cage for a few nights?"

There was a giggle behind him, and Oz turned to see a pair of young girls—twins, by the look of them—perhaps twelve years old, walking by. They covered their mouths to whisper to each other, but they glanced at him repeatedly. He had no idea if they were American, but the girls certainly spoke English well enough to have understood what he had said. He raised an eyebrow and returned his attention to the phone conversation. "Sorry, Giles. Momentary distraction. What was that?"

"Simply that, given the time constraints, it seems imperative you make your way to Sydney and then fly to Hong Kong if you've got the money. If he's willing, I'm certain Qing will be able to handle your transformation this month. He has more than one aspect himself, in fact."

Oz didn't know whether to cringe or cheer, though he wasn't really likely to do either. It was an enormous relief to think there might be someone who could shelter him—or shelter the world from him—for the three nights of the full moon. But blowing most of the cash he'd brought along on a single plane ticket was a painful thought. On the other hand, he knew a couple of guys who had followed the Allman Brothers Band across the country until they ran out of money, then washed dishes in restaurants and painted houses until they had enough to come home.

"Qing sounds like my man. How do I find him?"

"I'll tell him you're coming. Write this down."

"Hang on," Oz replied. He reached down between his legs and hauled up his pack, trapping it between his body and the phone so that he could root around for the black Sharpie marker he had in there. It was at the bottom. He had nothing to write on, so he pulled out the frayed paperback copy of *The Brothers Karamazov* he'd been reading and used the inside cover.

"Go."

Giles gave him an address and telephone number for Qing in Hong Kong. Oz would have to get his own map of the city, but that would be easy enough.

"Thanks," Oz said. Simple. Final.

"Will you keep me apprised of your progress?"

"Doubtful. If things work out, you'll see me again before you hear from me. If not, not. Favor, though?"

"Not to worry," Giles assured him. "I've not mentioned a word to anyone. That's best, I think, until you've got it sorted."

For a moment, neither of them said a word. The silence seemed to stretch long over the phone line, and it was almost eerie how nearby the two ends of that conversation seemed then. Sunnydale seemed so close, Willow not so far away at all. He ought to say something, have Giles pass along word that he was all right, that he loved her, that he hoped—

"Take care of yourself, Giles," Oz said.

"And you as well."

Oz hung up the phone. Passing messages back to Willow would probably make him feel a little better about himself, make him feel a kind of connection to her. But it wouldn't do her any good. Giles was right: It was best to say nothing at all, until he had something to say. He had not even asked Giles how Willow was doing. As much as he loved her, part of him did not want to know. If she was taking things badly, he would feel even guiltier than he already was, and if she was recovering, moving on with her life, that might be even worse.

With a shake of his head, he shoved the book and pen back into his pack and slung it over his shoulder. *Cease fire,* he told his brain. *You never used to think this much. It's unhealthy.*

The Outrigger Reef was a first-class hotel, the sort of place Oz felt awkward just walking through. Sigatoka itself was beautiful, but the village where locals shopped and did their business and the sprawling resort seemed like two completely different worlds. The hotel was a tourist destination, pure and simple, and he could see why. The fountains and greenery in the lobby made it peaceful as well as sophisticated, but the real selling point was the fact that the hotel itself was only yards from the sand, a stone's throw from the ocean.

Oz had not been drawn here by the hotel's status as a tourist mecca on the island, however. Rather, he had needed a phone he could use his calling card on without too much trouble, and he had a feeling that the little restaurants and shops in Sigatoka were likely to charge him just to dial out. He had to save as much money as he could at the moment.

Now he strolled through the comfortable air-conditioned lobby of the Outrigger Reef and stepped out into the humidity and heat. The sky was a faded purple now, darkness coming on, and the air was not quite as oppressive as it had been earlier. By the time he got back to the *Sargasso Drifter* it would be well after dark and Mr. Ostergaard was not going to be a happy man. But the chief steward would probably have been a lot angrier if he hadn't returned at all.

He had parked the Jeep about halfway across the parking lot. As he slipped the key into the lock, Oz paused. He glanced around, a frown creasing his forehead. The wind had blown a familiar scent to him. Just the hint of it, there one moment and gone with the next breeze. There were a number of people in the lot, mostly leaving their cars and walking up toward the hotel, but none of them were paying him the least bit of attention. Already even the memory of that scent was leaving him, and he realized it must have been his imagination.

After all, what were the chances he was going to run into someone he knew in Fiji?

With his backpack on the seat beside him, Oz drove back to the main village of Sigatoka as quickly as he dared.

Night came quickly to the island, and by the time he pulled the Jeep into the lot behind the combination gas station and rental agency, it was full on dark. The clouds had cleared off again, and the stars were spectacular. The gibbous moon was a fat and misshapen thing, still growing, sliding toward perfection. A rim of light surrounded it like an aura of frost. Oz stood beside the Jeep and stared up at the moon for a moment, breath catching in his throat. It was so beautiful, he wanted to shout to it. When he closed his eyes a moment, though, he had a flash of dream memory, the feeling of Veruca's blood-soaked fur beneath his lips, her flesh tearing in his jaws.

Chilled, he scowled and turned his eyes away from the night sky, away from the moon. Inside the rental agency, the man who had rented him the Jeep made a few rumblings about wear and tear as though he might try to charge even more money, but one glance from Oz and he fell silent. He did not even walk outside to check on further damage on the Jeep, just ushered Oz out the door and was visibly glad to see him go.

As he walked through the village, headed back toward the pier, the hairs on the back of his neck stood up, and he felt the moonlight on his skin the way others would the sun. It was always like this when the full moon drew close, but he never spoke of it to anyone, never discussed that or how acute his sense of smell was, never talked about any of the things that made him different. Oz did not want to be different. He was just a guy, that was all. Human.

Nights like this, though, it was harder to believe that.

After several blocks he saw a shop he recognized from that morning, then the restaurant he, Alf, and Robideau had discussed dining in today. Thinking of his friends, he slowed his stride. They were going to be pissed off that he'd ditched them, and he did not blame them. It was inevitable, just as Mr. Ostergaard's scorn was, but Oz was suddenly not in so great a rush. Still, he could not take too long. If Ostergaard fired him, he'd be trapped on Fiji when the full moon rose.

The soles of his high-tops scuffed the road as he picked up the pace again. He put both arms through the loops of the backpack now. The street he was on had turned westward, and he was meant to be going south toward the port, toward his ship. Oz frowned. He must have gone farther than necessary in the dark. Back along the street there was a turn he was supposed to have taken. What was important, though, was that he reach the ocean. Finding the ship then would be simple. There was a moonlit alley ahead, and he turned left and started down it, picking his way around empty fruit crates that littered the broken pavement. He could see the other end already, a squat little shop or office, and beyond that, the ocean.

His mind began to wander into the future, to Hong Kong and beyond, to Tibet. When he heard the soft snickering behind him, he cursed himself for not having paid more attention.

Street punks. Even in paradise, he thought as he turned around.

There were two of them about thirty feet back, and his first thought was that they did not look Fijian. The one nearest him, whose face he could see clearly in the available light, was thin and pale, with ragged cut hair and angular features that made him look almost comically severe. The other he could not see as well, but he was built like a linebacker, broad shoulders silhouetted at the end of the alley. He held a large knife in his right hand, and it glinted in the moonlight.

The gleam off that knife's edge was what made Oz take a step backward. He turned to glance toward the ocean again, and not far from the other end of the alley two more dark figures dropped down to the pavement, blocking his retreat.

Oz crouched low, adrenaline surging through him. Without realizing he was doing it, he curled his fingers over as though they were claws. He had been in tight scrapes plenty of times, mostly back in Sunnydale, with the Slayer, but a couple of times with the Dingoes. This wasn't his first back alley brawl. But the odds sucked.

He sniffed the air, and he froze. His mind flashed back to the parking lot at the Outrigger Reef, and he knew it had not been his imagination then. This was a scent he knew. "Oh, crap," he whispered.

The linebacker stepped farther into the alley, knife gleaming in his grasp, and the moonlight fell fully on his face now.

"Take him alive," the big man said. "I can't skin him till he's got a pelt to sell. But don't worry if you have to break him a little."

Oz's gaze darted to the thug nearest him, the one right in front of the linebacker. His face changed, and Oz's heart skipped a beat.

Vampires.

Cain heard the kid whisper to himself, and smiled. It

was almost worth the commission he was going to have to pay the Pierrault brothers to see Oz's reaction to the vampires' presence. It had gotten under Cain's skin to bring in extra muscle—especially extra muscle that could only work at night—but the Osbourne kid was no ordinary werewolf. He ran with the Slayer. There had been no way for Cain to know why he was going to Fiji, or who he expected to meet up with there.

Caution. Cain had survived as long as he had because he was damn good at the job—it was his calling—but also because he wasn't a damn fool. Better to err on the side of caution, that was the saying. And this Fiji trip was the perfect example. Cain had been tracking the werewolf all day and managed to stay out of sight, unnoticed, even up in the mountains. Oz had been hanging around with a tribe of Litoka demons. They were peaceful creatures, normally, but it wasn't a good idea to rile them up. Hell, they were demons, after all.

If Oz had stuck around with the Litokas, Cain would have needed the Pierraults' help in a big way. That was exactly the kind of possibility that had led him to call in the vampire brothers in the first place. As it turned out, he hadn't really needed them. He could track Oz on his own, run him to the ground easily enough. Under normal circumstances he would have waited until the moon was full—that was the real hunt. But the kid was on the move, and Cain needed to recoup some of his losses on the Veruca situation. He had to capture Oz when the opportunity presented itself and then hold him until the moon was up.

Now the opportunity was here, and he was paying the Pierraults, anyway, so he figured he might as well put them to work.

"Take him alive," Cain said. "But don't worry if you have to break him a little."

• • •

Vampires.

Now that he recognized them for what they were, Oz realized that he could smell them. Their scent was cold and visceral, like raw beef about an hour away from rancid. They didn't all smell like this; mostly they just smelled *stale.* But these three had a scent that was almost identical, and it occurred to him that they might have been related even before death.

Twisted, Oz thought. Someone had vamped a trio of brothers. *At least they aren't triplets. That'd be perverse.*

The two behind Oz who were blocking his way to the pier began to snicker. The one with the human guy muttered something in French, but Oz had forgotten most of what he had learned of that language the second he graduated from high school. Plus, he figured he didn't have a heck of a lot of time to spend trying to translate. The only thing he had going for him was that the guy in charge—the human—didn't want him dead. At least not yet.

Not yet. But why not? Who the hell was the guy and what did he and his vampire lackeys want with Oz? The answer came to him almost immediately. The basic physical description matched the only person in the world who had ever tried to hunt Oz before—Gib Cain. Which meant the reason Cain didn't want him dead yet was because he was waiting for the full moon, so he could skin Oz alive.

Oh, joy.

Again he felt the moonlight on his skin, felt the beast striving within him, waiting for the moment when it could break free. Veruca had said that he was the beast all the time, but Oz was not willing to accept that. Maybe, though, well . . . maybe he *was* more than human.

"Cain . . . ," he began.

"Smart boy." The hunter smiled. "Grab him," Cain said casually, almost tiredly, as though it were a done deal already.

Oz crouched, picked up a broken fruit crate in each hand, and heaved them at the nearest vampire. One of the splintered slats clattered to the ground, and he snatched it up, thinking *stake.* The vampire tried to bat the crates away, but they were falling apart and shattered around him. A shower of broken wood forced Cain to shield his face, but Oz only caught a glimpse of that. He was already in motion.

The alley ran between two long buildings. There were shops on either side of him, and they all had high windows—too high for him to reach. There were, however, several doors on either side of the alley belonging, he imagined, to shops both on the street he'd just left and the one he had been heading for.

In the eye-blink moment in which Cain and the nearest vampire were throwing aside the remains of the fruit crates, Oz turned toward the other two bloodsuckers. As he rushed at them he could see the ocean beyond them, and his heart ached. The sea wasn't his life, but at the moment he missed it an awful lot.

The two vampire brothers hissed, their eyes glowing a sickly, unnerving yellow in the light from the moon and stars. They grinned, exposing glittering fangs like murderous diamonds, and they waited for him, cruel eyes daring him to try to get past them.

Oz altered his course in an instant, the weight of his backpack almost making him lose his balance as he shifted his momentum. With all the speed and strength he could muster he cut to the left and threw himself at a tall wooden door with a fat knob and a rusty keyhole. After all the time he'd spent in Sunnydale, he would have thought the vampires would not be able to frighten him. But he had seen too often what they were capable of and so he said a silent prayer to whatever cosmic forces were out there in the universe, listening in.

He plowed into the door, and it gave way with a screech and a puff of rust, slammed open with a splintering crash. A spike of pain drove into his shoulder and sent echoes all down his arm and up his neck, but he barely felt it. He was in.

Out in the alley there was loud cursing in French, then Cain hissing at them to keep it down. Oz ignored them. He clutched the broken wooden slat in his hand and hurried through the store, trying not to think about that door and what would have happened if it had not opened. In L.A., even in Sunnydale, he probably would have bounced right off. *Materials here must be cheaper, people don't worry so much about security,* he thought.

Yet that was not how it had *felt.* He had felt faster and stronger than he ought to be, and it wasn't the first time. Oz pushed that line of thought away. *It was the rusty lock, that's all.* It had to be, of course. Otherwise he would have to conclude that he had drawn on the strength and speed of the wolf, of the beast, and that would mean . . . something he would not even consider.

He hustled through the back room of the store, pushed through curtains out into the front. Behind him he heard a crash as Cain and the vampires pursued him. Oz's heart thundered in his chest, and he felt fear, yes, but he also felt exhilaration. He could still feel the moonlight, though he could no longer see the sky.

Oz dodged showcases and display stands. It was a gift shop filled with things tailor made for tourists: T-shirts and knickknacks and island jewelry.

"Wolf!" snarled a vampire behind him. "Heel! Heel to your betters!"

There was a crash as a display stand went down, barreled over by the vamp in the lead. Oz bristled at the leech's words, wanted to cuss him out, but he kept his head down, not daring to lose even a fraction of a second.

His stomach clutched and churned, and his whole body seemed cold despite the heat of the night. The dead were after him; he could practically feel their icy claws upon him.

As he passed the counter at the front of the store, Oz reached out and grabbed hold of a marble statue that he imagined represented a volcano god or something. He hefted the stone icon but barely slowed down as he cocked his arm back and hurled it through the glass front door of the shop.

The glass exploded out into the street. Oz pulled in his arms and legs and ducked his head as he leaped through the frame of jagged glass teeth that threatened to close around him. Then he was out on the street.

"'Allo, wolf boy!" a voice called from above him.

Oz started across the street but faltered and nearly took a spill as he twisted to look around and up. On the roof of the shop stood one of the vampires, this one thinner even than his brothers, his hair longer. With a soft, chuffling laugh, he dropped off the roof and landed on the street perhaps seven feet away from Oz.

Nowhere to run, Oz thought. The vamps were too fast.

So he lunged at the vampire, brought his makeshift stake up. The vamp slapped him a vicious backhand, almost too swift to see. But Oz was pretty fast himself. He took the blow, let it spin him around, and when the vampire came at him, arms extended, he knocked its hands away and rammed the broken slat through its skinny chest.

It dusted, a look of surprise and fear on its raven-like features.

That's it. Ravens. They remind me of ravens.

Oz was no Slayer. He had hunted vamps before, but never alone, and tonight he'd gotten lucky. But there were two others, not to mention Cain, and—

Even as the thoughts went through his head, the other two vampires—he had begun to think of them as *ravens*—emerged from the shop and faltered, staring gape-mouthed at him with the stake in his hand, putting it all together in half a second.

"*Non,*" one of them whispered. Then his voice rose. "*Henri, non!*"

Oz turned and ran. He was on the main thoroughfare now, the road he'd meant to turn down in the first place. He could see the pier, the lights on the various ships moored there. One of them was the *Sargasso Drifter.* The sailors lived onboard, but it wasn't a privately owned ship. He had no idea if the vampires would be able to get onboard or not. And he didn't want to endanger his friends. But at least there he would have allies, the odds would be better.

"Stop!" a voice roared behind him.

Oz did not look back. It was Cain's voice, he knew that much. In his mind's eye he had an image of the hunter standing just outside the shattered glass door of that shop, calling after him. The guy had to be an idiot if he really thought Oz was going to stop just because he said so.

A horn blared suddenly, and Oz caught the glint of headlights over his left shoulder. Instinct made him dive forward, but the grill of the car still clipped his foot. He hit the pavement and rolled, but even as he did so he heard a loud, wet thump, and the car screeched to a halt.

People began shouting, moving toward him out of restaurants and off the sidewalks. Somebody tried to help him up, but Oz barely registered the guy. His eyes were glued on the dark sedan that had nearly run him down. A pair of expensive Italian shoes stuck out from under the car. One of the legs was broken, twisted up the wrong direction. But those shoes . . . all he could think of was the Wicked Witch of the East and her ruby slippers, Dorothy dropping a house on her.

The Mercedes wasn't a house, but it would do.

It struck home to Oz just how close behind him the vampire had been, and he shuddered. His ankle hurt, but he didn't think it was broken. Frantic, heart pounding, breath coming too fast, he glanced over at the storefront with its shattered glass door. There in the darkness, just inside, he saw Gib Cain standing, arms crossed, staring at him.

So that was it. Too many people around. Cain wasn't giving up, but the hunt was on hold for the moment.

Then someone screamed, and Oz looked over to see that the legs beneath the car—one whole and one twisted and broken—were moving. The vampire who'd been run down by the car was down, but not out. A chill went through Oz, rippling up his back, and he glanced all around him, looking at the faces in the crowd. There had been three of them. One was dust, one was going to have a hell of a limp for a while, but where was the third one? The third brother?

The vampire was nowhere to be seen. Oz began to back away from the scene. People asked him in half a dozen languages if he was all right. He plastered a false smile onto his face and moved more swiftly, walking backward. Though his ankle throbbed, he turned and pushed through a couple of people and began to run. The backpack seemed heavier than ever. If it had been just his clothes in there, he probably would have dumped it back in the alley, but all his money was in there, and the book with the information about his contact in Hong Kong.

Oz clutched the straps of the pack tightly as he ran. He glanced side to side, watching for a fleeting, birdlike shadow closing in, but there was nothing. Only tourists looking at him oddly, faces staring through the glass of restaurant windows.

In his mind he could still see the dark shape of Cain staring at him from the shadowy interior of that shop, could remember the way the moonlight glinted off his knife in the alley.

Moments later, Oz ran up the gangway to the *Sargasso Drifter.* Jim Armstrong was on the deck, supervising several crewmen as they battened down the doors of the hold where the containers had been offloaded. At the top of the gangway, Oz turned to look back at the village of Sigatoka. There was no sign of Cain, nor of the brothers. No vampires, no hunters.

He let out a long breath, but there was not an ounce of relief in it. For that, he would have had to feel safe, and he did not. Far from it. He knew that the hunt was not over.

It had only begun.

Three Nights Until the Full Moon

Oz had finished his shift twenty minutes ago. Now he sat in a hard wooden chair in the chief steward's office and suffered the disappointment of the man who had given him his job. Despite Mr. Ostergaard's obvious disapproval, Oz did not squirm. He deeply regretted the way he had taken advantage of this man's kindness and goodwill, regretted that he had let him down and planned to do so again, but he had done the job to the best of his ability. That was something, at least.

They had left port at Sigatoka shortly before midnight, and the hours between Oz's return to the Sargasso Drifter and their departure had been nerve-racking ones. Even now he knew it was possible that one or more of the vampires had come aboard. Not Cain. It would be too difficult for him to hide. But one of those vampires? He'd given some thought to it, and even though they lived on the boat while at sea, it wasn't their home. They probably wouldn't need an invitation. So it might be possible to hide down there in the bowels of the ship, with so few windows to let the sun in. That would be very, very bad.

Oz wished he could avoid thinking about it, but that could cost lives, not least his own. He was on edge, starting at shadows, spooked by every door he had to open. Ostergaard noticed it even now, saw the way Oz glanced around constantly. The old man stroked his walrus mustache and frowned.

"I hope you apologized to Canfield and Robideau," Mr. Ostergaard said, his tone much like that of a teacher correcting a wayward student. "When you disappeared on them yesterday, they feared something had happened to you. Spent most of their liberty trying to figure out where you had gotten off to and if you were all right."

Oz nodded. He had apologized to Alf and Robideau, explained that he'd gotten turned around, lost track of them, and then surrendered to the island's beauty and wandered the beaches all day. Both men had accepted his apology, but it had been clear in their eyes that they did not believe him and they had been cool to him when he had seen them at breakfast this morning. Oz felt badly, but there was nothing to be done for it. Just as there was nothing to be done about Ostergaard's mistrust of him now.

"I talked to them about it," Oz told him. "They're pretty ticked."

Ostergaard raised an eyebrow. "Do you blame them?"

"No. Not any more than I'll blame you for not wanting me on your crew."

The ocean rolled beneath them, and the ship swayed. Ostergaard seemed not to notice as he rose and went to the window. The sun shone on his face then, making his hair and mustache look thinner, whiter, making his face ashen and drawn.

"I'm angry because I vouched for you. I had no reason to. It was only that I had a feeling I could trust you. If we were somewhere else, somewhere you could legitimately have been delayed for a few hours, I might have understood. It was sheer irresponsibility, disappearing the way you did."

Mr. Ostergaard turned toward him. "But I'm not going to deny you a return trip home. You're a good worker, Oz. I'll pay you your wages for this trip, and for the journey back to California as well. But if shore leave comes up for you, it's going to be curtailed. Only a couple of hours, just to get your feet on dry land and a meal that isn't from the mess. I'd say those conditions are more than fair."

Oz blinked in surprise. Ostergaard stared at him, awaiting a response.

"Well?" the man said.

"Yes, sir. More than fair. And I'm grateful for the opportunity you gave me. The thing is, I've made other plans."

"What?" Ostergaard's cheeks reddened, and his eyes narrowed dangerously.

"I won't be continuing on with you after we reach Sydney."

The man simmered with anger. Oz could only imagine the things that were going through the chief steward's head, the presumption that he was ungrateful and untrustworthy. But he had spent enough time feeling guilty for things that weren't in his control, and he had honestly never imagined Ostergaard would let him stay with the crew.

The chief steward shook his head and turned back toward the window. "Good luck with whatever it is you're hunting for, Oz. Clearly, this isn't the line of work for you."

Oz rose from the chair. "Sorry."

Ostergaard did not look at him again.

Regret followed him out of the room, but already, Oz's mind had returned to what lay ahead, to Hong Kong, and to the full moon, only three nights away.

Trust me, he thought. *You don't want me to stay.*

Chapter Six

Three Nights Until the Full Moon

A child was missing.

The people in the mountain village of Lingka went about their lives much as they always had. They had little choice in the matter, of course, for if they did not work the land they would have no food. But there were few smiles as Kangri walked through the village that day in search of Wei the glassblower. Even the children who played in the dirt road that ran through the village did so without the laughter that had always followed them like thunder after lightning.

The construction of his house was coming along well, but no longer did the prospect of its completion fill him with the joyous anticipation it had once upon a time. His wedding to Shisha had been postponed. It was her brother Dawa who was missing. Dawa was seven years old and a bright, healthy boy smart enough not to go afield without his parents or his sister.

He had not needed to.

Dawa had disappeared from his bed, snatched in utter silence during the night. Shisha had been the one to discover his absence at first light the next morning, the one to notice the three small drops of dark blood on the wide, rough-hewn boards of the floor and the sticky ink-black residue on the windowsill that might have been oil but most assuredly was not. More of that substance had later been found around the boy's bed.

Beyond the window, several feet from the bed, Dawa's parents had found a small puddle of blood and a small length of bone and muscle that they soon realized was Dawa's finger. It had been gnawed upon, flesh stripped off it, a tiny delicacy for the thing that had stolen him from his bed, this beast so excited about its prize that it could not help but have a taste right away.

Still, no one had heard anything. Not a scream or a cry or the creak of a board.

Dawa had not been the first, nor would he be the last. There was talk in the village that they should leave, abandon their homes with only what they could carry upon their backs and settle again closer to Lhasa, where they might be safer. But there was talk as well of setting a trap for the child-stealer, of eviscerating it and leaving its corpse out for the vultures, so the demon of the eastern mountain would know that his creatures had trespassed where they did not belong.

Kangri was afraid to hunt demons. But he was also afraid to leave. He kept his head down and worked on his new house and prayed that no more children would be stolen, that the monsters would move on, that he could at last marry Shisha. But his love for her, their future together, had been forever tainted by the loss of her brother and the dread that hung like a shroud over Lingka.

When he crossed the bridge over the narrow river that bisected the village, Kangri did not look at Shache's small house. He did not want to remember the gory scene he had discovered there. Someone had put wards around the house—carved, meticulously decorated wooden faces that were meant to protect it from the forces of darkness, from creatures of evil nature. The absurdity of this did not seem to occur to anyone else—*why ward off evil when the entire family had already been slaughtered?*—so Kangri kept his thoughts on the subject to himself.

The wards were a product of superstitions that had lingered for centuries or more, but now it seemed that superstition was reality. *Perhaps,* he thought, *every house ought to have such wards.* And as he glanced around he realized that many of them did. A shudder went through him then. He would have to make some for his new home to keep dark things from slipping in through windows at night.

Windows.

To his right was the small hut where Wei the glass-blower lived alone. He was called this because he made windows for the village. As Kangri approached the door, it creaked open slowly as though a breeze had blown it. And there was a wind down off the mountains that day. But a shadow fell across his mind then, and he remembered the door to another silent house he had entered.

Kangri hesitated.

When Wei appeared in the partially open door, the young man let out a long breath and smiled at his own anxiety.

"Wei, you were supposed to come to see me today," he said. "You were going to measure for my windows."

The old man walked with a stoop from his work. Now he glanced up at Kangri and scowled. "Windows? What are windows? They are not important. We should all have houses without windows, without doors. How else to be safe? Do not bother me with such things now."

Kangri stared at him, blinking back his surprise. "But . . . my new house."

"Ah, windows," Wei muttered, waving Kangri away. "When the monsters are dead, we can talk about windows."

Before Kangri could plead with him further, Wei turned to go back into the house and shut the door. He could hear the old man muttering still and the click of a lock as it was slid into place.

With a sigh, mind awhirl as he tried to figure out what to do without windows, Kangri turned to walk back toward his new home. Even as he did so he heard shouts from farther up the river. Alarmed, he ran to the bridge and looked to the north. On the bank of the river nearest him a small band of nomads was approaching. They were dressed as always in leather and fur, thick hats upturned on either side. All but the youngest had thin beards.

In all there were eight of them, though the last two were dragging a wooden cart with two burdens in the back. They shouted loudly to rouse the attention of the village as they followed the line of the river into the center of Lingka. By the time they reached the bridge, Kangri had been joined by perhaps a dozen others, including Tsochen, the father of his intended.

The nomads seemed more gaunt than usual, and grim. The only one Kangri knew well was Ritsu, who was small and much more talkative than the others in his tribe. With them was also Ganjin, to whom most of the nomads looked for leadership. He was larger in stature than most of them and so was often called "son of the mountain."

Ganjin approached Tsochen and bowed his head to the man. "I am sorry that you have lost your son."

Tsochen inclined his head, but his eyes were on the

cart and the two long lumps there, covered in yak skin blankets. But it was Kangri, angry that his village seemed poisoned now by the terror that had been visited upon them, who first spoke to the nomads.

"What have you brought here, Ganjin?" he asked.

The huge man, the son of the mountain, looked down upon him with eyes as cold as winter. He glanced at Ritsu, who stared first at Kangri and then, out of respect, turned his attention to Tsochen. Ritsu walked back to the cart and pulled back one of the skins to reveal a human corpse. So ruined were its features that it would have been impossible to recognize. For a heartbreaking moment in which he could not breathe, Kangri thought this was Dawa. But though the corpse was splashed with blood and large portions of its flesh and bone missing as if torn away by enormous jaws, he realized that it was an adult body, and the clothes were the traditional garb of the nomadic people.

"It is Ken-de," Ritsu said, glancing at Kangri. "And here is what killed him."

The nomad pulled back the other blankets, and all those villagers who had gathered around moved forward, muttering and whispering to one another and to themselves at the sight of the thing that lay there. It was no animal they had ever seen. Its features were long and flat, its mouth impossibly broad and lined with hundreds of teeth so small, they might have been a baby's were it not for how sharp they were. Soft folds in its slick flesh might have been wounds or some hideous formation upon its body. It was long and thin, with three fingers on either hand. They looked strong, those fingers, though there were no claws to speak of on it. One of the hands was open, however, and on the leathery palm of the demon were a pair of small pits, ridged openings that had teeth of their own.

From those openings oozed an oily substance that Kangri was certain must be the same as that left behind in Dawa's bedroom.

All eyes turned to Tsochen, father of the missing boy, who had been stolen from sleep by this thing, whose finger had been eaten. Who would never be coming home again.

Tsochen's face was like stone. He stared at the demon and at the dead nomad on the cart, and then he turned to Ganjin. "Thank you for showing this to me. You killed it?"

"No," the son of the mountain said, shaking his head so that his shaggy hair flew around him. "The holy men at the monastery, they killed it and left it for us."

"It is dead now, the thing that came into the village?" Tsochen said, voice faltering.

"Yes," Ganjin agreed, nodding slowly. "But there are many demons in the mountain, and perhaps now in the valley as well. Far too many."

One Night Until the Full Moon

Oz had a list of places he wanted to go before he died. Not an actual list, of course, for that would have required picking up a pen and writing things down. The list was in his head, and Hong Kong had always been very near to the top, right beneath Australia, Brazil, and Constantinople circa A.D. 1100. Given that the last one was impossible, he had managed to hit two of his top three places in as many days. Unfortunately, his visit to Australia had consisted of less than twenty-four hours in Sydney, most of which he spent asleep in a dingy hotel near the airport.

Just before he had gotten onto the plane that morning he had promised Australia he would return. He doubted

Australia had taken any notice, but it was a promise he planned to keep.

It was after dark when he had landed at Hong Kong International Airport, a stone's throw from Victoria Harbor. Now he sat in the backseat of a taxi and gazed out the neon-splashed windows at a sparkling wonderland of light and commerce. Everywhere he went there were flags with small pink flowers on them, and he wondered if they were the reason it was named Hong Kong, which was Cantonese for "the fragrant harbor." He'd read that in a book at some point, though now that he thought of it, there had been something about incense factories, too.

All of the things that weighed so heavily upon him—the people he'd left behind, the coming full moon, the knowledge that Cain was tracking him—seemed somehow less important as he gazed at the towering steel and glass of Hong Kong Island. He knew that there was more to Hong Kong than this—that the mainland portions were mostly rural, like much of China—but in his mind, *this* was Hong Kong. This island was where the action was, high finance and rampant consumerism and wild nightlife.

When his mind registered the phrase *wild nightlife* he shook his head in wry amusement. He had a feeling that was true in more ways than one. The way this city had grown up, it was a crossroads of the world in ways that even New York and London were not. The British had taken a slab of barren rock off the coast of China and created from it the ultimate modern city, a place that was about indulgence, with hardly any historical or cultural landmarks. And yet all through the city, in the shadow of those gleaming spires, there were streets and districts that catered to the Chinese population and to their culture and traditions.

Hong Kong was the glittering jewel of the Orient, but between the skyscrapers and the marketplaces were deep and ancient shadows. From all Oz had heard about it, Hong Kong was a city where almost anything could happen and where things were often not what they seemed. The denizens of this city ranged along the social and moral spectrums. According to Giles, it had more than its share of demons as well. Oz wondered as he stared out the windows of the cab into a dark alley if he were the only werewolf in Hong Kong. It was both troubling and exciting for him to think that perhaps he was not.

The taxi driver was Chinese, as was nearly everyone else on the streets. *He's remarkably clean cut for a cabbie,* Oz thought, *even uses gel to spike his hair.* Oz spoke only a couple of words of Chinese, *thank you* and *hello* being pretty much the extent of his linguistic abilities in most languages that weren't English. Fortunately, in Hong Kong, that wasn't an issue. With its status as one of the world's major centers of commerce, most people spoke some English, and a great many spoke it fluently. Or so he'd read on the plane from Sydney.

That would change when he got to Tibet.

It wasn't impossible for an American traveler to get into China these days. But there was paperwork, documentation, forms with the embassy, especially if it wasn't a business trip. On the other hand, even though Hong Kong was part of China now—at least officially—Americans could travel for up to thirty days in Hong Kong, pretty much no questions asked.

From there . . . well, if one was willing to break the rules, getting into mainland China was simple enough. There was nothing simple, however, about traveling to Tibet from Hong Kong without knowing Chinese and without the appropriate documents. It was a long way, too many opportunities to be stopped and thrown out of the country or imprisoned.

So he had to find another way.

That was a concern for another day, however. Tonight, his one worry was in the sky above Hong Kong. Though the lights of the city obscured much of the sky, he could still see the moon, not quite full but oh so close. He could feel it up there and his heart beat faster every time he glanced at it. Full as it was, he tried his best *not* to look, but it drew his eyes.

Talk about cutting it close, Oz thought. The following night would be the first of three when the moon would cause his transformation, would draw out the wolf.

"Bonham Strand," the cab driver said, breaking Oz out of his reverie. "You wanted east or west?"

Oz consulted the book in his hand, inside which he had scrawled down the information Giles had given him.

"West," he said. "It's a side road, though. Yeun Po Street."

"Right," replied the driver.

The cab's interior was silent again as the man navigated the traffic in Hong Kong. Bonham Strand seemed to appear suddenly. Thus far they had driven through districts with professional buildings and, near the harbor, some less than desirable streets with warehouses and fish markets. But Bonham Strand West was something else entirely. It was as though they had stepped back in time. Both sides of the street were lined with open shops. Merchants stood in front of some of them, hawking their wares. Oz spotted a place that sold live snakes, and he doubted they were meant to be pets. He saw bookshops and herbalists and restaurants that were little more than alcoves.

To a lot of people, Oz knew, Bonham Strand would have seemed charming. But there was something sinister about it as well, some dark truth that seemed to lurk behind the store fronts just out of reach. If there was a place in Hong Kong that he was going to find answers, he felt suddenly certain this was it.

"Here. Yuen Po Street," the driver said.

He pulled to the curb and Oz paid him, tipping what he thought was reasonable even though he hadn't remembered to check to see what was customary. Backpack over his shoulder and duffel in his hand, he got out of the cab and barely noticed as it drove away. Bicycles flashed past him, and people milled about. Merchants called to them as they passed.

There were plenty of shops on Yuen Po Street, but compared with the thoroughfare of Bonham Strand West, it seemed even more archaic, a narrow little way where fewer pedestrians strolled and where the scents of food and spice and herbs were stronger and more exotic. Oz's stomach rumbled, and he vowed to get something to eat as soon as he was settled.

Halfway down Yuen Po Street he found what he was looking for: a butcher shop with a wooden sign painted bright crimson with black letters. Oz took a breath and paused in front of the door, then pushed inside. A bell above the door rang. Behind one of the huge display cases—in which cuts of meat gleamed a rich red—stood a girl perhaps seventeen years old with ribbons in her hair. She was tiny, very pretty, and dressed in styles he might have seen in L.A.

The girl greeted him brightly in Chinese and then looked at him expectantly. Oz regarded her a moment and then raised his hands in a gesture that he hoped indicated how stupid he felt for being in her country and not speaking her language.

"I'm looking for Qing," he said.

Her lips turned upward in a sweet smile. "You must be the werewolf."

Oz dropped his duffel. He stared at the girl, completely at a loss for words. It had barely registered with him that she had spoken to him in English. To have someone be so friendly while they were talking to a complete stranger about something so inconceivable . . . well, it had thrown him.

"I'm Oz."

She came around the display case and put out her hand. "Jinan. Qing's my father. He's out back. So you're going to be staying with us for the full moon, huh? Kind of cool."

"It is?"

Jinan rolled her eyes. "*Sshyeah.* Never met a werewolf before."

Oz stood awkwardly in the middle of the butcher shop. Jinan gazed into his eyes as though searching for the wolf in him and mystified because she couldn't find it. After a moment she shrugged. "Guess I should get my father," she said.

"Thanks."

As Jinan turned, she tossed her head so her braids flipped behind her. Walking back into the rear of the shop, down a hall that had a number of heavy doors on either side, she glanced back and smiled. A ripple of awareness went through Oz and suddenly he was sure she was flirting with him. He found it both flattering and disquieting.

Jinan disappeared into another room at the back of the shop. Oz heard low voices but he did not think the language was Chinese. It certainly wasn't English. A moment later the hall was filled by an enormous, bald Chinese man with an amiable smile and the broadest shoulders Oz had ever seen. He wore a white shirt with no sleeves, and on his left shoulder there was a small tattoo, a dragon partially hidden behind its wings.

"I am Qing," the man said. "You are the friend that Rupert Giles told me about?"

Only when Oz heard his accent did he realize that Jinan had none.

"Oz. That's me. I'm sorry to cause trouble for—"

Qing gave him a good-natured pat on the shoulder that nearly knocked Oz over.

"No trouble, my friend. I owe my life to Rupert Giles. To keep you from harming yourself or someone else for a few nights, that is little enough to pay for my life, don't you think?"

"When you put it that way—"

A voice interrupted them from the hall speaking rapid Chinese, and Oz glanced past Qing to see Jinan returning alongside a fortyish woman who could only have been her mother. The woman strode into the middle of the store and crowded Qing, ignoring Oz except to point at him. It was obvious she was cussing her husband out, and Oz scratched idly at an ear as he waited for it to subside. But when the woman stopped, Qing started in, quieter but with just as much weight to his tone. He did not so much as glance at Oz.

After more than a minute of this, the woman took a deep breath, then turned and beamed at Oz with the brightest and yet somehow least genuine smile he had ever seen.

"Welcome to our home," she said with a quick nod, forming the words the same way he would have spoken the same ones in Chinese, like someone who only knows what they're supposed to mean and doesn't really understand them.

"Thank you," Oz replied.

But Mrs. Qing—Oz had no idea if Qing was his last name or his first—was already turning away. She marched down the hall and was met outside that back room by a skinny old man who took one look at her and then glared at Oz. Then they both disappeared into the back once more.

Oz picked up his duffel. "I'm sensing it might be better if I found somewhere else to stay."

"No," Qing said, frowning deeply. "That will not be

necessary. I owe a great debt to Rupert. And it would not be right to let you go now. It would be . . . irresponsible. My wife is nervous, that is all. But you will be safe. And so will we."

Jinan sighed and rolled her eyes. "We'll be *fine.* My mother and my grandfather are always freaking out over something."

She beamed at him, and Oz did not have the heart to tell her they were right to be afraid. This time tomorrow night, if they did not have him locked up good, he might well be ripping all their throats out. It might have made Jinan just a little less welcoming.

Qing nodded as though that put an end to the discussion. "Now, my friend, would you like something to drink? Or to eat? Have you had dinner?"

"I haven't, actually."

The big man said something to his daughter in their native language, and Jinan nodded happily, then reached out to grab Oz's duffel.

"Come on, I'll fix you something."

"Thanks, but that's kind of—"

He had been about to say *heavy.* The duffel was kind of heavy.

Jinan carried it as though it weighed nothing at all.

First Night of the Full Moon

Oz was cold.

Outside, the sun was going down and darkness was stealing across the city. Inside Qing's butcher shop, Oz had stripped down to just his boxer shorts and now he paced the small room. He was self-conscious about being so close to naked in the home of strangers.

Nice people, though, Qing's family. Even the mother and grandfather, once they had gotten used to the idea that they were going to have a werewolf for a houseguest whether they liked it or not. And Jinan, she was a sweet kid. *Kid*? he thought now. The girl might have looked younger, but he had discovered she was twenty. It wasn't just her appearance, though. She had a kind of energy that made her seem younger. Jinan wasn't immature, though. Just sort of excitable. She had played tour guide for him all day, giving him the whirlwind look at Hong Kong. The nights were going to be terrible, but Oz was already enjoying his days here. It really was an extraordinary place.

And the meals . . . Jinan's mother might not want him here, but she fed him like she didn't ever want him to leave.

Oz smiled even as he shivered, wrapping his arms around himself. He paced the little room, a dozen steps in any direction. Again, he shuddered, exhaled and saw the plume of his breath.

It was cold.

But that was what you got in a meat locker.

At first he had been hesitant about being held in this room, but Qing had explained that he hoped the cold would make the wolf tired. The walls were thick and there were no windows and the single huge door was steel. They had chained and padlocked the handle from the outside about ten minutes ago.

Oz felt itchy. It didn't happen every time, but a lot. Right before the change, he felt itchy. He scratched at his belly and his legs and felt the hair standing up on the back of his head again. Right before the *Sargasso Drifter* had docked in Sydney he had shaved off what little beard he'd grown, but now there was stubble on his face again, and that itched as well.

The air was cold. But his skin grew hot to the touch.

"Oz?"

Jinan. Her voice came from just outside the door.

He stretched his arms out as if unfamiliar with them. With a snort, he began to pace again, faster than before. His heart raced, and he felt as though he might explode, as though he would tear himself apart. The horrible truth was, he was about to.

"Can I get you anything? Do you have enough water?" she asked, sweet voice now tentative, even a little afraid.

Of course she's afraid. She should be.

Oz wasn't sure if those thoughts were his own.

"The moon's rising, Jinan. Go away," he growled, still pacing quickly back and forth, prowling the floor of the meat locker.

"It's not totally dark yet," she said. "If you need something, I can still—"

Not totally dark, he wanted to say, *but the moon is up. The moon's full in the sky and* in *me, now. Slicing right through me.*

But all that came out was a low snarl. His tongue ran over his fangs, and he dropped to the ground, went down on all fours, skin burning as the fur grew there.

With a roar, he threw himself at the steel door. His skull thunked against it, and he was dazed a moment, but he slunk back into the room and then raced at it again, the muscles in his haunches working like pistons as he crashed into the door again.

"Oz?" Jinan called, voice cracking.

But Oz was gone.

The moon had come, and with it, the wolf.

Jinan flinched when the wolf hit the door the first time. She stepped backward, raising a hand to her mouth. Her tongue snaked out and wet her lips, for they had gone dry. She found it hard to swallow. Quickly she glanced toward the front of the shop, toward the windows. There was still a faint glimmer of light, but the night had come on fast.

When the monster slammed into the door a second time, Jinan let out a small yelp of surprise, despite herself. The door shook on its frame and the metal bulged slightly, a rounded dent that would be barely noticeable later but shocked her profoundly now.

"Oh," Jinan whispered, staring at the door, at the chains on the huge steel handle to the meat locker. But the thumping against the door did not come again. The werewolf seemed to have settled down, at least for the moment.

Oz was so quiet and sweet. Jinan had seen extraordinary and horrible things in her life, knew many beings who had more than one aspect, but usually the good ones were good and the bad ones bad. Werewolves were something else entirely.

A noise behind her made her start, and she turned to find her father standing there watching her.

"Troubling, is it not?" he said to her in Chinese.

"Yes," Jinan replied. Though there was something compelling about it as well. In her mind she saw Oz's features and tried to imagine what he looked like now.

Qing nodded grimly. "These three nights will seem very long."

Chapter Seven

Third Night of the Full Moon

The shop was closed, but the work went on. Jinan stood shuddering inside one of the meat lockers in the back of her father's butcher shop. These past few nights had been difficult, and not merely because it was nerve-racking having a werewolf on the premises. To make room for Oz, her father had been forced to overload the other three coolers, which meant that restocking the display cases in front was a much more complicated job than it normally would have been.

The days she had spent showing Oz around Hong Kong had been a lot of fun, no question about that. But he was hardly the ideal houseguest.

Jinan stood in the meat locker and glanced around in search of a box of chicken parts she had just put in here a few days earlier. At length she located it and then piled two frozen ducks on top before hefting it and turning toward the door. Her mother and grandfather were cleaning the front of the shop, the floor and windows, the display cases, while she and her father restocked for the next morning. Often Jinan wished they could put the task off until morning, but it was simply easier to take care of it at night. Then she did not have to wake up as early in the morning.

She stepped out of the cooler, burden in her arms, and pushed it closed with her back. Immediately across the hall was the door to the empty meat locker—though "empty" wasn't really accurate. It didn't have any merchandise in it, but it was most certainly occupied. There were more dents now, and the previous morning Oz had helped her father install brackets and a heavy iron bar across the door.

Jinan had not been sleeping well thanks to the sounds that came from within that meat locker. She doubted any of her family had gotten a good night's sleep of late.

As these thoughts skimmed through her mind, she paused and glanced at that barred door. A frown creased her forehead. Only now that she was thinking about how noisy it had been the previous two nights did it occur to her how quiet it seemed in that locker tonight. For a moment she cocked her head and simply listened, but the box in her arms, weighted down by the frozen ducks, seemed to grow heavier. She grunted as she resettled it in her arms and then started toward the front of the store.

A noise from beyond that door made her hesitate. Jinan turned toward the door just as it quaked with a loud thump that echoed in the hall and the crack of splintering wood.

Jinan whispered a prayer and stared at the door. *Wood, where is there wood? The door's made of steel.* Then she realized what it was. The hinges were bolted to the wall. Now one of them had separated from the wood by half an inch.

"Oh, no." Jinan backed away from the door.

The werewolf crashed against it again and it shook, the bar across the door bending slightly, the dent much larger than before. One of the brackets had begun to tear loose just like the upper hinge. Jinan backed away. "Father!" she called.

It struck the door a third time, harder than before, and the shriek of splintering wood and dull thump of warped metal made her hold her breath for just an instant. Then Jinan dropped the box and the frozen ducks and turned toward the front of the shop. "Dad!" she called again, screaming this time.

Qing was standing at the other end of the hall staring at Jinan as she ran. The loudest crash yet came from behind her, a rending of wood and bang of metal that made her heart beat even faster. Despite all her anxiety about the werewolf, there were images of Oz in her head, and she had found it difficult to separate the two. Now, terror did that for her.

"The door is giving way!" she shouted in Chinese as she ran, nearly stumbling, into her father's arms.

"I suppose it was too much to expect it to withstand the wolf's strength for three nights," Qing said, resignation and sadness in his voice.

With a horrible crack that Jinan could feel inside her chest, like being too close to the fireworks, the door of the meat locker tore free of its hinges and crashed to the floor. Just inside the door, the werewolf howled and Jinan suddenly felt very tiny. It stepped forward and she saw that its face was bleeding from its collisions with the door, bright red blood matting its fur and dripping from its snout.

"Stop him!" her father shouted to the rest of the family. "He must not be allowed to leave the shop!"

Even as Qing spoke, Jinan's mother came up beside him.

"Leave?" she said, voice tinged with panic. "I'm more worried about him *staying*."

The werewolf snarled and advanced slowly down the hall. Blood and saliva dripped from its maw, splashing the wood floor. Jinan cursed under her breath and braced herself.

Her flesh began to ripple. To change. Muscles bulged, and her skin turned bruise-black, became slick as oiled canvas. Her hands grew and lengthened into claws, ears turning up and out, long and pointed. From her lower back, bone and flesh flowed outward into a long, powerful tail.

Jinan's skull split open, and a furnace of flames erupted from within, fire flickering from eyes as well.

She glanced over at her parents and her grandfather and saw that they had all transformed as well. All her life she had loved her family but been disturbed by what she was. Not because she was ashamed of her heritage as a Kaohsiung demon but because she spent all her days pretending to be something else. Now as she stood side by side with them she knew she had never felt more like they were a family.

The werewolf hesitated, letting out a low, curious growl.

Then it attacked. At first it ran on four feet but as it neared her father, the beast stood. It lunged at Qing and he grappled with it, just as fast as the wolf itself. His huge, thick tail whipped around and staggered the wolf, but then it was on him again, roaring its lunatic hunger. Qing pummeled the wolf twice in its wide, hideous, terrifying head. Bloody slobber flew, and the raging light in its eyes dimmed a moment.

Then it attacked again. Qing tried to stop it, and the wolf raked its huge claws across his obsidian skin.

Jinan gasped as her father cried out in pain.

"He is too strong!" Qing said.

"We'll help you, Father. But try not to hurt him. It's Oz!"

Her mother scowled, slithered in her demon form across the floor and looked for an opening in the bloody struggle. "Perhaps, Jinan," she snapped, "you should be more concerned about your father's blood than the monster's."

A sad chill passed through Jinan, despite the fire blazing from her open skull. The idea that something might happen to her father was awful. If she had to choose, she would of course choose her family. But Oz was an innocent, not to blame for the savagery of the wolf.

She tensed, ready to attack him. The flames on her head roared higher and it leaked from her eyes. Qing lashed at Oz with his tail again, and when the werewolf tried to claw it, he struck the beast again. That moment was enough distraction that Jinan's grandfather was able to get behind the monster, behind Oz. With a hiss, her grandfather leaped upon the monster's back and wrapped his legs around its chest, his arms around its throat. He began to choke.

The wolf snarled and staggered, trying to tear him off. Jinan's mother latched onto one arm, and her father to the other, and together the three of them drove the beast to the ground. Its snout hit the wood floor with a bloody thump.

"Wait!" Jinan said. "Hold on."

She turned and fled from the room back to the meat locker she had just come from. Hanging from the ceiling were sides of beef and pork, impaled on hooks that dangled from thick iron chains. With inhuman speed and strength, Jinan tore the chains down from the ceiling, ripping them right out of the wood. She pulled off the meat and then ran back to the front of the shop.

Her father was on the werewolf's back on the ground. Her mother and grandfather were helping him keep it pinned to the floor. It lashed out with its claws, bucked against them, and Jinan could see that, despite her family's strength, they would not be able to keep the monster down much longer.

"Here!" she cried.

Qing glanced up, saw what she had, and grinned. Fire flickered in the recesses of his mouth, inside that smile, as he reached out to take the chains from her and began to bind the werewolf.

"We need your weight here, too, Jinan," he told her.

And so she threw herself into it, helping to hold Oz down as her family wrapped it in heavy steel chains. Her grandfather rapped the wolf on the skull hard enough to stun it a moment. When it bucked again, nearly throwing Qing off despite the chains, he wrapped his right arm around the bound wolf's throat and choked it until it began to slip into unconsciousness.

The werewolf slumped to the floor.

"I am sorry, my friend," Qing said. "But you will thank me in the morning."

Jinan stared at the wolf—at Oz—so still, save for the rise and fall of his massive chest. She shifted her form again, the fire sputtering out as her flesh reformed. With a shudder, Jinan tossed back her braids and stared down at the slumbering werewolf.

"Morning seems so far away," she whispered.

But no one was listening. Her grandfather and her father dragged the wolf by its chains along the hall back to the open meat locker. They could not afford to empty another, and the door to this one was destroyed. Jinan knew her father would end up staying up all night, keeping an eye on Oz, despite the chains, and she felt badly for him. But her heart ached for the beast as well.

"Come then," her father said, when he had settled the unconscious wolf down in the meat locker. "Let's clean up the shop. We have to be ready to open for business in the morning."

As they turned away from the monster, Jinan's mother stopped Qing in the hall. "Never again. Promise me, husband. Whatever your debt to Rupert Giles, it has been repaid."

Exhausted and battered, weakened by wounds sustained both in its attempts to escape and in its melee with the Kaohsiung demons, the wolf stirred back to consciousness for only a moment. It sensed its confinement, and then surrendered to the chains and to the encroachment of sleep.

The wolf was a monster, but even a monster could dream. The dreaming mind was a strange landscape, littered with fragments of imagery from the consciousness of the wolf, and that of the man.

In the dream, Jordy is running.

Past the piano in Aunt Maureen's living room, around the coffee table, fleeing in abject terror, panting, eyes wide . . .

Jordy shrieks. "It's gonna get me! The monster's gonna get me!"

The little boy is prey. The wolf hunts him through the house. Jordy has run through the living room. Now the wolf, swift and deadly, makes a hurried circuit of the house and lurks in the dining room, just out of sight. When Jordy barrels into the room, the wolf pounces on the tender-fleshed child and drives him to the floor, fingers hooked into claws . . .

Tickling him.

"No one escapes the tickle monster, Jordy!" Oz declares mercilessly.

He touches the boy's belly and neck, under his arms, the crook behind his knee, and Jordy howls and squeals with tortured laughter.

"Stop! Quit it, Daniel! I'm gonna bite you!"

On the edge of panic, the boy snaps at him, bites his finger . . .

The skin is broken. Oz is bleeding.

Jordy has passed on the curse.

Oz holds up his hands, and what is a tiny cut, the smallest spot of blood, blossoms suddenly. The blood flows out over his hands, warm and rich, its copper scent tantalizing, delicious. He relishes that blood on his hands even as he recoils from the sight of it, from the knowledge that though that small cut was on his flesh, this blood all over him is not his own.

A shudder goes through the great sleeping body of the wolf and through the soul of the young man hidden within it.

In his dream, the blood on Oz's hands becomes fur, and the fur spreads. He is the wolf now, and the wolf desires only more blood.

The forest sprouts up around it, and black lips curl back from razor-sharp fangs and the wolf turns its head up to the night sky and there she is, its mistress. The moon gazes down upon the beast, and it opens its throat and lets loose a howl that echoes back across the ages, joining with the cries of its ancestors.

It drops to all fours and begins to prowl the woods, picking up speed as it goes. Branches whip the wolf's back and haunches as it bounds through the forest . . . and then it pauses. Again it lifts its head, but this time the moon has not drawn its attention. The wolf raises its snout and sniffs the breeze.

Prey. It has caught the scent of prey. The sheer joy it had taken in its surroundings dissipates. The wolf crouches low to the ground, a rumble in its chest audible only to the beast itself, and it begins to slink through the trees. By scent it tracks its prey.

Then it hears music. It stops, startled by the sudden intrusion. After a moment, a dark anger rising up in it now, it continues on, over a small crest within those woods. It finds itself looking down upon a paved path that winds through the woods . . . a park . . . perhaps. Its prey sits on a wooden bench on the other side of that black paved ribbon and strums a guitar, picking out notes with an expression less of frustration and more of curiosity.

The wolf hesitates. It knows this prey.

When the girl comes striding across the grass to the guitar player, the wolf takes several steps back, hiding itself beneath overhanging branches, behind a screen of leaves. Not because it does not want to be seen, but because it does not want to see.

Her. The wolf does not want to see her.

Willow.

It turns to flee noisily through the undergrowth, crashing along blindly, panting, snapping at shadows.

It reaches a clearing and discovers it is not alone.

Veruca is there. It can feel the desire radiating from her.

Oz is not the wolf. No matter what Veruca says, he will not allow himself to be the wolf. His body is a cage for the wolf, not simply a different face, like the crescent moon masking its fullness. But why, then, is the wolf attacking Veruca when they should be mating? Why does the wolf, a simple, stupid animal, tear out her throat and feel the warm splash of her blood on its snout?

"Oz?"

The wolf stands, turns quickly, and Willow is there on the other side of the clearing. But he is not the wolf anymore. He is just Oz.

Just Oz.

With Veruca's blood smeared on his chin and painting his cheeks.

And he is still hungry.

Twenty-eight Nights Until the Full Moon

With a grunt of terror, Oz opened his eyes, breathing quickly, the world around him thick with the surreal quality that always lingered when he woke from the midst of a dream. A terrible dream.

He glanced around at the walls of the meat locker, at the ravaged doorway, steel door propped just inside the room against the wall. It took him several moments to realize where he was, to push away the remnants of his dream and piece together where he was and what had happened. There was a moment of relief as the knowledge that it was over for another month washed over him. But then he considered that door and wondered what the cost had been.

The beast had escaped.

Do I have more blood on my hands?

Oz began to sit up and then slumped back to the floor. He glanced down and saw that he was loosely draped in thick iron chains. They stank of meat. The chains were wrapped around his chest and arms and legs. Otherwise, he was naked.

"This is different," Oz muttered.

He began to slide out of the chains. The wolf was much larger than he was, and so it was a simple thing to extricate himself from the heavy iron bonds. Heart heavy, afraid to leave the locker because of what he might find, he located his backpack and got himself another pair of boxers, then dressed in the same clothes he'd had on the day before. There was noise out at the front of the shop. A bell rang, indicating that someone had entered. A customer, he hoped. If it was business as usual for Qing and his family, that had to be a good sign.

As Oz buttoned his shirt, he heard footsteps in the hall, and then Qing appeared in the doorway.

"Good morning, my friend," the big man said.

Oz could not meet his eyes, though relief washed over him at the man's use of the word *friend.* It meant no one had been seriously hurt, despite the wolf's escape.

"Morning. And thanks."

"I am sorry about the chains, but you gave us a bit of trouble last night."

"So I saw," Oz replied. He took a deep breath and finally looked at his host. "Don't apologize. I'm grateful for your help."

Oz ran both hands through his hair, then stashed as much as he could carry in his backpack. He glanced at the duffel. "Would it be all right with you if I left some stuff here? Hopefully I'll pick it up on my way back to the States. And if I don't come back . . . you can just dump it. Sell it or whatever."

"As you wish," Qing replied, with a small nod.

With a slow nod of his own in return, Oz picked up his pack and walked with Qing to the front of the shop. Though he liked these people very much, he felt terrible now and wanted nothing more than to be away from them, out of their lives as quickly as possible. He'd imposed himself—and his curse—upon them long enough.

The front of the shop was testament to that. Qing's wife and her father were wrapping packages for a customer, but he didn't see Jinan anywhere. One of the display cases was shattered. Its debris had been cleaned up, but it was empty now, and he wondered how much meat they had lost in the process. *What did I cost them between that door and the stock?* There were gouges in the wall big enough for him to have put his head into them.

Oz sighed. "Guessing most of your honored guests don't trash the place. Whatever you owed Giles? Pretty much paid in full."

Qing rose up proudly at these words, but he seemed gravely serious. "It is a debt that can never be fully repaid. It has been our pleasure to watch over you these past nights, and to aid you on your journey."

The bell rang again as the customer departed. Qing's wife looked at Oz and instead of the anger he expected to see on her features, he found sadness there. Her father, however, glared at him.

"On . . . journey," the old man said in heavily accented English. "You understand, American boy? Moon is gone. You be gone, too."

"No argument," Oz said.

He shook Qing's hand, but the two said nothing, understanding each other well enough. Then Oz went to the door and pushed it open, bell ringing again.

"You have map and address for Wuxi shop?" Qing's wife asked.

Oz nodded.

She smiled. "Come back to see us. After you cured, okay?"

"With bells on," he told her.

Then he left the butcher shop behind, shouldering his pack and making his way along Yuen Po Street, out onto Bonham Strand, and east, walking fast.

The moon was gone for another month.

But the clock had started ticking again.

In the doorway of an herbal medicine shop on Bonham Strand, Jinan watched Oz walk away. He should have looked so out of place, this short American guy with his red hair and his high-top sneakers, yet Oz walked as though he were completely unaware of his surroundings, or totally comfortable with them. Jinan thought it must be the latter.

Oz passed a small clutch of teenage poseurs Jinan knew. They acted tough, wanting more than anything to be noticed with their slick hair and dark glasses, minds full of imagery from too many Tsui Hark and John Woo films. Under normal circumstances they would have harassed Oz, stepped out in front of the lone American guy with the faded backpack and menaced him, just for their own amusement. One of them, a guy whose hair fell in long bangs across his face, did start toward Oz, but then he paused and turned back toward his friends, waving a hand in the air as though he'd changed his mind.

And change it he had. *But why?* Jinan thought she knew. They sensed something off him, something they did not want any part of.

She was fascinated, both by Oz himself and by the journey he had undertaken, this trip to a fabled monastery in Tibet where masters practiced mystical arts away from the prying eyes of the world. With a last, regretful look down Yuen Po Street, Jinan snatched her own heavy pack from the ground, slung it over her shoulder, and started after Oz, careful not to be seen.

Oz walked for miles, carefully following the map of Hong Kong that Qing had given him the day before. There was public transportation he might have taken, but it all seemed to get him where he was going by very circuitous routes. And he really didn't mind the walking, the exploration seemed just another part of his journey. From Bonham Strand his path took him into an eccentric neighborhood that seemed far more Westernized in its bid for tourism. Retail shops and nightclubs lined the streets, and he passed a number of non-Asians as he made his way through the morning rush.

Soon he found himself on a long, busy road lined with old but elegant apartment buildings. Oz had an image in his mind that suggested everyone in Hong Kong lived in shining steel high-rises, the wealthier they were, the nearer the top. But these perfectly maintained buildings told him otherwise. If he had a lot of money and wanted to live in Hong Kong, he would certainly choose this neighborhood over the more modern neighborhoods.

He passed a number of museums, both art and science, and stood and gaped, dumbfounded, in front of the Museum of Tea Ware in Hong Kong Park. It was a beautiful building on Cotton Tree Drive. A plaque in Chinese and English announced it as the former official residence of the commander of the British Forces and the city's oldest colonial building, having been built in 1846.

But . . . it was a museum of tea ware.

Vaguely amused by that sight and marveling at the other parts of the city his journey took him through, he was able, at last, to shake the dark shadow of the previous night from his mind. Qing and his family had known what they were getting into. He owed them, certainly, but there was nothing he could do to repay them now except to stay away the next time the moon was full.

Now, though, he let himself forget about them. He had to get to Tibet, and to do that, he had to find this demon halfling, Wuxi, that Qing had told him about.

Hours after he had set out, tired and hungry—having eaten nothing all day but a muffin and a juice he had bought in an American franchise store—Oz passed through several blocks of office buildings that housed law firms, investment brokerages, and tech companies and reached the darker part of the city. Fewer people walked here, though there were food vendors on the sidewalks to serve those who did. A flower shop on the corner was the brightest spot on the street. Though the sky was clear and blue, it seemed almost as though the sun did not reach all the way to this street—this street that had no marker declaring its name.

Halfway down the block he found the number he was looking for, an occult bookshop with filthy windows and plants hanging under the awning in front. Oz paused a moment outside, studied the map Qing had given him again, and confirmed that this was indeed his destination. He hefted his backpack and went through the front door.

No bell announced his entry.

"Hello?" he called as he stepped inside. "I'm looking for—" Oz blinked, alarm bells going off in his head.

"Wuxi?" he finished.

In the middle of the dark shop, whose walls were covered with shelves loaded with books and mystical artifacts, stood a short, ugly vampire with a cigarette dangling from his lips. But it wasn't the vampire Oz was looking at. It was the eight-foot demon with a face like a tiger and horns like a ram. His ears and lips were pierced, and gold rings dangled there; his fur was striated with black zebra stripes. In his hands, the big demon held a skinny, bespectacled, red-skinned demon with white hair and Yoda ears and two pair of stubby little horns on his scalp past which his hairline had long since receded. The little old demon guy looked terrified.

Oz regarded them coolly. "Got a feeling this is a bad time," he said. "I'll come back."

Chapter Eight

Twenty-eight Nights Until the Full Moon

Oz had no idea what kind of demon it was, and he didn't really care. *Big* was pretty much the only classification he needed at the moment. No way was he going to be able to just leave and let them give Wuxi a beating or even worse, but he needed half a minute to retrench, figure out the best way to proceed.

The ram-horned demon and his vampire sidekick weren't about to give it to him.

Oz took two steps back toward the door. He reached behind his back, trying to grab hold of the handle without turning away from them.

"Bad timing, kid," the vampire muttered with a snort of laughter that sent plumes of cigarette smoke shooting from his nostrils. Then he turned to the huge, stripe-furred demon. "Toss him out, Kenny."

The demon tossed Wuxi across the room, and the

scarecrow-thin old halfling crashed into a bookcase. A shelf broke with a loud crack, and when Wuxi hit the ground, books cascaded down on top of him. Oz turned around, grabbed the door handle, and yanked it open just as a hugely powerful hand clutched his shoulder and spun him around.

He was face to whiskers with the snorting demon, and his stomach gave a nauseous twist as he realized he was going to have to fight this thing. His life might even depend upon it. Oz's right hand tightened into a fist before he even realized he was doing it, and he slugged the stinking, filthy beast in the side of the head.

The demon let out a cat-like hiss.

Oz stared at it in disbelief. "Your name is Kenny?" he muttered.

"Kennu," it snarled.

"Canoe?"

With another horrible hiss, Kennu reached down between Oz's legs and lifted him easily off the ground. Oz swore loudly, beat at the demon's head, tried to kick himself free, but it was no use. For a single moment he stared down at the demon's head and realized he could be impaled on those horns in a second. Then Kennu roared and threw him through one of the plate-glass windows at the front of the store.

The impact hurt like hell, but the glass gave way, shattering into a million shards that sprinkled to the ground with a sound like an orchestra of wind chimes. Oz hit the pavement with a grunt, and all the air was knocked out of him. As he rolled, tiny bits of glass cut his hands and face.

Some of the people on the street scattered, disappearing into stores and crouching behind vendors' carts. Others just stood and stared. Oz ignored the spectators.

When he stood, shakily, in full view of a couple of dozen people out on the street and a vendor selling dumplings, Oz was growling low in his chest. The moon was gone, but down deep inside him, the beast remembered. He felt it there in him, the wolf. His tongue snaked out and licked the blood off his chin, sliding over a sliver of glass that sliced him there. Oz sucked in a painful breath. Then he reached inside his backpack and pulled out a stake. After what had happened in Fiji with Cain and the vampires, he had vowed to make sure he never left home without one. He had no idea how the bloodsucker had gotten to the shop without torching in the sun, but Oz figured he'd stake first, ask questions later.

The wood felt good in his hand. The tip was very sharp; he had whittled it himself.

Someone called his name.

Surprised, he glanced up to see Jinan standing by him. She came to him, began to help him brush glass off his shirt and pick it from his hair.

"What happened?" she asked. "You okay?"

Though aware of the shouts and sounds of things breaking that came now from inside the darkened shop, he frowned and stared at her. "What are you doing here?"

Jinan glanced away, unwilling to meet his gaze. "You're going to that monastery you told us about. I want to go, too. I want to learn the secrets of the dark arts. Plus, I want to get the hell out of Hong Kong."

"I'm not big on company," he told her. Jinan's brown eyes narrowed, and she flinched a little. But Oz didn't have time to worry about hurt feelings. He handed her his backpack. "Watch this for a second, will you?"

Heart hammering wildly in his chest, Oz sprinted back into the store with the stake in his hand. As he ran in, the vampire glanced over at him. Kennu didn't bother. He was too busy slamming Wuxi's head against the wall.

"Let's try that again," Oz muttered.

He ran straight at the vampire and, just as the leech

tried to grab him, Oz ducked low and lunged upward in a bone-crunching tackle that propelled him and the vampire over a display case filled with ornate urns and crystals. They crashed down in a cluster of flying limbs, but Oz was on top.

"American dog!" the vampire snarled. "Who do you think—"

Oz slammed his forearm against the vampire's throat, cutting off his words.

"Not dog," he said.

Then he punched the stake through its heart, and it exploded in a small cloud of cinders. The vampire had been arrogant and stunned that he would attack. Oz had gotten lucky. He hoped there was more luck where that came from.

Kennu's heavy boots stamped in a monstrous tantrum as he lifted Wuxi off the ground by his throat, still choking him. The halfling's glasses flew off as he batted at Kennu's grip. The massive demon pointed a long, clawed finger at Oz and snarled.

"You!" he said, tiger-face pinched with fury. "We let you live. You could have just walked away."

A thousand images flashed through Oz's head of Willow and Buffy and Xander. He shook his head.

"That's not how we do things back home."

The stake still in his hand, hoping to at least hurt Kennu, get him to drop Wuxi, Oz launched himself at the demon. It was a monumentally stupid thing to do, and he was well aware of that. But he wasn't about to walk away. Wuxi was a friend of Qing's and seemed innocent and harmless enough. More than that, though, there was a selfish reason.

Wuxi was his route to Tibet.

Kennu was faster than he looked. Without even putting Wuxi down, the big demon backhanded Oz hard enough to make him black out for a moment. He felt it as he hit the floor and rolled, but he was disoriented.

"This is Hong Kong. A whole different set of rules here," Kennu hissed. "You came a long way just to die."

Slowly, painfully, wiping blood from his face with the back of his hand, Oz rose once more to his feet. There was no way he could beat this thing. It was going to kill him. Oz was weighing his options when he saw movement behind Kennu, and a smile twitched at the edges of his lips.

"Actually? Still got a ways to wander," he told the demon. "You, though . . ."

Kennu roared in pain as the blade of a sword punched through his back, its bloody tip splitting skin and fur and protruding from his chest. The demon went down on his knees, stared at Oz a moment, and then the light went from its eyes and it fell to the floor.

". . . pretty much done," Oz told the dead demon.

Jinan stood behind the corpse, wiping the blade of the sword on its fur. "You could thank me, you know?" she chided him.

Oz nodded. "Thank you."

"You're welcome," she said. Then she turned a radiant smile upon Wuxi, who was tsking and clucking with his tongue as he surveyed the damage to his shop. "Here, old man. This belongs to you."

Jinan handed him the sword, and Wuxi brightened considerably, charmed by the girl. He thanked her, then proceeded to ignore them almost completely as he continued to examine broken artifacts and displays.

"So, where were we?" Jinan asked, arching an eyebrow as she looked at Oz again. "Oh, right. Talking about how I'm going with you to Tibet."

Oz shook his head, still feeling a bit muddled. "Bad idea. Things tend to get freaky around me."

Jinan scowled. "Please, it isn't like I'm human or anything. I can take care of myself."

At last Wuxi seemed to be paying attention to them. Oz realized that he must have been searching for his round little glasses, which were now set on the bridge of his nose again.

Wuxi did a courtly half-bow in front of Jinan with a flourish of his hands. "So we see, young Jinan." He gestured toward Kennu's corpse. "Your father will be very proud . . . after he punishes you for running off. Not that I'm going to tell him."

Then the skinny demon halfling turned to Oz. "You are the American that Qing told me about, yes? This is a big adventure you on. Must have been hard for you to leave your life behind you, eh?"

Wuxi had an accent even thicker than Jinan's mother's but it sounded bizarre coming from him, with his mottled red skin and four little horns. Qing had revealed that his entire family were Kaohsiung demons the first night Oz had stayed with them, but they *looked* human most of the time. Hearing English spoken in that accent was oddly surreal, almost as if Wuxi was putting him on. Clearly, though, that was not the case.

"Didn't have a choice," Oz told the shopkeeper.

"Getting back to me coming with you," Jinan prodded, her scarlet lips parted just slightly in that perfect smile, eyes twinkling.

Oz stared at her a long moment, rolling it over in his head. Wuxi obviously knew Jinan's family, was fond of her. He was willing to cooperate with the girl. Without Wuxi's help, getting to the monastery was going to be a good deal harder, but the last thing he wanted was someone else around to have to protect . . . from himself.

He turned his back to both of them and walked toward the door. "I'll find another way to Tibet."

"You forgetting something?" Jinan called, voice tight with anger.

When he glanced back he saw that she was holding his backpack. Oz went to take it from her, but the little demon halfling blocked his way.

"Don't be a fool, you," Wuxi said in his chittering voice. "Maybe you find another way, but not soon and not fast. You got a month before the moon come back. I can get you to Tibet *today*."

Today, Oz thought. *Today.* It was almost too good to believe.

Wuxi nodded as if he could see how attractive that prospect was to Oz. "But you wanna use Wuxi Travel Agency, you gotta take Jinan. She wanna go, it not up to you to tell her she can't."

It was well over an hour before the shop had been returned to some semblance of organization. Oz and Jinan had offered to help sweep up broken glass and put things back in order. Even though Oz had had to pay the old halfling nearly a third of the money he had left over from buying the airplane ticket from Sydney, that was a bargain considering the service Wuxi was about to provide. Oz figured the least he could do was help the old guy clean up his shop.

While he swept a bunch of broken glass from a dustpan into a trashcan, Oz heard Jinan speaking to Wuxi in Chinese. When he glanced over she gave him an apologetic look.

"Sorry. I just wanted to know why, if Wuxi's such a powerful magician, he can't just cast a spell to clean all of this up."

Oz nodded. It was a reasonable question.

Wuxi scowled. "You young people think you know everything. All kinds of magic. You think if I big sorcerer

I need to run shop? I got talent for translocation. That about it."

"I meant no offense, Wuxi," Jinan said. "I wish I could do half of what you do."

"You spend enough time with Master Shantou, you learn plenty," Wuxi promised.

When the cleanup was completed, Wuxi made a phone call. He nattered on in Chinese for a while, and though Oz could not understand him, he assumed the old man was complaining about the damage to the shop. When Wuxi hung up, he brushed his hands together.

"Good. They coming to fix window in an hour. Plenty of time. First, we get you something to eat so you not have to stop in Lhasa."

Oz stared at him. "Plenty of time? You mean you can get us to Tibet and be back here in an hour?"

"Maybe ten minutes," Wuxi explained. "But you two gotta eat something first."

And so they did. The shopkeeper sent Jinan and Oz back out onto the street to retrieve a late lunch for all three of them. While they were out, Jinan chattered incessantly about Tibet and the things she hoped to learn in the monastery. Jinan had interrogated her father on the subject after discovering that it was Oz's destination, and that had prompted her running away from home. After they were gone, Wuxi would tell Qing where Jinan had gone so that her parents would not think she had simply been stolen off the streets. Oz doubted that would make them worry any less, but as Wuxi had so firmly told him, it was not his place to say so.

Thanks to the information Jinan had gotten from her father, Oz confirmed that, as he had suspected, the monastery was not Buddhist. In truth, the adepts and students there couldn't be considered monks at all. But given that those in the valley below and any of the nearby villages thought of it as a monastery, it had come to be known as such.

By the time they returned, Oz carrying two large brown paper bags loaded with steaming chicken and noodles redolent with delicious scents and Jinan carrying a six pack of Coca-Cola, Wuxi had completed preparations for their departure. In the slanted light of early afternoon that splashed into the shop through the shattered window and filtered through the grimy plate glass that had not been broken, Oz could see that Wuxi had used chalk to draw a broad circle on the floor. Around its circumference the halfling had added Chinese characters and strange symbols that formed their own rings around the inner circle. Nine white candles burned at equal intervals on the outer rim.

As they entered, Wuxi glanced up proudly from his handiwork. "You ready? Good! Let's eat!"

Twenty minutes later they had scarfed down their entire meal. Oz was very full, and even a bit sleepy. He never felt fully rested after the nights of the full moon. Oz glanced at his watch. "Are you sure you don't want to wait until after they get here to repair the window?" he asked.

Wuxi frowned. "I thought you in a hurry?" Then he waved the exchange away. "Listen, you two gonna be cold. You don't have better jackets than that, you take a couple of old Wuxi jackets."

Oz had a sweatshirt in his pack, but it had already occurred to him that it might not be enough. He had assumed that as a Kaohsiung demon, Jinan's own fire would keep her warm. Now he glanced at her in concern. "How cold will it get up there?"

Wuxi laughed. "You going to the roof of the world, American boy. You don't have jacket, you freeze your ass off."

For a moment, the three of them stared at one another. Then Jinan giggled lightly, and Oz shrugged. "I guess I'll borrow that jacket," he said.

"Borrow?" Wuxi asked. "You *buy* the jacket. Jinan borrow. She coming back eventually. You, I don't know."

"Appreciate the vote of confidence."

The old halfling cackled and fetched them both heavy, wool-lined jackets. Oz slipped into his and found it too large for him, but he wasn't going to complain. He did wonder, however, if the jacket actually belonged to Wuxi at all, or if he had just given the demon twenty dollars for something that had been left behind by a customer.

The candles had burned down about a quarter of the way. They gave off an herbal scent that Oz had given up trying to identify five minutes after they had returned with the food. Wuxi ushered them inside the circle. Oz and Jinan both put their backpacks on. He glanced around, wondering exactly what was involved with this spell. Willow was a novice witch herself, and Oz had seen some magic. But with the sun streaming in the window, and the sort of broken down appearance of the magician in question, with his spectacles up on his forehead and his pants drooping a bit . . . it was hard to imagine any big magic was about to happen here.

Wuxi stood with them inside the circle. The moment he stepped within its boundaries, a kind of purplish smoke began to unfurl from the wicks of each of the nine candles. The halfling shopkeeper scratched himself, settled his specs down upon the bridge of his nose once more, and exhaled loudly. He placed his hands on his hips, and the purple smoke began to swirl around the outside edges of the circle like a gentle whirlwind.

"Keep hands and feet inside circle," Wuxi instructed them. "In event of emergency, scream really, really loud."

"That's reassuring," Jinan muttered. She shifted the weight of the pack on her back and turned to the magician. "Is this gonna take long? 'Cause I kind of have to—"

The world falls away around Oz, and he feels like his stomach is left behind. He gasps, inhaling purple smoke, and the backs of his eyes hurt. The pressure on his skull is intense, and his skin is suddenly very, very cold. He flails his limbs in the purple darkness, feet trying to find purchase on something solid, hands reaching out as though his arms might become wings upon which to glide through this unknowable ether.

There are things in the cold abyss. They caress him as he hurtles past, clutch at him. Something sharp stings his cheek, the leg of his jeans snags on some outstretched tendril jutting at him in the void.

His fingers touch something warm. A glimmer of light, of heat, in the nothingness. Another hand slips into his own. It is soft and human, an anchor to what is real. Oz feels his stomach churn again and he shudders, convulses. If not for the velocity and his efforts to maintain some kind of equilibrium he would bend and vomit up the spicy chicken and noodles and pray that it didn't get all over him.

Warmth from those fingers. Heat. Light.

Oz glances to one side and sees Jinan. Her eyes are wide with terror, but her jaw is set with determination. She will not give in to her fear. He realizes that it is her hand that he is holding, and his gaze goes to where their fingers are twined together.

Jinan smiles tentatively.

As if yanked from behind, Oz was brought up short. His head snapped back, and he stumbled slightly, letting go of Jinan's hand. Nauseated, he fell to his knees and breathed air greedily, doing his best not to throw up. Jinan was beside him. He saw her boots and then his eyes traveled up her denim-clad legs to her porcelain doll face and the sweet smile there. She glanced down at her hand curiously, and then her eyes ticked back toward him.

Oz struggled to stand, taking long breaths. Jinan didn't seem nearly as affected by their trip—*translocation,* Wuxi had called it.

"Lhasa, Tibet," Wuxi said. "Last stop. All passengers on their own from here."

Jinan turned toward the frail old demon, nearly awestruck. "That's amazing, Wuxi. You have to teach me how to do that."

Wuxi waved at her in false modesty, then straightened up. "Thank you for using Wuxi Travel," he announced, then lowered his voice. "Try not to get killed, Jinan. Your father never forgive me."

"I can take care of myself," she repeated.

With a grin, the demon halfling disappeared in a puff of purple smoke. Oz stared at the spot for a moment and then turned around. His eyes went wide as he took in the view before them. The city of Lhasa sprawled before them, rising up the side of Red Hill with a mystery and magnificence that made Oz wonder quite seriously for a moment whether Wuxi had transported them back in time as well as through space. It looked far more majestic in real life than it had in the travel guide. Oz wished that Wuxi had been able to get them a little closer to the monastery—the little demon had explained there were limits to how far he could translocate, especially with passengers—but he was glad he had had a chance to see Lhasa.

The site was breathtaking, first because of the ancient, massive, imposing structure of the Potala Palace that loomed over the city thirteen stories high. Oz had read about it, even seen pictures of the former residence of the Dalai Lama—the spiritual leader of Tibetan Buddhism—

but to see it in person was something else entirely. Below it, in the city proper, tourists wandered amidst monasteries and temples, flower gardens and trees integrated into the city's design as though nature and structure had grown together.

Oz had been interested in visiting Lhasa before. Now it pulled at him like the song of some mythical siren. He forced that longing away, however. He would have to visit Lhasa on the way back, when he had the luxury of wasting time.

He glanced to the north and saw the hills rising there, the mountains beyond them. The map in his backpack was quite specific, but only now did he truly understand how long and difficult the trek was going to be. A tremor of anxiety went through him. He never should have agreed to let Jinan come along. As much as he understood her desire to learn from Master Shantou, he could not afford to be slowed down. He hoped that the fact that she was a demon meant she did not tire as easily as a human.

"Watch your step. Let me know if you need to rest," he told her.

"I said I can take care of myself," Jinan reassured him.

"I hope so."

Twenty-seven Nights Until the Full Moon

Their journey on that first afternoon had taken them over small hills and a low mountain range, across grasslands and small rivers. On the first night they had camped in a small, narrow valley and though it was cold the hills around them had provided some shelter from the wind. They had gathered two separate piles of branches and brush. With the touch of her finger Jinan had lit one of them into blazing fire, then had woken up during the night when it had burned out to light the second.

The next morning was uneventful, even pleasant with its extraordinary vistas of distant snowcapped mountains. They passed a tribe of nomads herding yaks and saw a family of musk deer as well as a number of other animals, though mostly from a distance. At midday, Oz saw something slinking through the high grass far off and he sniffed at the air. Jinan glanced at him curiously, and he frowned.

"Company," he said, rucking his pack up higher on his shoulders and pointing out across the grass. "It's got a weird scent. Maybe one of the big cats. I've smelled tigers at the zoo. This is similar."

"It's probably a leopard," Jinan replied, lips pursed in contemplation. After a moment she shrugged. "Yeah. A leopard. I'm pretty sure they still have 'em wild here."

Oz did not like the sound of that, but when the wind shifted, the animal turned and fled across the grassy plateau. He assumed it had caught Jinan's demon scent and thought better of trying to hunt them. But it did cross his mind that it might have been his own scent that frightened the leopard.

Feeling's mutual, he thought.

Over the course of that first full day, Oz slowly began to adjust to the thinner air at this elevation. They were, after all, at the roof of the world, just as Wuxi had said. Tibet was the highest region on Earth. Even the plateau, though surrounded and interrupted by mountain ranges, was nearly three miles above sea level. It was the most extraordinary place Oz had ever been.

Fiji had been paradise, there was no question about that. But Tibet was its own kind of perfection. Cold and utterly, completely wild, but beautiful. The night before, when he had looked up, Oz had thought the sky had never looked so clear, the stars had never been so close. For the first time in a very long time he had even been able to appreciate the beauty of the moon . . . but that might have been because it was on the wane and would not be full again for four weeks.

The hiking grew more strenuous over the course of that day, but both of them were up to it. The only mistake they had made was not bringing the kind of food supplies they would need for such travel. Thankfully they passed a village in the afternoon. At the edge of the village they were met by an old man plucking fruit from an apricot tree. Oz urged Jinan to talk to him, to ask him about buying some food and canteens, or even calfskins that they could later refill from mountain streams.

"Why me?" she asked, giving him an odd look.

Oz stared at her a moment. "Not personally a speaker of Chinese."

Jinan chuckled and shook her head. "Neither are they," she said, pointing a thumb toward the old man.

"But this is China."

"Not as far as they're concerned," she explained. "They speak Tibetan. I don't."

Though Oz had educated himself quickly about Tibet when he learned he was to come here, he had somehow missed the fact that Tibetans spoke their own language. Fortunately, they were able to find a couple in the village who spoke Han Chinese and to make their purchases without too much difficulty. The experience was sobering for Oz, though. Though he had balked at having Jinan along, she was a nice enough girl, and good company. She could light a fire with the flick of a wrist. But, selfish as it was, one of the reasons he had not fought harder to keep her from joining him was because she spoke Chinese.

Which was, apparently, going to be useless to them as they traveled into areas that were even more remote than this.

It was too late to worry about such things, however.

Too late to do anything but keep moving forward.

As the shadows grew long that afternoon, they started up into a mountain pass. Oz hoped to make it through to the valley on the other side before they camped for the night, but they were still in the pass when the sun went down. Rather than protecting them from the wind the way the surrounding hills had done the night before, the pass was cut between the mountains at an angle that seemed to invite the wind, to bolster it, so that it whipped at them and sliced right through their clothes. They were forced to find shelter for the night between two large outcroppings. Though they tried to find enough brush for a decent fire, the search was fruitless, and he and Jinan slept huddled together in the shelter of the rocks.

Twenty-six Nights Until the Full Moon

In the morning she was quiet—almost as quiet as he was.

As they moved farther north and west they saw many wild sheep, goats, and even donkeys, as well as the occasional nomadic herders.

Throughout their journey Jinan had kept up a conversation with Oz—his participation mainly limited to one-word replies or polite inquiries where they seemed required. He learned as much about her life in Hong Kong and her years in high school than he probably would have even by reading her diary. Jinan had spent her entire life pretending to be a normal girl. As close as she grew to her friends, and to the two guys she had fallen in love with in high school, she could never truly open herself up to them.

Oz understood.

As much as he had wanted to make this journey free

of complications and without anyone around that he might hurt, he had to admit, at least to himself, that he was glad to have Jinan with him. Even if she was around when the wolf came out, she was a fire-demon. Chances were, she'd light his furry backside aflame, and he'd howl and run for the hills. It was his good fortune that back in Sunnydale he had friends—and a girlfriend—who weren't afraid of him. But that didn't mean he wasn't afraid *for* them.

Oz liked things quiet. Part of him would have liked to explore this terrain in silence. But he found he did not mind Jinan's loquaciousness at all, and she did not seem to mind his laconic nature. He figured she barely noticed how quiet he was. She had an audience, and that was enough.

Over the course of that long day Oz stopped many times to consult the directions Giles had given him and the map he had gotten from Qing. Those stops grew longer and longer as they crossed another mountain ridge and found themselves descending into a picturesque valley. They had eaten what passed for lunch quite late, so they did not bother to stop to eat again until the sky had turned a deep, rich shade of blue laden with the whisper of the encroaching night. The last thing they wanted was to be stuck on the mountainside for the night, so they pressed on until, shortly before dusk, they reached the valley.

To the east and west, jagged mountains jutted into the darkening sky. Oz and Jinan had stuck to the passes and ridges as much as possible, avoiding climbing directly up the face of a mountain to try to skirt the snow and ice. Some of the trails had taken them across light, snowy terrain, but they were soon back down again. The mountains to the east and west of this valley were some of the highest they had seen, and their peaks had a sort of halo around them that might have been windblown snow.

Oz paused again and checked his map.

"You think we're here, don't you?" Jinan asked.

"Might be. Let's try to go a little farther before we camp. I'd like to look for the village that's on the map. Then we'll know."

For another hour they hiked across the verdant valley, but as the night grew darker it became colder. They pulled the collars of their heavy wool jackets up high. Oz would have stopped then, except they had come to a small river that wound gently across the valley. The grass burned, but it was oily, so the two of them decided to head north along the course of the river and pick up whatever wood they could find along the way.

"One more hour," Oz told her.

Jinan looked as exhausted as he felt, and he knew she must also be hungry, but she did not argue. Soon they collected enough small sticks and branches off of the trees they passed to make a fire. Oz dropped his pile on the ground and slipped his backpack off. He sat down hard and exhaled loudly. But when he looked up at Jinan, she did not seem prepared to rest just yet. The girl had narrowed her eyes and was gazing farther up river.

Oz rose and tried to see what it was that had drawn her attention. After a moment, he could make out several dark shapes perhaps half a mile away, like huge beasts asleep on the grass. And above those shapes, like cutouts in the night sky, he could see the outlines of vultures circling beneath the stars.

Without a word, Oz slipped his pack on again, then picked up the sticks. Jinan glanced at him once, and they walked on. The muscles in his legs burned with exhaustion, but he barely felt it now. The vultures were a kind of dreadful punctuation above the scene they were approaching, which quickly revealed itself to be a nomad camp, the dark shapes the tents of the wandering herders.

At the edges of the encampment someone had hammered posts into the ground and placed small icons, like demon faces carved from stone, atop each post. They were facing outward, away from the tents. Oz reached out to touch the first one they came to. The stone was smooth, the eyes of the thing were wide and cruel. The sculptor had done a hell of a job.

Like scarecrows, Oz thought. *Warding off . . . what?*

They walked farther into the camp, into this circle the nomads had created where they had thought they would be safe. A single dead yak lay near one of the torn, ragged tents. Beyond it, at odd intervals throughout the encampment, they discovered the corpses of three nomads, one of whom had been torn into pieces.

"The nomads . . . ," Jinan began. She shook her head. "Even their herd. All gone except these few dead ones. What could do something like that, all the way out here?"

The vultures circled overhead, dropping lower as if not at all put off by their presence. Oz took another glance around the camp.

"Whatever it is, I'm thinking we vamoose. Probably better if we're gone when it comes back."

Chapter Nine

Twenty-six Nights Until the Full Moon

The nomads had brought guns.

Kangri stood at the eastern edge of his village with both hands gripping the carbine rifle that was slung across his shoulders. It was gas-operated and held ten rounds. The nomads had said these rifles were used by militia in China, but Kangri had never seen a weapon like this before. Rifles, certainly. They used them to hunt antelope and deer for food, or bear and leopards if such beasts threatened the village or livestock.

This carbine, though, this was a powerful weapon.

Yet even with the guns the nomads had brought, Kangri did not feel safe. The carbine held ten rounds; there was no way to know how many monsters served the demon of the eastern mountain, or how many rounds would be required to kill even one of them.

It was cold enough that he wore his thick wool hat pulled down over his ears, and yet Kangri's hands were sweating, making his grip on the rifle slick. The night was clear, the moon still fat as it dwindled above them. Wooden posts had been planted all around the village, and torches burned in them all night long, replenished constantly by those whose turn it was to act as sentries.

When the nomads had brought the corpse of the horrid creature into the village, the people had all thought it was over. Messengers were sent to ask the monks to come down from the monastery and bless their dwellings again, to place wards all over Lingka.

But the messengers never returned, and the monks never came. It was assumed that those sent to solicit their aid had never reached the monastery, and it was considered unwise to send anyone else out of the village.

Several nights later, the bloodshed began again. Late at night, women and children, even grown men, plucked from their beds. No blood, no screams, just gone, as though ghosts had come and stolen them away. Seven villagers missing in three days. Two men had been chosen to go to the monastery and beg the monks to intervene, but they had never returned.

Now each evening the darkness stole upon them like an accomplice to the evil things that lurked in the night. The torches had been put up, and the entire village took turns at sentry duty. But even those who were not on duty did not sleep well, if at all. In the mornings the people of Lingka were sluggish, their work suffered. They were sullen and bitter and jumped at every sound. But Kangri thought that perhaps it would get better now. Since they had posted sentries and lit torches there had been no sign of the creatures, nothing moving in the shadows of the night, and no one else had been harmed.

But each time Kangri stood sentry, he felt a kind of terror he had never imagined before. His impending wedding was forgotten. Work on the nearly completed home he was building for his bride-to-be had been put aside.

The village was in the midst of a mountain wilderness, its people working and living simply, close to the earth and beneath the heavens, nothing but the expanse of the valley around them as far as they could see. Yet now that valley had become their prison. They were afraid to stay and terrified at the thought of trying to leave. The nomads had brought the guns days ago and had not returned since then. A messenger had been sent to the nearest village, but he, too, had not returned.

It was possible, of course, that the danger was passed, that life would return to normal. But Kangri did not believe it. The predators had not been destroyed. They were out there still, in the mountain caves, roaming the valley after dark. The torches and sentries might put them off for a time, but not forever. Without the monks' help, Kangri believed it was only a matter of time before they were forced to flee. Someone would have to try again to get a message to the monastery.

A hard wind came up then, and Kangri pulled his jacket further up around his face, the carbine dangling in his left hand. The torch to his left swayed but remained rooted in the ground. Its flame guttered in the wind but did not go out. He gripped the rifle firmly with both hands once again and peered out across the valley. His eyes itched, and Kangri yawned broadly.

Something moved out in the dark.

A surge of adrenaline rippled through him, and Kangri stood up straighter, peered into the night, suddenly very awake. He brought the rifle up and lodged the stock against his shoulder.

No doubt, now. Something was there.

He opened his mouth to shout. His finger tightened on the trigger. Time to sound an alarm, bring the whole village running with guns ready. The demons were coming at last.

Demons, yes, because there were other shadows out there now. Three that he could see, walking upright like men, coming across the valley in the dark, slowly, as though they cared not at all if he saw them.

Kangri took a breath, was about to shout, when the voice came from the shadows, speaking his language.

"Boy, you look like you're about to have a heart attack."

Taken aback, Kangri hesitated. He narrowed his eyes, and a moment later he realized that the three figures approaching the village weren't merely walking like men, they *were* men. The one in front was very large and carried a massive pack strapped across his powerful shoulders. A rifle was slung there, a gleaming black deadly thing that made Kangri's own carbine look like a child's toy. It alarmed him, the sight of that gun, but the man wore it as though he had forgotten it was there. His hands were empty and open as he approached, a gesture of peace.

Behind him were two men who must have been brothers. They were thin and pale, their skin almost iridescent under the light from the moon and stars, and their hair was black. Westerners, all three of them. Kangri had only seen a handful of Westerners before, all headed for the monastery, and he found them fascinating. But he was on sentry duty.

"Come no farther," he said nervously, finger still on the trigger of the carbine. "You are fortunate that you speak Tibetan, or you might be dead already."

The large man with the rifle paused, and his companions followed suit.

"Calm down, friend. We're just passing through. Didn't figure a place like this, out here in the wild, would have a need for armed guards. Do you have leopards raiding your livestock or something?"

Kangri took a breath, began to relax. He realized that from the perspective of this wanderer, he must look almost foolish. But what should he say?

"There have been . . . attacks, yes," Kangri began cautiously. "This is not a good time for strangers to come to our village. Particularly not strangers who travel by night. You say you are passing through. I'm afraid we are not going to be very hospitable. I would advise you to pass around us rather than through."

He stood up straighter and took a breath, hoping his expression would communicate to the strangers how serious he was. The two pale men moved in the shadows, just beyond the reach of the torchlight. He tried to get a better look at them, but it was almost as though the night had draped itself over them, obscuring their features.

A shiver went through Kangri.

The man with the black rifle stared at him. A smile curled the edges of his mouth, but Kangri did not think it was genuine.

"Fine," the man said. "We'll go around. Tell me, though, which way to the monastery?"

A wave of menace emanated from the man, and Kangri hesitated to reply. It was crazy. The man was empty-handed, and Kangri held his carbine. He could have shot the stranger where he stood, and his friends—*shadows and moonlight shifting in pools upon their pale faces*—he could have killed them all. But he felt danger coming off of this man, and it unnerved him.

"There," Kangri said, pointing to the mountain to the west.

The man's eyes narrowed. He stared at the western peak and then, slowly, his gaze ticked toward the east, to the jagged face of the home of the demon.

"So Muztag's fortress is up there, then," the stranger said.

Kangri could not breathe. The stranger knew the name of the demon of the eastern mountain.

"You . . . you do not want to go up there."

"Don't I?" the man replied. Then he turned to the two shadow men who traveled with him. "I don't want anyone to know we came this way. Kill him."

"No," Kangri whispered.

The bone structure and flesh of their faces seemed to flow and contort, and now the shadow men swept toward him with the grim visages of monsters, mouths wide, fangs gleaming in the light from the moon and stars. He raised the rifle, finger tightening on the trigger. But the shadow men were too fast. One of them tore his arm off before he could fire the carbine. The other tore out his throat before he could scream.

His vision went black—there were no stars in the endless night he gazed into now—but he could still hear them. He died, accompanied by the sound of them sucking at his veins, drinking his blood.

Twenty-five Nights Until the Full Moon

The face of the eastern mountain sloped gently upward at first but soon became a jagged and forbidding incline. Cain and the Pierrault brothers—Andre and Max—made good time in spite of the difficult terrain. The werewolf hunter was determined to reach the end of this particular journey, tired of traveling, eager to bring the hunt to a conclusion. The Pierraults just wanted to be certain they could outrun the sun.

Several times Cain had suggested to the vampires that they stay behind. Traveling only at night had not been a big deal in getting from Fiji to Lhasa, but once they were in the mountains it was a major pain in the ass. The first day they had managed to find a cave to sleep in, but after that they had been forced to pitch the tent Cain had brought along, and then the hunter himself had stood guard for the vermin. He was tired now and very much on edge. But they were nearly at their destination at last.

It had been simple enough to track the werewolf back to the Atwill woman's settlement in Fiji with the filthy demons she was playing nursemaid to, like some Jane Goodall wanna-be with monsters instead of gorillas. Things had gotten pretty bloody before she gave up the werewolf's latest destination, but Cain had let her live. So he and the Pierraults had gutted a few of her pet demons; who the hell was she going to tell? *Police! Help! A bad man and two vampires killed some of my hell-spawn friends!*

Even now, freezing his butt off climbing a damn mountain in the middle of the night, Cain smiled at the memory.

When the Atwill woman had first started spilling about the monastery in Tibet, he had nearly cursed loudly. He had figured the hunt was over before it had really begun, time to head home. How much farther was he going to have to chase the Osbourne kid? But then she had let slip why Oz was going to Tibet, looking for someone to help him control the wolf side to his nature. That was a good laugh as far as Cain was concerned. The kid still thought he was human or something, but the hunter knew better. A werewolf was a werewolf, as much a monster as a vampire. The only difference to him was that there was no percentage in killing vampires. Even if someone had wanted to buy a vampire's skin or stuffed head or something, it was impossible. You killed a vampire, you could sweep up what was left of them with a dustpan and brush.

Not that it mattered what Oz *thought* he was. His pelt was still worth a mint to Cain's clients. And if the Atwill woman was right, and this monastery had other werewolves in it . . . he could be looking at a gold mine. Suddenly a trip to Tibet had begun to sound very, very promising. And the Pierraults wanted revenge for their brother's death, so he would have all the muscle he needed if there were a lot of werewolves.

It was not until he'd gotten into Lhasa and the Pierraults had taken the opportunity to sample the nightlife that they had learned of Muztag. The nomads that roamed the mountains north of the city referred to him as "the demon of the eastern mountain," but to them, Muztag was a myth. According to the sources Andre and Max had consulted, though, the creature was all too real, a hideous, ancient thing that had prowled a fertile valley on the Tibetan plateau for centuries and whose influence spread far beyond his mountain fortress.

Muztag and the master of the monastery were ancient enemies.

Cain didn't like the sound of that. He was walking into the middle of a battle decades, maybe hundreds, of years old. But the lure of wealth was strong, and he figured maybe Muztag could use someone whose whole life was about hunting werewolves.

In the early hours of that morning, the dawn still far away, Cain and the Pierraults struggled up the craggy face of the mountain with a cold wind battering them against the cliff. The hunter's fingers grew numb as he found handhold after handhold, managing to scale the rock with great effort and few setbacks.

Perhaps a third of the way up the face of the mountain the cliff became worn and smooth and too steep to scale without pitons and other climbing equipment.

"Damn it!" Cain whispered. Then he shook his head and laughed softly to himself.

"What's funny?" Andre hissed.

"I wanted to do the right thing," Cain replied. "Like getting permission from a mob boss before doing a hit in his territory. But we're not getting up to that fortress. Not tonight, anyway. Looks like we're going to have to forget about protocol and head for the monastery instead, hope this Muztag doesn't mind me poaching on his land."

"Tomorrow," Max Pierrault said. "Dawn is too close. We cannot go to the monastery tonight."

"I look stupid to you?" Cain sniffed. Then he glanced at the horizon again. "Hell, you boys'll be lucky to make it down off the mountain by dawn."

He glanced down at them, began to lower his boot to get a better toehold so they could begin their descent, but Andre wasn't paying attention.

"Let's move. I'd think you two would be in more of a hurry."

Andre peered through the darkness. "My eyesight is better than yours, Cain. But take a look off to your left."

The hunter shifted slightly to a place where the ledge was wide enough that he could stand and glanced to where Andre was pointing. Cain rubbed his eyes, for in the dark, much of the jagged landscape looked the same. When he looked again, it took him a moment to realize what he was seeing. "Stairs," he muttered. "There are stairs."

They made their way north along the mountain face and in minutes found themselves standing on a set of broad steps that had been hewn out of the bare rock. The stairs were high and steep and extended only a hundred feet or so down past their location. They weren't meant to invite anyone up to the fortress but to ease the climb where the mountain became impassable.

"This is incredible," Max said, his accent thick. "How long must it have taken to do this?"

"They're demons. They've got plenty of time," Cain replied. "Of course, vampires do, too, but your kind are so damned impatient."

The Pierraults did not bother to reply. Cain had known them for a very long time, and they were used to his bluster.

Though the wind was still bitterly cold and his legs ached terribly, Cain felt a quickening of his pulse as they continued their climb. He had to stop from time to time to take deep breaths. The air was growing thinner the higher they climbed. Half an hour after they discovered the steps they reached a place where the angle of the mountainside became less severe. Snow had built up on the ground there and was slick across the steps. Their boots left fat prints in the snow, and it crunched beneath their heavy tread.

The three of them—hunter and predators—climbed in silence for a while longer. The sky began to lighten, dawn not far away. Soon, only the mountain itself would shield the Pierraults from the sun's rays. The idea disturbed Cain, despite the thoughts he'd had a short while before. The Pierraults were mercenaries and in this case they had a joint purpose, but they were not his friends. Still, it was good to have allies when entering a situation as uncertain as this one.

The wind blew harder, and Cain had to reach down and touch his gloved hands to the steps to keep from tumbling over. The sky continued to lighten, though they remained in shadow. The Pierraults were silent, but he sensed their urgency.

At last Cain saw the fortress above them. It had been built right into the side of the mountain. He imagined there had once been a network of caves there and Muztag had utilized those, created a lair within, and eventually constructed a stone facade for the place. Windblown snow whipped across the top of the steps. A massive door of wood and iron was set right in the center of the fortress. There were no windows.

On either side of the door stood a pair of hideous, leathery trolls wearing swords at their hips. The one on the left was smoking a fat cigar, a T-shirt emblazoned with the Union Jack stretched across his chest. The other had his arms crossed and was naked from the waist up, as if to better show off the tiger tattoo that covered most of his upper torso. The one with the cigar only looked bored, but the other, with the tiger tattoo, was glaring directly at Cain as he climbed the last dozen steps to the top.

"They're here," Tiger muttered out one side of his mouth.

"Yer point?" Union Jack replied in a rumbling voice that sounded like an avalanche, only with a twinge of a British accent.

Trolls always sounded like they had a mouthful of stones. Cain hated them.

Tiger sighed. "So can we kill then now?" he asked, as though Cain and the Pierraults weren't even there to hear.

"What the hell. Go 'head."

The troll with the tiger tattoo ran his tongue out over the two huge teeth that jutted downward from his upper jaw like tusks and grinned, drool sliding out of his mouth and steaming as it hit the snow. Then he drew his sword, sniffing the air. "Them other two are vampires," he said.

Max Pierrault hissed.

Andre muttered, "Damned trolls. What a stink."

Tiger started for Cain. In one smooth motion the hunter slid his rifle down off his shoulder, swung the barrel up, and fired a round through Tiger's forehead, blowing his brains and fragments of his skull in a spray across the snowy front stoop of the fortress.

Union Jack spit out his cigar and stared at the dead troll. Slowly his gaze ratcheted up toward Cain, but instead of fury there was only a dull kind of sadness there.

"Right," he said. "What the hell'd you wanna do that for? He wasn't all that bright, Stout, but he wasn't a bad sort."

"He was going to kill me," Cain replied, rifle trained on Union Jack's forehead.

The troll guard crossed his arms. "There's that, I s'pose. You're pretty quick with that gun. Now then, what can I do for you gents?" His gaze ticked toward the vampires again. "You two look a bit nervous. Don't blame you, it being sunup and all. Gonna have a shift change here meself in a minute. Rather not turn to stone if I can help it."

Cain took a step closer, drawing the troll's attention back to the rifle. "We want to see Muztag for a parley. Could be we have some information he'd like to have."

"'Course you do," Union Jack replied. "I'm afraid the boss is a bit busy at the moment. Had a little raid night before last, y'see. Got a lot of new arrivals to get settled. Or to eat. There's always some eatin' involved. Might just eat you, you're in such a bloody hurry to get in there."

Cain pulled the trigger. The bullet chipped a scar out of the stone facade of the fortress.

"Got it," Union Jack noted. Then he shrugged and went to the huge wooden door, banged on it three times. "Me shift's nearly up as it is."

The vampires slunk quickly up behind the troll, anxious to be inside and away from the blossoming dawn. Cain considered keeping his rifle at the ready, but he didn't like his chances of surviving this if he went into the place shooting. Bad enough he had already killed one of Muztag's guards. That might be enough to cost them their lives, but there was no way they were turning around now.

He slid the rifle strap over his shoulder again and watched as the massive door to the fortress of the demon swung open.

In the darkness within, the shadows seemed to writhe.

Oz and Jinan had been climbing all morning. They had slept at the foot of the highest mountain at the western end of the valley. Breakfast had consisted of coffee warmed over the fire and some cured meat he fried in a pan they'd gotten at the first village they'd stopped in two days before. It was the last of the meat, and though that meant they would soon have nothing to eat, Oz was not sad to see it go. They shared a bit of bread as well, and briefly discussed the possibility that they would soon have to catch something to eat if they did not find the monastery.

Though he thought they could do that if they had to, Oz doubted it would come to that. The previous night they had spotted torches burning around a village in the distance. Jinan had wanted to stop there, to see if they could get more food, even some blankets for the higher elevations of the mountain. Oz had insisted they press on. They could always go back to that village if necessary.

At dawn, as they ate breakfast, they stared up at the mountain. Perhaps two thirds of the way up was a dark shape that had to be some sort of man-made structure. Oz was certain it must be the monastery.

Now they climbed.

The way was not terribly difficult. When they came to a section of the mountain too sheer to scale, they simply retraced their steps and went around. There were trees on the foothills and even at higher elevations, and in time they found a rough trail that led up toward the monastery from the valley. Oz wished they had found it first thing that morning, but it was too late for wishes.

Well, perhaps not too late for one wish. But the truth of that awaited him in the monastery atop the mountain ledge high above.

More than an hour passed in silence. There was still some brush on either side of the trail, but a thin layer of new fallen snow covered much of it. The peak above the monastery was completely white, frozen in a kind of perpetual winter. It was beautiful, but Oz thought it was quite fortunate that they would not have to climb that high. The monastery was sometimes out of their line of sight, but as they drew closer, Oz could make it out far better. It was a simple structure, but large, constructed by timbers and stone. Smoke rose from somewhere in the building, and he assumed it was a morning fire, perhaps for cooking. The idea made his stomach rumble, and his skin felt warmer than he had been in days, just thinking about a real fireplace.

"You know," Jinan said suddenly as they rounded a turn in the path, which cut back and forth across the face of the mountain now, "we've been together for days and I still don't really know much about you. You don't talk much, Oz. About yourself. About home. Not anything."

"Better not to," Oz said, voice raspy from disuse.

She had gotten ahead of him and now she glanced back to make eye contact, but he said nothing more. Jinan turned her attention to the trail again and Oz followed her, but her words had come suddenly and, despite himself, he found his mind turning once more to home, to Willow and all that he had left behind.

All the things that mattered so much to him that he had traveled halfway across the world to safeguard them. Unbidden, a memory flashed into his head, of a night only a few months earlier, when he had watched Jordy so that Uncle Ken and Aunt Maureen could go out to celebrate their anniversary.

He and Jordy had been sitting on the front steps

watching the cars go by. The sky had been clear above them, the moon a crescent, sharp and dangerous. But to the two of them, it was as though it had disappeared completely.

"Oz, how long till the moon comes back?" his young cousin had asked him.

"We've got a few weeks."

Jordy had gazed up at the night sky and sighed. "Sometimes I wish it wouldn't ever come back."

Oz had put an arm around him and stared up into the darkness as well. "Me too," he had said, whispering without even really meaning to. "Me too."

"Hey."

He nearly slammed into Jinan, who had stopped on the trail to take a swig of water.

"Sorry," he said. "Mental vacation."

"I noticed. Did you ever think that maybe you'd feel better if you talked more? Talk to me," she said. Jinan laid a hand on his shoulder. "I know why you're here, but you know what? I don't need to be protected from you. I've seen what's in you and I'm not afraid."

Her hand slid down his arm, and her fingers twined with his.

As if her touch had burned him, he pulled his hand back and turned away, would not meet her gaze. He liked Jinan. A lot. But if she wanted to make more of it . . . that was something he just couldn't do.

"I've got another face, too, Oz," she said, disappointment in her voice. "I know what it's like to have a monster inside."

Oz gazed up, but they had come too close to the mountain now and he could no longer see the monastery. They were only minutes away now. Once they reached the ledge, they would be there.

"No, you really don't," he said. "What's in you? It's still *you*. The thing inside me? It'll kill you if you give it a chance, Jinan." Oz turned to her, met her expectant gaze, and this time did not look away. "As for . . . other things. You're running away from home when all I want is to finally be able to *go* home. This monk, Shantou? Maybe he can help."

Oz moved around Jinan as she put her water away and they continued up the trail, with Oz in the lead. The going was more difficult now, but they were so close to the top that he did not care. He dug his hands in to keep from losing his balance, ignoring the snow. When he glanced up again they were only a few yards from the ledge.

"What if he can't?" Jinan asked. "Help, I mean."

The ledge was just above him now, and Oz reached out and grabbed an outcropping of rock and began to heft himself up.

"Then I keep moving until I find someone who can."

He pulled himself up onto the ledge, Jinan right behind him. Oz could smell the smoke from the fireplace, and again he was warmed by the thoughts of a fire.

But when he looked up, that hope was dashed.

The tall doors at the front of the monastery had been shattered inward, and a corner of the stone structure had collapsed entirely. Gray smoke rose from that corner, pluming in the air, and the remnants of a fire still flickered there. If the place had been built of wood rather than stone, it would have burned to the ground.

The corpse of an eviscerated monk lay half in, half out of a first-floor window, its heavy shutter dangling loosely beside the dead man. A leg jutted from the rubble at the collapsed corner of the monastery.

Oz was paralyzed. He stared at the monastery, at the aftermath of some terrible act, and his hope began to evaporate. Whatever he had said to Jinan, in his heart he had believed that he would find answers here, that he would find a way to rein in the wolf.

Slowly Jinan walked toward the entrance of the

building. Without its doors it gaped like a wound. She whispered to herself in Chinese, and he could not understand her.

After a moment, he approached as well. Jinan paused just inside the ravaged entryway and stared within at blood-spattered stone walls and broken pottery, torn tapestries. A third corpse lay not far into the front hall.

"It's like what happened to the nomads," Jinan said hoarsely. "What . . . what will you do now?"

Oz had no idea where he would go next. The idea of retracing his steps was deeply troubling. "Keep asking the question until I get the answer," he told her, with a courage he did not feel. "We'll stay tonight. Tomorrow we'll start back down."

In the shadows of an inner room, something stirred. A small figure, no larger than Jinan, loomed from the darkness.

"You may stay if that is your wish," said a voice.

The figure stepped out through an arched doorway and into the hall. It was an old monk, dressed in a long, ceremonial robe that reminded Oz of the garb worn by a priest at mass. It was a deep, rich yellow, with designs stitched in gold around the edges and where the buttons joined the fabric along the front. He wore his white hair tied in a thick braid, but it seemed to have become partially unraveled. His robe was spotted with blood and torn in several places, and the right side of his face was bruised a dark, painful-looking purple.

His appearance had distracted them both for a moment from his words.

"You speak English," Oz said, more than a little surprised.

"So do you," the monk replied. "As I said, you may stay the night. But you should be warned. I will not be able to protect you if the evil returns."

Chapter Ten

Twenty-five Nights Until the Full Moon

"They came an hour after dark," the old monk said. "A grotesque menagerie of beasts, sorcerers, and demons in service to Muztag, known in this valley and whispered of across the plateau as 'the demon of the eastern mountain.' For generations, the legend of the demon lord Muztag has been a warning for wayward travelers, but our presence here has kept him from straying too far from his stronghold.

"The nomads whispered rumors that he had begun to gather the forces of darkness around him, into his service. I was a fool not to lend those rumors more credence."

Oz stared at him. Images of the ravaged nomad camp they had found down in the valley flashed through his mind. *Muztag.* At least the enemy had a name now. *But it's not my enemy,* Oz thought. *I've got troubles of my own. Priorities.* The words felt hollow in his mind.

Jinan went to the old man in the blood-spattered ceremonial robes and gestured as though to offer him her arm. He held up a hand to indicate that he was all right, but favored her with a grateful nod. The demon girl let her backpack slide off and dropped it to the floor, glancing around again. She shoved her hands into her pockets and studied the old monk again.

Just inside the front door, Oz made no move to come farther inside the monastery. Despite the selfish thoughts he'd had a few seconds earlier, he did not like the idea of turning his back on someone in trouble. But he had three and a half weeks before the next full moon, and he needed to find someone who could help him, someone who would know something, or who had been through what he was experiencing.

His mind was elsewhere, on what he ought to do next, so it took him by surprise when Jinan spoke again.

"Are you Master Shantou?"

The old monk gave a polite half bow. "At your service." He raised both hands, indicating their surroundings. "As much as I can be, given the circumstances."

Oz narrowed his eyes, studying Shantou. "Where'd you learn English?"

The monk raised an eyebrow. "From books. Many of my students have been English or American. I taught an Australian once. I speak many languages. Is my English acceptable?"

"Better than most of the Americans I know," Oz told him.

This earned Oz another subtle bow and a broad grin that seemed out of place in the aftermath of the horror that had happened here. Oz figured the old monk was just being polite.

"You have sought me out," Shantou went on, quite serious now. "Just as so many have done before you. It is possible that I may be able to help you, but you should be aware of the danger you are in every moment you stay."

Jinan took a deep breath and glanced at Oz expectantly. He said nothing but she was undaunted by the lack of support. Instead, she stood a bit taller and faced Shantou again.

"We can take care of ourselves."

A shiver went through Oz. Every time Jinan made that claim, it felt more like she was whistling in the dark, daring fate to prove her a liar. He had planned to stay the night here and head back in the morning, but if he started back down now he could camp in the valley overnight. From the looks of this place, he wouldn't be in any more danger in the open than he would be in here.

Though it might be nice to sleep with a roof over his head for a night.

"So what's the story on Muztag?" Jinan asked the old monk. "The real story, I mean. Not a myth or a legend. If he's been like a bogeyman for so long, why get ambitious all of a sudden?"

Oz reached for his backpack. If Jinan wanted to come back with him, she could. He'd make it clear he thought she shouldn't stay, but in the end it wasn't up to him. He was not her father.

A hand on his pack, Oz hesitated. *Her father.* Qing had only really helped Oz because he owed Giles, but that did not free Oz from the feeling that he was now in Qing's debt. Jinan's family had gone out of their way for him, and he had cost them, damaged their business.

Reluctantly, he let go of the pack and crossed his arms, leaned against the wall to listen to Master Shantou, the little old man who represented his crumbling hopes.

"You do not understand," the old monk said softly. His gaze grew distant as though his eyes saw into another place, a faraway realm that brought him only sadness.

"Muztag is a Vastaghri demon. Very rare. By their terms he is not very old, either, which makes him even more uncommon. The race is nearly extinct. He is the youngest I have ever heard of, perhaps only five or six hundred years old. The young tend to slay their elders and their siblings for control of their land.

"Once upon a time, thousands of years ago, their kind thrived in Asia and Europe. They are born tyrants. A Vastaghri considers himself the lord of all he surveys, and once he has laid claim to that land, he will never leave it. Muztag does not want to set the world afire like some other species of demons . . ."

Shantou paused and focused on Jinan. "No offense."

She blinked. "None taken."

Neither of them asked how the old monk had known she was a demon, but Oz was suddenly more aware of Shantou's presence. He was some sort of magician or sorcerer to have gained the reputation he had. But for the first time since they had seen the damage to the monastery, Oz began to wonder exactly what kind of power Master Shantou wielded. Whatever else he might be capable of, he was the only person left at the monastery alive.

"You were saying?" Oz prodded.

Master Shantou inclined his head toward Oz. "Yes. Muztag. He settled here four hundred and fifty-seven years ago. For more than a decade he and those who served him—only a small group at that time—hunted the valley and the mountains and beyond with impunity. Antelope and bear and whatever else they desired, but people most of all. Nomads.

"Then the monastery was built. From time to time a drunken nomad will stumble away from his herd and not be heard of again. Or a rebellious child might leave the village and set out for Lhasa and never arrive there. Muztag might have been responsible. I suspect he was. But it was always possible that wild animals were the killers. I protected the village as best I could. Our mere presence here kept Muztag from growing too bloodthirsty. I am a humble teacher, and most of my attention must go to my students. But the demon has always feared me."

"Wait," Jinan interrupted.

Master Shantou gazed at her expectantly.

The demon girl raised a hand partway, as though she were in a classroom. "Are you saying you've been here for more than four hundred years. That you built the monastery?"

The old monk smiled. Some of his teeth were missing, and others were yellowed. His skin crinkled at the edges of his eyes and around his lips but otherwise was remarkably smooth.

"Not alone," Master Shantou told her.

"What are you?" Oz asked.

"I am Shantou," the Master replied.

There was a long moment of silence as the three of them stood amidst the debris of the shattered doors inside that entrance hall and gazed at one another. Then Shantou reached up and began to unravel his long braid, smoothing the sections that had been mussed and tightening them. When he began to speak again he was not even looking at them.

"I do not know what has changed. Perhaps the frustration of our conflict has finally driven him to risk all, or perhaps there is another Vastaghri encroaching upon his territory and he gathers these new lackeys and servants to combat that threat. It may simply be that his natural tyranny drove him to collect too many followers, and those followers are voracious and must be fed.

"In the end, it does not really matter why, though, does it?"

A great sadness came over the old monk then and if possible, he seemed even smaller to Oz.

"I was meditating in the courtyard. A light snow had fallen during the day. Not uncommon, but beautiful, and it was pleasing to be outside, to sit and breathe in the crisp night air. I was aware of my students. Their presence, their emotional state . . . I could always sense them. What sort of teacher would I be if I could not? Ferric and Shen were in their room asleep. They slept much of the day, awakening at night to spend the evening feeling the weight of the moon, moving with the tide of her influence."

A sort of bell went off in Oz's head. It sounded as though Ferric and Shen might have been werewolves. His throat felt suddenly dry.

"The rest of the students were in the great hall meditating and sparring, learning to focus with the aid of combat. Seven of them, men and women, Eastern and Western, human and demon. I had an alcoholic from Bonn and a teenaged witch from Kyoto who had become tainted by relying on dark magic. She was my most recent arrival. Miyu. How surprised she was to learn how many dark sorcerers have come to this place to cleanse themselves of the very same taint and temptation."

Master Shantou's voice lowered. "I sensed something else, then, something beyond the walls. Many somethings, in fact. In the midst of my meditation I could feel the eldritch power of Muztag's magicians approaching and sense the dull, cruel minds of the trolls and demons that serve him. I heard the hush of wings above me and I glanced up to see the dark shapes of *Draco Volans* gliding across the night sky."

"Hate those vicious little rodents," Oz muttered.

The old monk blinked and looked at him. "You have seen *Draco Volans* before?"

"Pretty much met everything hanging with the Slayer."

A light of understanding and interest flickered in Master Shantou's eyes. But he was not deterred from his story. It was as though he needed to tell it now, to make sense of it for himself.

The wind rushed through the cold stone building, whistling through narrow cracks and wailing in empty halls. Though all he had seen when they crested the hill had been the damage to the place, Oz could imagine what it had looked like before the previous night's attack. The various wings of the monastery each had their own peaked roofs, the elegant curl of Asian architecture visible in each one. There was a grandeur to it. And with every word Master Shantou spoke, his sense of that venerable old place became clearer until the monastery itself seemed a victim.

"There were several monks who had once been my students. They aided me in my teaching and in the upkeep of the monastery. Namcha was sweeping . . . just there, in that room . . . when they shattered the door, the magicians combining their power to tear down the mystic barriers I had had erected over the years. Namcha was the first to die.

"I should have been better prepared. Powerful sorcerers have walked these halls over the centuries, and I could have been better prepared for such an attack than I was. But I was arrogant enough to believe that Muztag feared me too much to attempt such a thing."

The old monk wiped his hands across his dusty robe as though he might erase the bloodstains there. He looked at the floor and then lifted his gaze again.

"I fought back, of course. But there were too many of them, and it was happening too fast. Never has Muztag fielded a host of beasts like this. Sothoth demons with massive eyes at the end of each tentacle, poison spines and crushing strength. Chitinuk demons with their horns and carapaces and clicking beak mouths.

"All I could do was defend myself, and now I am the only one left. I failed them. The other monks were slaughtered. My students were taken. Abducted. From the rantings of his beasts I have come to believe Muztag intends to force them to serve him."

Jinan hugged herself, suddenly more of a little girl than she had ever seemed to Oz before.

"That's . . . that's terrible, Master Shantou."

Oz swallowed. He knew without a doubt that what he really needed to do was put on his pack and get the hell out of there, just walk away. He took a long breath and let it out, ran his hands through his ragged hair.

"Anything we can do to help?" he asked.

Shantou stared at him as though the old monk could see right inside his head and heart. It was unnerving. Though his manner had been nothing but friendly thus far, now Master Shantou seemed grim, almost angry.

"In your current state? Nothing."

A heartbeat went by. Then a few more. Oz studied the old monk a moment, then he stood away from the wall, slung his pack up from the ground and put it on.

"Understood," he said. "Good luck."

And he headed for the door.

A chorus of voices in his head were telling him to turn around, that he was walking away from the one man who seemed to be capable of helping him. But the only guarantee if he stayed was that he'd be in the middle of a death trap, waiting for this Muztag and his goon squad to come back and finish the job they had started. It wasn't like he was back in Sunnydale. There was no Buffy around to do the really nasty work, no Scooby Gang to back him up, no Giles to break out the weapons and the research, find a spell to send all the monsters to some alternate dimension circus freak show.

In your current state, Shantou had said. So just like he had with Jinan, the old monk had intuited what Oz was and why he had come here. And Master Shantou himself had said there was nothing Oz could do to help. Not until he had dealt with the beast, put the reins on the wolf. The old monk ought to leave, too, but it was not any of Oz's business if he stayed.

"Oz, hey!" Jinan called.

He stepped out onto the snow-covered ledge in front of the monastery. The thin layer of snow was melting in the sunlight.

"You can't just walk away," Jinan said, her tone a mixture of annoyance and astonishment. "Oz! Where are you going to go?"

With a slow nod, he turned to her. Jinan ran up to him, and instead of the anger he expected to see on her face, he saw only sadness.

"Wherever's next," he replied.

At that, the sadness was burned off her features by a rush of righteous fury.

"So you're just going to leave me here?" she demanded, shaking a finger at him. "Master Shantou needs our help. And we need *his* help."

Face-to-face with Jinan, Oz neither saw nor sensed Shantou as he stepped out the front door of the monastery. It was not until he spoke that Oz realized he had followed them. He held a thick wooden walking stick in his right hand, and though he put some weight on it, somehow his need for it did not diminish his presence.

"We all have a journey, young Jinan," Master Shantou said. "Often the journey decides our steps for us. As I said, at the moment there is nothing either of you can do to aid me."

The monk held his hands clasped in front of him. There was a kind of mischief in his voice then, and he raised an eyebrow again. "But I may be able to help you."

He stepped out onto the mountain ledge then, walking toward Oz with a grace and strength that seemed incongruous with his obvious age and the presence of the staff he leaned upon.

"You have come to me to find a way to confront the beast. I sense the conflict within you, wolf."

A chill went through Oz, and he stiffened. "Don't call me that."

Master Shantou inclined his head. "Let your journey lead you, my friend. But, if you wish to remain, I may be able to help you control the beast. You would not be the first."

Oz hesitated. The surge of new hope within him was almost painful. "I'd be in your debt," he said at last.

Jinan whooped happily and jumped at Oz, kissed his cheek. Then she scampered over to Master Shantou and pumped his hand.

"Excellent!" she cried. "You won't regret this, Master Shantou. I'll bet we're a lot more useful than you think. We can start by helping you repair the monastery. Would you honor me by accepting me as your student?"

"All demons should have at least some understanding of magic, Jinan. Enter and be welcome in my home. Both of you," Master Shantou added, gesturing toward Oz. Then he turned and walked, staff in hand, back toward the shattered doorway.

"Come. Let us speak further, away from the eyes of the mountain."

Jinan glanced once at Oz and then hurried into the monastery after him. After a moment, Oz followed.

• • •

A wooden cup of water in his right hand, Gib Cain paced the length of the stone chamber where he and the Pierraults had been held since arriving—somewhat violently—at Muztag's fortress. Torches burned in sconces on the walls, and tapestries were hung where windows would have been if the place were not a warren of demons. There was even a pottery vase of flowers on a handmade table in the corner. Everything had been done to make the place look like it wasn't a prison cell.

But the door was locked.

"My patience is just about run out," Cain muttered.

The words were for himself, however. The Pierraults had retreated to the darkest corner of the room and there curled up on the stone floor together like a pair of old dogs. They slept the cold, motionless sleep of the undead. A couple of dozen times Cain had been tempted to go over and kick one of them in the face, if only to alleviate his boredom.

He supposed he ought to be glad they weren't already dead. After all, he had shot one of the big boss's troll guards and then trespassed, the other guard at gunpoint. They had not gotten fifty feet inside the door before they were surrounded by a motley group of demons and a bunch of little winged vermin that looked like a cross between bats and baby dragons. Cain had demanded that they be allowed to see Muztag. Demanding had not been his initial plan—always best to be more modest when tramping on the territory of a vicious demon lord—but after killing the guard he had thought it best to do some swaggering and hope that would keep him alive long enough to talk to the boss.

So far it was working, but he had not met Muztag yet.

On the table in the corner was a plate of bread, cheese, and fruit. Not much, but all in all, more than he would have expected as a prisoner in a stronghold that smelled like a barn and was filled with creatures who would rather eat human flesh than an apricot. Of course, they probably weren't all carnivores.

That was a comfort.

The sound of footsteps came from the hall. Cain frowned, stopped pacing, and stepped cautiously away from the door. Someone rapped softly. Bemused by the incongruous politeness, Cain shook his head. "Come in," he said.

The key rattled in the lock, and then the door swung open. In the corridor stood a woman in a black, hooded cloak fringed with red and gold. A dark veil covered the bottom of her face so that only her eyes were visible. A witch or a sorceress. Cain always got them mixed up; the designation had something to do with whether they came by their power internally, or if they drew it from outside themselves. From what he had seen, all the magic users working for Muztag wore the same outfits, cloak, hood, and veil.

From the corridor came the echoes of screams that tore through the halls of the fortress. They were frightening. Cain had hurt plenty of folks in his time, human and otherwise, but he'd never made anyone scream like that. Never even got a howl like that from a lycanthrope. The screams went on. In the deep shadows of the corner across the room, the vampires did not so much as stir.

The sorceress stepped away from the open door. Cain thought for a second she was beckoning him to come out, and he took a step forward. Then a huge shadow fell across the threshold in the torchlight that glowed in the corridor, and the hunter flinched and backed up.

Muztag had to duck his head to get into the room.

Cain knew it was he by the deference he received from the sorceress, but there was also an air of command about him. Anyone who saw this big, ugly freak could not for one second think anything but that he was in charge. Muztag's flesh was the purple-black of overripe plums. He was huge, with massive hooves and hands as big as Cain's head. His skin was lined with ropy muscles and tendons. Four horns jutted from his head, two at each temple, and after a second Cain realized they looked more like insect antennae.

The demon lord had five eyes. Two beneath the lower antennae, like a man's. Two above those, beneath the upper antennae. And one huge, Cyclopean orb three times the size of the others, right at the center of the top of his forehead. It was unnerving as hell to look at him.

Cain didn't say a word. He just stared at the demon lord.

It backfired.

"If you have nothing to say to me, why are you still alive?" the demon thundered in Chinese. He glanced back at the sorceress in the hall. "Why is he still alive?"

Muztag began to turn away.

"No, wait!" Cain called. He could understand Chinese relatively well, but spoke it badly.

Slowly, Muztag turned. "Do me the courtesy of addressing me as Lord Muztag. Otherwise I will eat your eyes."

Cain hissed air in through his teeth. *Big bad hunter,* he thought. *But you're scared to death.* And that was the truth. Muztag scared the hell out of him. That was the trick with prey, though. *Never let them get the scent of your fear. Hide it.*

Eat my eyes, Cain thought, and had to stifle a giggle. *Don't you have enough of those?* He cursed himself silently, forced the hysterical thoughts away.

"My apologies. Lord Muztag. Right," Cain began, taking a breath, steadying himself, trying to find the words in Chinese and knowing he was mangling them.

He only hoped Muztag would understand. "My name is Cain. I'm a hunter. I specialize in werewolves."

And so in his halting Chinese he told Muztag everything, that he was pursuing a wolf from America named Daniel Osbourne, that Oz was headed for Master Shantou's monastery, was probably there already, and that he had climbed the mountain to get Muztag's—Lord Muztag's—permission to hunt on his territory.

When he had finished explaining, Muztag stared at him for a full minute. The demon lord's face was so hideous that Cain had no idea how to read his expression. After a moment, the demon lord raised a huge fist and ran his long, clawed fingers over his chin. The four antennae twitched.

"You have killed many werewolves?"

"Ninety-one," Cain replied, standing a bit straighter. This was something he understood, having his credentials questioned.

"And demons?"

Cain hesitated. The last thing he wanted was for Lord Muztag to think he was interested in the demon lord's own head. But he also could not afford to insult him. After a moment, he nodded.

"Certain demons have horns that are of special value to some collectors. There are those who grind them down to make aphrodisiacs and the like. That is how I come to speak at least some Chinese."

Muztag grunted. "I have heard of such things." Then the demon lord backed out into the hallway and gestured for Cain to follow. "Walk with me, wolf hunter. It is possible that you will be useful to me. If so, you will live. And you might return with more than one werewolf pelt for your trouble."

Cain exulted, but he did not let it show. The vampires were still sleeping, so Cain left them there. As long as nobody decided to dust them, they'd be all right. Anyway, this was exactly what he had hoped. And Muztag hadn't even mentioned the dead troll. That was a pretty good sign.

With the sorceress walking a respectful distance behind them, Muztag led him along a torch-lit hall and then down a broad set of steps that seemed to descend forever into the bowels of the mountain. The screams Cain had heard before grew louder as they went downward. At a stone landing they set off along another corridor.

The screams were coming from a room guarded by a pair of trolls, one of whom was Union Jack, whom Cain had threatened to kill only hours earlier. The troll either did not remember—which Cain found hard to believe—or he was already over it. Union Jack was smoking another cigar, but he extinguished it the moment he spotted Muztag coming down the hall.

"Wish they'd stop that," the troll with the English accent muttered. "S'hurting me ears."

Muztag barked something in a guttural voice, and the trolls snapped to attention. Union Jack threw open the door. The demon lord made no motion for him to follow, so Cain stayed outside as Muztag went in. But the hunter could see inside. The room was large and well lit. Four humans in torn and bloodied robes—three men and a girl barely a teenager—knelt on the other side of the room. Their faces and eyes were slack as zombies' and one of them was drooling. It looked to Cain as though someone had taken a blender to their brains and then put them back in their heads.

But they weren't the ones screaming.

A pair of sorcerers had a demon spread out on a table and were pushing tendrils of magical energy through his skull and chest like some vicious, occult acupuncture.

Cain flinched at the sight and the sound of the demon screaming. He had green skin, sort of scaly, and long tapered, pointed ears. Red horns thrust up like small nubs from his skull.

Muztag snarled at the sorcerers and barked at them in that same awful language, like tires spinning on gravel. He was taking them to task for something, and Cain figured just from looking inside that it had to do with the fact that the demon—though clearly hurting—was not a drooling vegetable like the others.

Abruptly, the demon lord picked up the scaly demon and hurled him across the room. Scaly struck the stone wall and slumped to the ground, but as far as Cain could see, he was still breathing.

Lord Muztag swept out of the room and slammed the door behind him. He walked on without another word, and Cain followed. After a moment, Muztag glanced at him.

"For all the magic they supposedly wield, they can't break the mind of that half-breed. Can't make an obedient servant out of him without all that shrieking. They want me to be patient!" Muztag snorted. "I have explained to them that patience is a virtue. And I do not have any of those."

Cain thought it best to say nothing.

A short way down, they came to another room. Muztag barked at the sorceress, and she waved a hand. The door unlocked and swung open of its own accord. Cain noticed she hadn't been polite enough to knock this time.

"Have a look," Muztag said.

Cain did. Within the room, chained to the wall, were a pitiful-looking pair of men, one Asian and one who looked German or Scandinavian.

"Werewolves," Muztag explained. "Shantou has taught them to control the change. They have far greater willpower than his other students. They're no good for me except for meat. If you can force them to change, break their spirits, then you can kill them and take their pelts. In exchange for this, and for my allowing you to hunt on my land, you will do something for me. Another hunt. But this pelt I will keep."

A broad smile spread across Cain's features as he glanced back at the two creatures chained inside that cell. Then he turned and nodded to the demon lord Muztag.

"I think I'm gonna like this job."

Chapter Eleven

Twenty-five Nights Until the Full Moon

The day was half over, but they made the best of it. There were rooms for Oz and Jinan that had not been ravaged by the attackers, and the kitchen was in working order. That first afternoon at the monastery they turned their attention to the entrance hall. As exhausted as they were, Oz and Jinan worked with Master Shantou—who seemed far heartier than a man of his age with recent injuries ought to be—to remove the debris. Stone was piled outside to be discarded or used later, while wood was stacked against an interior wall to be utilized if possible or burned in the fireplace if not.

One of the massive doors had a cracked plank, and part of the iron strapping had been torn away. Oz located a hammer and a box of nails that looked ancient, as though a blacksmith had forged them. He put a broken piece of wood over the crack in the door and nailed it down. The iron strapping was impossible to set right, no matter how hard he tried to bend it back into place. It had a warp to it now. Finally he asked Jinan to heat the metal up.

A small but intense flame blossomed from the fingers of her right hand and she used her other to shield the wood from the fire as she worked the iron. When it had softened with the heat, Oz wrapped his hands in cloth to avoid burning them and bent the metal back down, hammered it flat, and then replaced a couple of missing nails to hold it flat. Heavy iron hinges had to be set anew in what was left of the frame, but that was simpler in a way than fixing the door.

By early evening they had rehung that door and the entrance hall was swept and picked up, the refuse of the battle removed. There was a large space over the repaired door where part of the stone in the upper frame had been torn away, but that bit of masonry was for another day. The second door was nothing but splinters and twisted iron now, so they were obliged to borrow one that led from the monastery into the inner courtyard to use in its stead. The hinges, ironically enough, were still in place, though the door was too small for the entryway. Still, it would do for now and could be barred.

Not that barring the door had helped much against Muztag's fiendish menagerie. But just the same, it seemed a silent agreement amongst them that it was important not to have doors open to the wild during the night.

Master Shantou made a simple stew on a woodstove in the kitchen, and they ate mostly in silence, save for the conversations they had about what other repairs would need to be made on the monastery. The wing that had suffered the most damage would simply be closed off for now. Rubble around several ruined interior walls had to be cleared away.

Only one chore had to be completed before they could sleep that night.

"I won't leave them to the vultures," Master Shantou said emphatically.

Oz, Jinan, and Master Shantou took turns with the shovel. In the guttering light of torches the old monk had planted outside, they dug graves for each of his apprentices whose corpses had been left behind. Not deep—just four feet or so—enough to keep the carrion birds away from them. But still it was nearly midnight when they patted down the dirt on top of the last of the graves for these dead men whose names Oz did not even know.

Every bone in his body ached. Despite all his travel, his time on the *Sargasso Drifter,* and hiking through the mountains these past few days, this had been the longest and most tiring day of his entire life. The muscles in his arms and back and neck burned; his eyes felt as though they had been rubbed with sandpaper. When he turned to walk back inside the monastery, his whole body felt so heavy that it seemed as though someone had tied bags of cement to him. Master Shantou seemed more mournful than sad, and Jinan seemed tired but still somehow filled with the energy, the fire, that always filled her. Oz would have been envious, but he didn't have the strength.

"Oz," Master Shantou said, his voice quiet but carrying across the mountainside with its subtle power.

He paused and turned to look at the old man. The torches still burned, and shadows flickered across his face and slid across the white hair bound in that tight ponytail that fell down his back. The moon and stars seemed very distant then, and for the first time Oz felt the full effect of the Master's presence. There had been no doubt of his natural charisma and command of his surroundings, even upon first meeting him, but now Oz felt the man's certainty, his knowledge of secret truths that gave him a kind of insight few people ever gained.

"Yeah?"

Jinan came to stand beside him, the two of them before the teacher, and for the first time Oz felt as though they truly were his students.

Master Shantou glanced at Jinan. "I will teach you what I know of herbs and potions. Of spells and charms. I am not a powerful sorcerer, but a magician of great knowledge and meager talent. But I shall teach you what I know."

Then his gaze fell upon Oz. "You are not the first man to come here searching for a way to cage the beast. Now I must tell you this: You cannot."

Oz shook his head, a sudden suspicion seeping into his mind that he had been manipulated. "But you said—"

"The first truth you must accept, my young friend," Master Shantou interrupted, "is that the wolf is not a part of you. It is *all* of you. You are no longer a man. Yet you are more than a beast. You must create within yourself a place of peace. In that place, you must seek out the wolf."

"Not really what I had in mind," Oz told him, bleary-eyed with exhaustion, the old monk's words hardly making sense.

"What is it that you fear?" Shantou inquired sagely. "Not that the wolf will do something terrible, but that *you* will. So, you see. You already know the truth."

Oz paled, suddenly colder by far than he had been. He wished for an argument, but none came to mind.

"There is an herbal compound that will weaken the hold that the moon has over the wolf. But it will not cure you. There is no cure. You must find a balance between the twin aspects of your nature. You must stop thinking like a man and allow yourself to evolve. To become what you are."

Jinan leaned into him, put a hand on his arm for comfort, and though he knew she hoped for more from him, in that moment he was grateful to have her companionship.

"I don't know if I can do that," Oz confessed, unable to meet the old monk's gaze. Instead, he looked off into the sky and found himself staring at the moon.

"In the end, magic and herbs and meditation can only smooth your way, but as always, the journey is yours alone. Until you have learned to trust the wolf, to trust what you are and find a balance in it, you will always be alone."

Master Shantou waved a hand, and all of the torches extinguished with a simultaneous rush of hot wind. Then, staff in hand, he walked past Oz toward the front of the monastery. Jinan looked at him with great longing and sympathy, and then she followed Shantou.

"Rest well," the old monk said without turning as he went into the ravaged building. "Tomorrow we begin."

Nineteen Nights Until the Full Moon

The days blurred one into the other. Oz rose early and with Jinan helped Master Shantou fix breakfast for the three of them. They ate sparsely, always fruits and grains and some meat, though he had never seen their host and teacher hunt. Still, whatever they needed always seemed to be available.

After breakfast they would all work together to continue repairing rooms in the monastery—though the badly damaged wing continued to remain sealed off. Other rooms, however, came together quite nicely. Oz had always been handy, but restoring stone walls was more complicated than he expected. He was no mason, but he was pleased with the work they all did, and Master Shantou appeared to be as well. There was furniture that could not be repaired and some materials had to be taken from other areas in the monastery—doors moved and rubble from the shattered section sifted for proper stones—but somehow they made it work.

After a small midday meal, Shantou would speak to him briefly, mostly reiterating the things he had said to Oz that first night. That he must come to peace by seeking out the wolf inside of him. And he tried; truly, he did. In his own mind he tried to draw out that savage thing and confront it, but he kept a tight leash on its urges and cravings.

Master Shantou spent a great deal of time with Jinan in a large chamber beneath his own quarters that the old monk referred to as his "herb closet." Though he understood that Shantou had taken them both on as students, Oz could not help often feeling abandoned. The monk spent hours teaching Jinan, and in that time left Oz to his own devices. He offered guidance, but too often it sounded to Oz like the kind of spiritual platitudes offered up by any New Age guru. He'd lived in Southern California his whole life. If all he'd wanted was this sort of self-help crap, he could have stayed home.

But he was here. And despite Oz's doubts, there was something about Master Shantou—something he could not quite put his finger on—that made him trust the old monk.

So he climbed down the mountain and took long runs through the valley—waving at nomads he saw tending herds of yaks. He studied a martial arts regimen that Master Shantou showed him on the second day. He hiked farther up the mountain to a beautiful spot amongst a stand of trees, where he could sit cross-legged and gaze down upon the monastery and the valley below and meditate. He could lose himself in that vista, or in the sky that stretched out forever there at the top of the world. Sometimes it snowed lightly, and one afternoon it came down so thick and fast with a hard wind that it felt like a blizzard . . . but it passed within a couple of hours.

It was beautiful, and more peaceful than anyplace Oz

had ever dreamed of. Though he feared the approach of the moon and he still had his doubts, he found in the rhythm of the days at the monastery a simplicity that obliterated everything he had thought he had understood about life. He had always been laid-back, far from excitable. But living as a student to Master Shantou gave him a sort of harmony of mind that he had not known was possible.

Whenever he looked at the eastern mountain he thought of Muztag. The demon and his dark servants were still there, and Oz wondered why they had not returned. Had Muztag thought Shantou was dead, or did he simply not care anymore? Did he think that the old man was beaten and no longer a concern?

From time to time he saw Shantou staring at the opposite peak as well, and the look in his eyes was far from peaceful.

Oz and Jinan often sat together by the fire after dinner, reading or talking softly. Though he was not much more talkative than usual, he had told her about Willow and about Sunnydale. She seemed fascinated but gave him the space he wanted, let him share only as much as he wanted. She, meanwhile, talked a great deal about Hong Kong and her family. So much so that Oz knew she was missing home, and at the same time, enough that he knew he wanted to return to Hong Kong at least for a visit someday. He had left some of his things there, so he had a convenient excuse.

Today had passed like they all had since he and Jinan had arrived here. Breakfast and repair work, noon meal, and then a run. It was one of those days when, despite the presence of the sun in the sky, the moon was still visible. A ghostly shade of it, but the moon nevertheless. As he hiked across the mountainside he found himself staring up at it again and again, like a child unable to shake the idea that the moon is following him.

Oz chuckled inwardly at the thought. In his case, it was true. The moon was following him. He was linked to it forever. And then his thoughts of children and the moon brought images of Jordy into his mind.

He paused, boots crunching snow, and tugged at the neck of his sweatshirt, which suddenly felt as though it were strangling him. Less than three weeks until the next full moon, and as content and relaxed as he felt being at the monastery, he did not believe he was any closer to mastering the beast within him. Master Shantou had begun to show him how to put together the compound that he would need to ingest to help him hold off the moon's influence, but that was untried.

Oz closed his eyes. He stood on the mountain, breathed the cold, thin air into his lungs, felt the chill breeze tugging at his too-long hair, and suddenly he thought of Christmas. He had missed it, and barely even been aware of it. Regret filled him, and he wondered what Willow was doing right at that moment, yearned to hear her voice.

But his mind came back to Jordy. The little boy opening presents on Christmas morning. The boy who was counting on him to find an answer. Oz wasn't doing this only for himself.

He reached back and touched upon Master Shantou's words. Pushed away everything, the feeling of the cold wind, the touch of denim on his legs and cotton on his chest and arms. Without opening his eyes he could feel the location of the moon. Inside of him was a hunger, a pair of red, glistening eyes that wanted to hunt, to stalk these mountains under the cover of night and root out the dens of other animals, to track musk deer and bring them down and spatter their crimson blood in the air so that it fell and steamed away the pristine snow.

Instead of pushing that bloodlust away, he reached down into himself and touched it.

Oz felt the hair on the back of his neck stand up, and a ripple of revulsion passed through him, along with something else. A delicious thrill. His lips curled back to bare his teeth, and he tried to open his mind to the wolf, to share his perceptions with it.

A scent caught his attention. Eyes still closed, he sniffed at the breeze and he knew it. An antelope. Snow crunched and small branches snapped and Oz opened his eyes and saw the animal moving through the trees toward him. He watched it, proud and yet innocent, pulsing with life. It was prey.

If he wanted it.

And of course he did.

But wanting and taking were two separate things. That was what he had to tell the wolf, what he had to show it. He had to put reins upon the beast.

The wind died a moment, and then shifted. The antelope had been moving steadily across the mountainside above his position, but now it paused, as frozen as if it had been crossing the highway and had suddenly been struck by the lights of an oncoming truck. Twitching, it turned its head to stare at him with enormous, wet eyes.

"It's all right," Oz whispered, both to the antelope and to himself, pushing the wolf down, putting the leash on it.

The antelope bolted in terror—terror he could *smell*—and disappeared into the trees back the way it had come.

Oz swore softly to himself. *Of course it was afraid. Instinct told it there was danger, and there is. From me.*

The ghost of the moon followed him as he started across the mountain again, counting the days.

Seventeen Nights Until the Full Moon

Lost in meditation.

Trying again to touch the wolf.

Oz sat upon the mountainside perhaps two hundred yards above the monastery, in the place he had become accustomed to meditating. His eyes were closed so that he might better listen, both to what was inside of him, in his heart, and to the world around him. The whisper of the wind and the swaying of trees. He could taste the deepening of winter on his tongue, smell the fire from the monastery, and hear the burble of a mountain stream that ran not far off toward the western face. It was slower now, and it rippled with the ice that had formed over sections of it.

"Are you a monster?"

"Yaaahhh!" Oz snapped, recoiling from the whisper in his ear.

He fell sideways and scrambled across the snow, his hands cold on the ground, his eyes wide. It was only Shantou, and yet the monk had appeared without a sound—not a footstep or an indrawn breath—as though he had simply arrived from nowhere.

"Where did you learn to walk so softly?" Oz asked, heart still beating fast.

"I did not learn. I became what I am. Just as you must. Close your eyes, Oz. Touch the wolf. Let it come forward. Let it roll over you."

His mind went back to that time two days before with the antelope. Reluctantly he reached within himself again, tried to connect with the wolf, with the beast. He felt its yearning again, its desire to run free, to hunt. He shook off his reluctance and tried to bring the wolf out, to share its awareness, or merge his own with the wolf's. He crouched low, and his hands curled into claws as if play-acting.

But he was not play-acting.

A low growl escaped his throat.

It was not on purpose.

Its suddenness startled him so completely that Oz stood up straight, eyes open, unable to breathe a moment. Shantou was staring at him curiously, nodding gently.

Oz shook his head. "Sorry. Surrender, just not me."

The old monk sighed. "Oh, my friend," he said, "have you listened to nothing I've said?"

Before Oz could argue, Shantou put his weight upon his staff and turned soundlessly. "Return to your meditation. Tomorrow we have an errand to do. One I ought to have taken care of days ago. I have been remiss, but it seemed important to take care of things here first."

"What is it?"

"Tomorrow," Shantou replied. "Meditate."

Oz sat back down and closed his eyes. He tried for over an hour but he could not get back to that peaceful place in his mind.

Sixteen Nights Until the Full Moon

After lunch, Oz and Jinan accompanied Master Shantou down the mountain along the path they had discovered on their way up the first time, and which Oz had used to get down into the valley nearly every day since. From the base they set off due east across the valley, where tall grass thrust up through several inches of recent snowfall. Winter had come to the mountains of Tibet, and it seemed unforgiving.

"So what's our agenda today?" Jinan asked as they walked side by side behind the monk.

Master Shantou did not pause, even continued on several steps, walking with his staff but not putting much weight on it. How much he depended upon it seemed to change from day to day.

"The village of Lingka. We have spoken about it before."

"Muztag's houseguests have been hunting down here?" Jinan asked.

Now the old monk did pause to glance back at her. "I am uncertain," he said, resting a moment on the staff. Then he turned and began to walk again. "A nomad of my acquaintance, Ganjin, informed me that a demon had killed several of the villagers. I destroyed the demon when it came down into the valley again.

"I have heard nothing more from the village since then. This is not unusual. I assumed that it meant the attacks had ceased. But now I wonder if the silence has been because nothing has happened, or because something horrible has. Surely after what he did to my students and apprentices, Muztag has no fear of reprisal should he attack the village."

They made the trek across several miles of grassland with only the wind and one another for company. Oz found it curious and somewhat unsettling that save for the occasional bird he spotted no wildlife at all. Not an antelope or even a yak that had wandered from its herd. He said nothing about it, though he thought that even if Master Shantou and Jinan had not noticed, they certainly seemed ill at ease. It was as though the wind carried with it a foreboding sense of disquiet.

When they stopped briefly to take a drink of water, the old monk lowered his head. "I ought to have done this sooner," he said. "I wanted to see to the monastery and to the onset of your studies, and I have occupied my mind night and day with attempting to find a way to destroy Muztag once and for all. But I should have looked in upon the village before this."

So Oz knew he wasn't the only one who was feeling it, the sense of dread as they approached Lingka. He also had a persistent prickling on the back of his neck, the hairs standing on end. It was a familiar feeling, but it took him a while to place. He realized after a time that it reminded him of being a small boy, of waking up in the middle of the night and going to the kitchen for a drink of water, of forcing himself not to glance at the window above the sink, at the black night beyond, for fear that he would see someone looking back in. That was the same feeling he had now.

That someone was watching.

Some forty-five minutes after they had set out, he, Jinan, and Master Shantou arrived at the village. At first he was relieved to see that the village was still standing. There were no plumes of smoke, no fires. But as they drew nearer he saw sentries with rifles on the outskirts of the village and noticed the absence of children. Even the demon village back on Fiji had had children playing outside during the day, but not here. Oz had seen Lingka only from afar, while out hiking or jogging across the valley. In his mind he had an image of what its people would be like. The reality was far different from his imagination. There was no laughter. In fact, there were very few people outside at all, save for the guards. To the north of the village he caught sight of a tall stockade fence that was under construction; a new addition to Lingka.

When the nearest guard caught sight of Master Shantou, he began to shout. Oz was not certain at first if he was challenging their approach, but a moment later the other sentries joined in the shout and he realized they were simply conveying the news of the old monk's arrival.

"The town crier," Oz muttered.

Jinan glanced at him. "What's that?"

He shook his head. "Nothing. Just a little too *Road Warrior* for me. They're under siege here."

Master Shantou said nothing, but to Oz he appeared somehow diminished by the condition of the village.

Then, as if by magic, the old man stood up straighter, and the despair drained from his face to be replaced by a kind of quiet dignity that was more in keeping with the way he usually carried himself.

A trio of guards approached them and bowed. After Master Shantou had passed them, however, the three men glanced up warily at the monk's companions. Oz nodded gravely to them, not willing to look away but wanting to acknowledge their attention, no matter how unfavorable it was.

Another guard escorted two older men toward them. One was tall and somewhat portly, nearly bald. The other was compact, a diminutive man an inch or two shorter than Oz, his size belying the quiet power that rippled through his body with even the smallest motion. Immediately the two men launched a dozen questions at Master Shantou in a staccato barrage that must have been Tibetan, for Jinan looked just as puzzled as Oz felt. As the old monk spoke to the two men, other villagers began to emerge from their dwellings and come toward the monk. Just as the guards had done, these men and women bowed to Master Shantou, but their faces were tentative, their eyes haunted, as though they had only the shadow of belief that he could be of any real help to them.

The two men—the closest thing to officials the village had, by Oz's guess—did not so much as glance at him and Jinan. But the other people had no such compunction. Oz's unease on the way to the village was forgotten, the instinctive discomfort at the thought that he had been watched replaced now by the tangible distress of being stared at with such bold and naked suspicion. There was fear in the acute glare of these people as well, and Oz liked that no better than he did their wariness. His entire agenda coming on this journey to begin with was to alter his life in such a way that no one would ever have cause to fear him again.

A light touch on his arm drew his attention. Oz turned to find Jinan gazing at him with concern.

"You look spooked. Jumpy. Are you all right?"

Her hair was in braids again, her perfect Cupid's-bow lips painted with screaming red lipstick. She could not have seemed more out of place if she had made an effort. Oz raised an eyebrow, amused by her seriousness given the incongruous image of her amongst the dour, rural villagers.

"No," he confessed. "Should I be?"

Jinan smiled. "No. Just wanted to make sure."

When Oz turned back to look around for Master Shantou, the old monk was still entrenched in Tibetan mutterings with the village elders. But his own attention was drawn quickly away from Shantou to two of the guards. They were young, no older than Oz himself, and possibly younger, and they were glaring at him with open disdain. They also had rifles, which gave him no comfort at all. The two guards stood with a trio of older women who whispered to them.

After a moment, one of the guards approached him, rifle slung across his shoulder. His eyes were narrowed and his lips pressed together to a slit, and he crossed his arms as he glared at Oz. He barked something at Oz in Tibetan. Though the words were gibberish to a Californian, their tone had an immediacy that clearly demanded a response. The guard towered over him, but Oz thought that turning away might set the man off. His gaze ticked toward Master Shantou, but the old monk had not seemed to notice the sudden friction.

"You getting any of this?" Oz asked Jinan in a rasped stage whisper.

Growing angry, the guard shouted at him now, pointing furiously—possibly even accusingly—at Oz's head, which made absolutely no sense to him at all.

"I'll get Master Shantou," Jinan said quickly.

She had started to walk away, when a large, austere man stepped between Oz and the guard. He snapped at the boyish, armed sentry in Tibetan, then turned and reached up to Oz's head. Before Oz could react, the man tugged on his hair.

"Ow?" he said, quite reasonably he thought, as he stared at the man.

But the grim-faced new arrival was busy glaring at the guard, who turned after a moment and returned to the trio of women and his fellow guard. They all stared at the man who had intervened and then began to whisper amongst themselves.

The austere man who had pulled Oz's hair turned to smile at him and Jinan. He took a long breath and studied Jinan, and then began to speak to her. When Jinan quickly—and most happily—replied, Oz realized the man was speaking Chinese rather than Tibetan. After a couple of minutes, the man patted Oz on the shoulder and then walked over to join the conversation Master Shantou was having with the elders.

Oz turned to Jinan. "What was with the hair?"

"Apparently none of them have ever seen a redhead before. They thought you might have been a demon in disguise." Jinan let a beat go by before snickering softly. "Kind of ironic, don't you think?"

"Irony isn't what it used to be," Oz replied. "My sense of humor, pretty much surgically removed."

"You had one?" Jinan asked, straight-faced.

Oz regarded her coolly. After a moment, he looked over at the man who had spoken to Jinan. "So someone here speaks Chinese, at least. Too much to hope for English, I guess. Did he tell you anything?"

The mischievous light in Jinan's eyes went dim. "His name is Tsochen. His daughter was to marry soon, but her intended husband was killed a week or so ago. There have been a lot of deaths. The demons have been poaching on the village in a big way."

Oz glanced around at the people who still stared at him and Jinan. "Who'd have guessed?" A shiver went through him. "Master Shantou was right. This Muztag guy thinks he can get away with anything now."

Jinan moved closer to him, their shoulders touching. "Maybe he can."

Chapter Twelve

First Night of the Full Moon

A single high window filtered the afternoon light into the private sanctuary where Master Shantou prepared most of his potions and did much of his research. The old monk was absent at the moment, however, meditating in the courtyard as he did most every afternoon.

Jinan sat alone at the single wooden table in the room. Dust motes swam in the splash of light from the window, and the sun warmed her. The monastery was huge and drafty and now that winter was coming hard upon the mountain, it was always cold. Even with her own internal fire, the chill on her skin was noticeable. She wore a thick, turtleneck sweater of red wool, and black wool pants.

She loved this room. It seemed a treasure trove of endless possibility, with its shelves of dusty books and occult artifacts, enchanted amulets and other objects she was not yet allowed to touch. A stuffed bird sat atop a shelf in a far corner, and she reminded herself for perhaps the twentieth time to ask Master Shantou if it had more use than merely as a display. Jinan suspected it did. The place was a sort of archaic laboratory as well, with racks of herbs and bottles filled with oils and powders made from the flesh and bone of various animals and plants. On either side of the window were two tall cases whose shelves were filled with boxes and bottles that were laden with dust, forgotten ingredients for spells Master Shantou had apparently not had reason to perform in a very long time.

Before Jinan on the table lay a book of herbal spells that could be worked on human physiology. It was written in Chinese, though the style was so old that she had trouble deciphering the meaning of some of what was written there. Though she was meant to be studying healing spells—Master Shantou had insisted that these were some of the most difficult and yet most useful potions—she had come across a section on concoctions that could influence human emotion, and her mind kept drifting to those pages even if she would not allow her fingers to turn the pages.

Love spells. There were love spells.

The warmth of the sun through the window and her disinterest in focusing upon the work she was meant to be doing combined to make her sleepy. With drowsy eyes, Jinan entertained just for a moment the idea of learning some of the love spells in the book. *What could it hurt?*

A smile played at the corners of her mouth. Her hair—loose, for once—fell down across her face, and she pushed a hand threw it, flipping it back. She picked up her headband from the table and slipped it on, yawning.

"Keeping you awake?"

Startled, Jinan spun around to see Oz standing just inside the door. He watched her curiously and then, as though realizing he had erred, backed up a step and knocked twice. Jinan laughed softly, but then an alarm bell went off in her head. She glanced quickly down at the book on the table. Though it was not open to the love spells and though it was written in Chinese, still she flushed with embarrassment and flipped it closed.

"Hey," she said, standing up, hands twined nervously behind her back.

Oz came into the room and leaned against the end of the table. He wore jeans and boots and a tattered hooded sweatshirt that smelled of incense and he seemed more distant and preoccupied than ever. Not that Jinan could blame him. The afternoon was moving deathly slow for her, but she imagined the minutes were flying for him.

"Tonight's the night, huh?" she began awkwardly. "First night of the full moon. Are you ready?"

He ran a hand through his shaggy red hair. "I don't know." After a moment he shook his head and focused on her again. "Master Shantou asked me to come see you."

Jinan nodded, smiling, a flush of excitement rising within her. "He showed me how to make the compound you have to drink for tonight. I guess it's sort of a test for me. He wants me to teach you how to do it."

Oz nodded thoughtfully, the weight of the past month bearing heavily upon him. Jinan could see it in his eyes, and her heart went out to him. Where he leaned upon the table, his hand was propped on the wood and she reached out to cover it with her own to reassure him. He flinched in surprise at her touch. For a moment he only gazed at her, and she felt a connection then, saw in him an acknowledgment of her own feelings and evidence that he felt at least something for her.

Then he pulled his hand away with a regretful glance.

At the door to the sanctuary, Master Shantou cleared his throat. Jinan felt herself blush even more deeply, but the monk's arrival seemed to make Oz only that much more distracted.

"The night approaches," Master Shantou said.

Oz nodded. He glanced at Jinan. "After I'm gone, bar the doors."

Master Shantou narrowed his gaze sternly. "We cannot bar the doors if we are outside with you. Now prepare the compound. Jinan will instruct you, but you must do it yourself. And learn quickly. There is little time."

Oz wrinkled his nose in revulsion at the smell that wafted up to him from the wooden bowl. For the better part of an hour he had worked with Jinan, collecting the ingredients on the English translation she had scrawled on torn parchment paper and then combining them in the bowl. It wasn't as simple as just dumping them all together, however. The preparations were intricate and had to be painstakingly followed. It was, to his surprise, much like following a complicated recipe. Unfortunately for him, the results were not nearly as appetizing as the sorts of things one usually concocted in the kitchen.

The oils had been measured and poured. Ash from an immolated wolf was sprinkled into the bowl. Most of it was herbs, some common and others quite rare. Oz crushed them first with a pestle and mortar and then stirred them into the mixture. The entire time he was working on the compound he thought of little other than Willow. She had an instinct for this sort of thing; it would have taken her ten minutes to complete.

But Master Shantou had been specific. Oz had to prepare it himself. Maybe that was part of the magic.

"Not so much of the valerian," Jinan cautioned as Oz began to sprinkle it into the bowl. "It'll put you to sleep and that would sort of defeat the purpose, wouldn't it?"

He hesitated. The idea of simply drugging himself—drugging the wolf so that it slept through until morning—was more than a little appealing. But that would be avoiding his problem rather than confronting him. He was never going to get home that way.

At last he raised the wooden bowl in both hands and stared down at it. It had a greenish tint to it not unlike pesto sauce. The odor reminded him equally of skunks and stale laundry. He was hardly aware of the small groan that uttered from his throat then.

Master Shantou appeared in the doorway again, as though he had known that the compound was complete. He rested on his staff and waited, somewhat impatiently.

Oz wrinkled his nose again. "Nobody thought to make a pill for this," he said. "Weird."

Quickly, so that he would not be able to change his mind, he lifted the bowl to his lips with both hands and drained the thick, vile fluid in several huge gulps. When he had swallowed the last of it he scowled and wiped his sleeve across his mouth, the bitterness of it making him shudder.

It was awful. *Stuff better work if it tastes like that,* he thought.

But he knew that the compound was only meant to alleviate the moon's pull upon the Wolf, not sever it. The rest was up to him.

As the light began to die and the blue horizon deepened ominously, they climbed the mountain above the monastery to the spot where Oz had meditated every day for nearly a month. He had found a place of peace there, but it was within himself, not the location. Sitting cross-legged there he had found it possible to ignore the freezing cold wind and even the occasional snow squall. Several days before he had meditated there for two hours while flakes piled up on his head and shoulders, accumulating on him, sticking to his thick jacket.

At peace. It was an inner harmony he had never

imagined he would be able to attain, and he knew he owed Master Shantou for that. The old monk's teachings were simple, yet forceful, and they and his surroundings forced Oz to reach within himself for balance and confidence.

All of that was pretty much out the window now. It felt like a load of crap to him at the moment, with the sun's rays dying in the sky and the night crawling across the mountains. Dusk was his undoing.

Oz sat now in his familiar spot. His eyes were closed, but he could feel Master Shantou's eyes upon him, could smell Jinan's scent, like lilacs. His pulse was too fast, their nearness distracting. In moments the change would be upon him, and they would be in jeopardy. An old monk with a wooden staff and a tiny slip of a girl. Granted, she was a fire-demon, but it had taken her whole family to subdue him the last time the moon hung full in the sky.

He blew out a breath. Tried to focus on his other senses. The cold wind bit at his cheeks with a stinging caress. Oz steepled his fingers together and laid them across his lap. He took long, deep breaths and felt his chest rise and fall, skin brushing against the cotton of his T-shirt. The wind ruffled his hair. He smelled the smoke from the monastery's fire.

Damn it, he thought, and blew out a hot breath of frustration.

Dusk was here. The wolf was waking inside him. The moon was huge and pregnant with awful intent above. He did not have to open his eyes to see it; he felt it. The wolf snarled, began to yearn for the moon, to reach for it the way a flower turns toward the sun.

Oz tried once more to focus.

Master Shantou's voice carried through the twilight, though he spoke in a whisper. "Jinan, perhaps you should go inside."

That's good, Oz thought. *At least she'll be okay.* But then he realized that Master Shantou intended to stay alone out there with him, and Oz felt torn.

"Wait," he said quickly, opening his eyes. The sky was more black than blue, stars glittering above. Oz was startled. He ought to have changed already, or any moment now. He felt it coming on, but the rage and hunger was not as strong as it should have been.

"Maybe you should stay."

The smile that flickered across Jinan's face was heartbreaking. She had misunderstood his desire for her to remain.

"Well, if you're going to insist," Jinan replied.

Oz gazed at the ground. "Y'know, just in case. You can help protect Master Shantou."

He did not see the change in her expression, but when she spoke again her tone was cold, clipped.

"Sure."

There were things he knew he had to say to her, but now was not the time. Not when he had finally reached the moment for which he had traveled all this way and worked so hard these last weeks. He closed his eyes and tried to regulate his breathing again, falling into the meditative trance Master Shantou had taught him to achieve.

The wolf was there waiting for him.

Oz growled low, unconsciously, and the sweatshirt suddenly felt irritatingly tight around his neck. He breathed evenly, soothing himself, the winter wind crisp as it numbed his skin. The mountain was silent save for the breeze in the trees and the distant gurgle of the water under the frozen surface of the stream.

Then all external stimuli seemed to disappear.

Oz is onstage with Dingoes Ate My Baby at the Bronze. The lights are hot and bright, but he exults in this, the place where he belongs more than almost any other.

His guitar, stenciled so long ago in lipstick with the name Sweet J, thrums in his hands with electricity pouring out of the amplifiers. The song isn't even one he recognizes, but that doesn't matter. The beat of it gets under his skin, a primal thing matching the rhythm of his heart, and he kicks the wah-wah pedal on the stage and picks his way through a blistering solo. The kind of solo his mind always composes but that his fingers can rarely reproduce. Tonight, though . . . every note goes right from his mind to the guitar, through the amps and out to the audience.

They roar. They love it. Beads of sweat pour down Oz's forehead as he bends over the guitar.

He finishes the solo, and Devon starts singing the next verse in a wail that sounds more like some kind of wild animal than a human voice. Oz grins broadly, his usual reserve melting away. Everything around him, including the rest of the band, seems indistinct.

He looks out at the crowd in the Bronze. The whistles and shouts meld into a wave of sound, but Oz frowns. There are so many of them, mostly kids from the high school, but also some from the college as well . . . at least he thinks they are. But he cannot tell, for none of them have faces. They are as gray and indistinct as everything else around him, but it is as though their features have been blotted out, or Oz has a blind spot where each of their faces should be.

He plays one last chord, but he plays it wrong. It is loud and jarring and it interrupts the music and suddenly the rest of the band falters. Oz can feel them staring at him, but he barely registers it. Out of the corner of his eye he sees color and movement, and when he turns he finds that not every face has been obscured.

At the foot of the stage, just off to his right, stand his girlfriend and his nephew.

"Willow?" he begins, confused and afraid. Something is wrong here. Terribly wrong. "Jordy?"

Their faces contort with terror, and both of them turn and shove through the crowd in silent, frenzied panic. Oz doesn't understand, but he feels it as well. Hot breath on his neck, eyes burning into his back. He feels it in the core of his being, in that primitive, reptilian part of his brain, and the terror inhabits him as though he is merely a new skin it has slipped into. And yet the terror is as much for them as it is for himself.

"Wait!" he shouts after Willow and Jordy. "Come back!"

Oz leaps down from the stage, dropping his guitar to shatter on the ground. He takes off into the crowd, shoving through the faceless throng who murmur and growl and reach out to touch him and pinch him and shove.

"Jordy, don't!" he shouts.

The crowd blurs around him. The world tilts under his feet, and he stumbles into two faceless, gray girls who shove him backward. Oz gets turned around, his throat and eyes dry and burning with desperation. He reaches out, shouts again for his cousin, pushes past people, and finds himself suddenly in a clearing in the midst of the crowd, an open circle of bodies. Somebody must be dancing, he thinks. They've all stepped back to give them room. He's seen things like that before, at clubs and in the movies.

A presence looms behind him.

Oz shivers. "Jordy?"

He turns and sees it, the wolf, towering over him. It is hunched there, pointed ears twitching, yellow eyes burning in the gray mist. Everything else is blurred, but not this. Not the Beast. Saliva steams and drips from its jaws, and its teeth snap and gnash at him.

"It's not Jordy, Oz," the wolf snarls. "You know who it is."

And it begins to howl.

• • •

It was full dark. Night. The moon was fat and gleaming above, the snow on the mountain glistening in its light. Jinan doubted she had taken a single breath in the minutes since night had fallen. Her heart thundered in her chest so loud that she was sure Master Shantou could hear it. For his part, the old monk merely stood there, one hand on his staff, eyes narrowed as though he were peering through a microscope.

Jinan was almost afraid to smile, afraid to accept what she was seeing. Oz was doing it. He was actually doing it.

And then he wasn't.

He had been sitting so peacefully, rocking ever so slightly, humming a fast melody she did not know. Jinan had no idea what the music was, but it had been helping, she was sure of that.

Now the rocking and the humming stopped, and the growl began. It sounded low and distant at first, as though it might just be hunger pangs in his stomach. But then his lips curled back, and she could see that his teeth were lengthening, sharpening.

Jinan shook her head, sadness welling up within her.

Oz hunched over, fingers curled into claws, and he *changed.* Fur tore up through his skin even as his limbs and muscles stretched and grew, his face thrusting outward with a crack of bone, his ears elongating, his brow lowering over eyes that snapped open now, gleaming with malice and hunger.

He opened his gnashing jaws to reveal long, needle fangs that glistened in the moonlight even whiter than the snow. From deep within the throat of that beast came a long, ululating howl, and it sprang to its feet. The wolf focused on Master Shantou immediately, as though it recognized him as an enemy, as though it knew he had been helping Oz to cage it.

"Oz, no!" Jinan cried.

And then she changed as well.

It looked painful for Oz. For Jinan, shape-shifting was as simple as flexing a muscle, an exhilarating experience she had relished all her life. This was her true face revealed. She shook her head and shuddered as her tail grew out from the base of her spine, her skin turned an oily blue-black, and her skull split open so that the fire that smoldered within her always could erupt volcanically from within. It scorched the very air around her, and she felt tendrils of flame licking from her eyes, spitting from her throat, as she cried out again.

"Oz!"

Jinan leaped at the werewolf, afraid to hurt him and terrified of the consequences if she could not. Muscles rippling with demonic strength, she latched on to his back with both hands and tried to pull him away from the old monk, whose face only registered disappointment.

"Try to understand me! Leave him—"

The werewolf bucked and shook her off, snarled at her, and then cracked her across the face with a vicious backhand that tumbled Jinan end over end onto the snow and across the ground. She started to roll down the mountainside but grabbed hold of a rocky outcropping to stop herself.

But when she stood again, the wolf had already forgotten her. She was a nuisance, an afterthought. Master Shantou was its prey. It lunged at him.

The old monk sighed and lifted his staff, which began to crackle with blue-white energy. The wolf slashed its claws at him, but Master Shantou sidestepped the attack easily, brought up the staff, and struck the beast's furry head with a resounding crack. Sparks of that blue-white electricity flew from the point of impact, and the thing howled in pain and reeled. The werewolf was anguished and enraged, and it turned slowly on the old monk.

Master Shantou struck it again in the skull.

The werewolf crumpled to the ground, unconscious.

Jinan walked over and stood beside the old monk, gazing silently down at the still form. The fire that blazed up from her open skull was diminished slightly, and though only another Kaohsiung demon would have realized it, the drops of liquid flame that slid from her eyes now were akin to tears.

Second Night of the Full Moon

When Oz came to that morning, he felt as though his eyelids had been pasted shut. There was dried blood on his lips, and somehow he knew it was not that of prey, but his own. His head ached like he'd been on an all-night drinking binge and now had the mother of all hangovers. And in some ways, this was a hangover. But it had nothing to do with drinking.

Wincing at the pain in his head, he forced himself to open his eyes, shading them with a hand. Sun streamed in the window of his room at the monastery. His mind was dull save for the pain, but images slowly began to rouse themselves in his head. Sitting on the mountainside, Jinan and Master Shantou watching over him. The moonrise. He had held the wolf at bay.

But only briefly.

"Crap," he muttered.

He rose and dressed slowly, then went out into the monastery. It was late, and he assumed Jinan and Shantou had eaten without him. She would probably be in the sanctuary, but he did not want to face her just now. For that matter, he did not really want to face Master Shantou, either. Reluctantly, however, he found his way through the maze-like interior of the massive stone structure and walked out into the central courtyard.

Master Shantou sat in the snow, arms raised as though in supplication to the sun. His eyes were closed tightly, but his eyebrow went up as Oz approached.

"I have done all that I can," the old monk said without opening his eyes. "If you cannot embrace the beast, you will never control it."

As dusk approached, Oz sat in his accustomed place. Master Shantou was nearby, looking over him, staff in hand. Jinan was inside somewhere. She had not offered to come up with him tonight, and he could not blame her. He had enough disappointment in his own heart without having to bear the burden of hers.

He focused, he meditated. He tried. He really did.

And he failed.

In the village of Lingka, Tsochen drank vodka that burned his throat and grimaced as it went down. His daughter had not left their house at all in the weeks since Kangri's murder. Their neighbors were disgusted, Tsochen knew. Were he a proper father he would force her from her room, from the house, force her to do her part to feed and protect the village. But he could not bear to do that to his flower, his little girl.

He understood.

Were it not for his great pride, this bear of a man might have walled himself up within the house as well. Kangri had been a good boy and would have made a fine husband for Shisha. More than that, though, it was simply not safe in the village. They had to work, to farm and to weave and to live and move on, but the shadow of the horror that had been visited upon them was long upon the valley. The eastern mountain loomed ominously above, but the nightmare creatures that crouched in the tall grass or crept on spider legs into their homes, those were the real fears. The mountain was just a mountain. It symbolized a predatory evil that Tsochen knew none of them would escape.

He choked on his vodka, startled by this subtle, silent admission to himself. The big man frowned and clinked his glass down on the table, furious that he had allowed himself to surrender.

"Enough," he muttered.

His wife glanced up from across the room, where she was fixing a hole in his sweater by candlelight. She said nothing, but her eyes were inquiry enough.

"We cannot stay here," Tsochen told her, his heart heavy but his decision made. "It may take days, but we must go. The valley is a place of death now, the air poisoned for us. I will speak to the others. We will gather our things and go south."

"But to travel in winter?" his wife said, caution and anxiety in her eyes.

"What is winter compared with a season in Hell?" Tsochen replied. He shook his head. "No, we will go. And the demons are welcome to anyone fool enough to remain behind."

His wife's gaze still upon him, Tsochen nodded with satisfaction and poured himself another glass of vodka. When he glanced at her again, she had gone back to stitching his sweater. He took a long breath and let his mind wander.

A thunderous pounding rattled the door in its frame.

Tsochen stood up, knocking the vodka glass over.

His wife dropped her needle.

The door crashed open, and Tsochen's wife shrieked at the sight of the hulking, red-scaled beast that stood on the threshold, tentacles erupting from its abdomen and reaching out toward them with a loud sucking sound.

Tsochen roared in fury and terror and grabbed for the tentacles.

They tore him apart.

Just outside the village, on the edge of the narrow river, the demon lord Muztag stood with two of his sorcerers and the hunter, Cain. Muztag's five eyes glowed in the dark, and he chuffed with bilious laughter as he watched the sorcerous fires begin to blaze below, consuming the dwellings and leaping from roof to roof as though alive.

Demons rampaged through the village, tore at the humans and their children, plucked small girls up and dropped them into heavy sacks they carried over their shoulders. *Draco Volans* flew down on leathery wings and tangled themselves in the hair of the women, nipped and scratched at their faces and throats, whipped into a frenzy by Muztag's hatred for these human cattle.

A chorus of screams lifted up over the roar of flames and the thunder of hooves and joined into a hellish disharmony that the demon lord relished above all else.

Yet none of that was the cause of his amusement. No, his great pleasure was born of another source. Down amongst the demons that served him, who killed and stole and burned, were the students of Shantou, human and demon alike.

They were his now, and Muztag had to laugh. It was truly delicious.

"So beautiful," he said in the tongue of his kin. "They are so pliable."

Cain looked at him curiously. The human looked bored, but Muztag had insisted upon his company. It was imperative that he realize what he was committing himself to. Fortunately, he seemed not at all bothered by the carnage and the screams.

One of Muztag's pet sorcerers stepped closer to him. "If old Shantou could see his students now, my Lord, it would kill him."

"Yes," Muztag replied, that chuffing laugh bubbling out of him again. "Shantou."

Third Night of the Full Moon

Oz lay in bed that morning feeling even more hung over than he had the previous day.

"Tonight," he promised himself.

At dusk.

Darkness creeping.

The ghost moon fat and looming.

Oz felt a calm within him unlike any he had achieved during any previous meditative session. It would have been easy to take comfort in that, to consider it progress. But to him it felt more like surrender, as though rather than coming to terms with the beast within he was getting used to the idea that he had failed to contain it.

Still, he tried.

Once again he let the world wash over him, let his senses flow with the wind and the cold and the power of the mountain, and he descended to the place inside of him where the wolf lived and thrived and hungered.

There is no waking dream this time, no imagined performance with the Dingoes, no appearance in his mind of those he longs to protect and longs to see and embrace even now.

Despite the sting of the icy wind, that place down inside of him is jungle humid, close and intimate. His ears ache with the snarl and the rumbling thunder of the breathing of the wolf. It is all around him, omnipresent now, the way he imagines he must be for it. It envelops and encompasses him as he moves through this primal place within him, pushes through low-hanging forest branches, knowing the peril he faces but curiously fearless.

Then it stands before him.

Towers over him.

Huge.

How can I be that big? *Oz wonders.*

Then he flinches as he realizes that he has recognized this monster as himself. For a moment he can neither speak nor really even think. The wolf breathes deeply, raggedly, its fangs gleaming. But it does not attack him.

Oz shakes his head, horrified and amazed. "You're not the most huggable guy, but . . ."

The wolf speaks.

"I am not a man," *it says.* "You are not a beast. Together, we *become.*"

Oz knows that it was not the wolf speaking but merely another aspect of himself. Still, the words unnerve him. As hard as he has worked to accept this as truth, as often as Master Shantou has insisted upon it, now he steps back from the slavering beast, the air damp and close and too hot around him. He shakes his head in denial.

The wolf lashes out and rips him open.

Twenty-nine Nights Until the Full Moon

And so it began again.

Oz woke late again the morning after the third night of the full moon. There was no hesitation, not even any real exhaustion. His eyes snapped open, and he knew instantly where he was and what had happened. A fury perhaps borrowed from the wolf raged in his heart, and he stared at the stone ceiling and the wooden beams supporting it with a gaze full of hatred, as though the architecture had somehow offended him.

For twenty minutes he simply lay there. When at last he sat up, he did so quickly, his every motion hinting at the frustration and rage he was barely suppressing. Down inside of him, where the wolf usually lurked, a small part of him wanted so very much to weep.

A stray thought swept through him and lodged in his mind, echoing there, banging about inside his head like a bird trapped in the attic.

What if I can never go home again?

A surge of adrenaline shot through him and—teeth gritted to hold back the animal growl he would not allow himself to utter—Oz launched a vicious punch at the wall. Loose molding around the stones cracked and sprinkled to the floor as pain shot up his arm.

Fuming, he glanced at his raw and bloody knuckles, wondering if the pain meant he had broken some of them. He cleaned up the cuts on his hand and bandaged his knuckles, dressed quickly and then slipped as quietly as possible out of his room. He was careful not to run into Master Shantou and Jinan as he took bread and cheese from the kitchen, and then he left the monastery.

There was no meditation that day. Instead, he hiked up the mountain, clad in his heavy jacket and a wool hat he had gotten from the villagers in Lingka, the sort of thing the nomads wore. The air grew thinner and the terrain more challenging and eventually he stopped to eat the food he had brought. Afterward he wandered aimlessly for hours. The snow was deep at this altitude, and there were icy crevasses that might be the death of a careless climber.

When at last his wanderings took him back down the mountain toward the ledge upon which sat the monastery, the night was coming on. He gazed at the gibbous moon with disdain. Like the tide, its power was receding now, and Oz could not help wishing—as Jordy had done on a night quite some time ago—that it would never come back.

Almost unconsciously, his steps took him back to that place where he usually meditated—where he had suffered three nights of failure. It felt all wrong to him there now, and Oz knew that he would have to choose another place if he was to stay, to try again. This one was tainted.

Footsteps crunched in the snow.

Oz sniffed the air. Lilacs.

He turned to find Jinan standing perhaps a dozen feet away, a great sadness in her eyes.

"I looked for you all day," she said.

His only apology was a tiny shrug. "Went up the mountain."

Jinan glanced up, and her exquisite features were silhouetted in the moonlight. "Did you find what you were looking for?"

"No."

She stepped nearer to him, her intensity forcing him to meet her gaze. "Next month," Jinan said in a rasp. "You were so close. I know you'll get it."

Oz nodded noncommittally.

Jinan reached up to run her hand across his face. "I know what Master Shantou said about you being alone. But you're not alone. Not really."

His heart nearly broke as he looked into those eyes. He was hurt, and she wanted to help him to heal. Jinan's heart was open to him. All she wanted was to be closer to him.

With profound regret, Oz took her hand away from his face.

"Nothing's changed, Jinan. Truth is, I am alone now. But there's someone I want to get back to."

Her lips pressed tightly together, and her eyes brimmed with moisture. She turned quickly away to hide the hurt on her face. Oz watched her, wishing he could say something more, but he had never been very good with words. As he watched her, though, Jinan stiffened suddenly, and her eyes widened as she gazed down toward the monastery.

"Oz?" she said weakly. "It may not be the moon that stops you from going home again."

Confused, he turned to look at the monastery, and again words failed him.

Winged silhouettes were outlined black against the night sky. A small army of demons and monsters scrambled up the face of the mountain toward the ledge . . . toward the monastery.

Chapter Thirteen

Twenty-nine Nights Until the Full Moon

Jinan stared down the mountain and shook her head back and forth, her mouth a silent little "o" and her heart thundering in her ears. From the moment Master Shantou had told them the story of Muztag, the demon of the eastern mountain, they had known this could happen. But as the days and nights had passed without a new attack, it had grown to seem as though it would never come. That Muztag considered his ancient enemy defeated, and that was enough.

Or so Jinan had come to believe.

Under the light from the moon and stars they swarmed over the ledge and rushed toward the front of the monastery. Wings and whipping tails, ice and fire, leather and scales and flowing tar for skin. Of the perhaps two dozen demons there were only a handful whose breed she could even recognize, could even guess at. As her mind instantly began to catalog, to gauge the monstrous force set against them, Jinan counted five trolls and a trio of dark sorcerers who floated on eldritch energies several feet above the ground. In the sky, amidst the several flying demons, there were *Draco Volans,* the vicious little dragon rodents swooping and circling more like vultures than bats.

They did not march, the things on the ground. Rather, they ambled and crawled and slithered and lumbered, and yet they moved far more swiftly than Jinan would have believed had she not seen them with her own eyes.

"Oh, God," she whispered.

The demons were horrible. A fiery tear leaked from her eye, and she shifted her shape without even realizing it. This was too much. It had been a glorious adventure, all of this—leaving home and running to Tibet, learning the rudiments of sorcery, watching Oz struggle with his curse, falling in love, no matter that her feelings weren't returned. She had relished every moment.

But this . . . how could she have prepared herself for this?

Growing up in a Kaohsiung family in Hong Kong, she had met her share of demons and halflings. Some of them were wonderful people, and others were absolutely vile. But the ghastly multitude that even now hammered the walls of the monastery was unlike anything she had ever seen. It wasn't merely that they were ugly—she had happily served the most hideous demons from behind the counter at her father's shop. It was the atmosphere they carried with them, a putrid miasma that she could sense, if not smell, even so far above the fiends, even with the mountain wind blowing across her face.

Snow crunched beside her. A rock was knocked loose and rolled six or seven yards before it came to rest at a jutting formation of stone. Jinan glanced over at Oz, and it was as though she came awake from a terrible nightmare to find that it was true.

Oz was scrambling down the mountain toward the monastery.

"No," she said, shaking her head.

Images flashed through her mind of the horrors down there on that ledge tearing through the monastery, defiling the place and her things, beating Master Shantou, even tearing him apart. . . .

"No!" Jinan shouted. "Oz, stop!"

Her thoughts were a whirlwind of urges and fears and loyalties. Everything she had inside her screamed at her to protect the old monk and that benevolent place of learning. But she could hardly breathe, she was so terrified of the filth down there. Jinan had spent a great deal of time the previous month talking about how she could take care of herself. But now she wished desperately that her family were with her.

If she threw herself into that battle, she would die.

Oz stumbled, nearly lost his footing, and then only barely regained his balance as he rushed down the mountainside unmindful of her hesitation.

Jinan stared at him. Oz was going to die. Her gaze ticked back toward the monastery, and though she could not see the front doors from her vantage point up on the mountain, she heard the crack of wood that echoed across the valley and the cacophony of roars that went up as the fiends began to rush inside, rampaging through the place.

"Fathers protect me," she whispered in her native tongue.

Then Jinan ran after Oz. Fire blazing up from her open skull, she descended the mountain face in long leaps, the weight of her tail a comfort and an aid in keeping her balance. Each time she landed, sliding in snow, she slapped the earth with her tail, using it much like a rudder. By her fourth leap she had nearly caught up with Oz.

"Wait," she called after him. "Maybe you should let me—"

Oz was scrambling haphazardly, gaze upon the monastery, not paying any attention to his footing. He did not even slow down as he cut her off.

"They're going to kill him! I'm not just going to watch."

A flash of guilt went through Jinan, for she had considered doing exactly that. Oz hit a severe downgrade then and he began sliding on his boots as if skiing. Twenty-five feet or more he slipped that way down the mountain, and then his right foot hit something under the snow and he went over, tumbling hard, limbs flying, gaining momentum.

There was a narrow ledge below with outcroppings of stone jutting from it. If Oz collided with them—

Jinan leaped. Fire trailed behind her from her skull and eyes and the tips of her fingers. She would be like a flare to the demons below had they glanced up the mountain in that moment.

She landed in a crouch atop two jutting rocks, tail swishing as she spun around and dropped to the ledge, where she caught him, stopping his momentum before he could shatter bones on the rocks. Oz shook himself, disoriented and dizzy, and he gazed up at her.

Each time previously he had seen her in her real skin, Jinan had felt embarrassed, almost as though he had walked in upon her coming out of the shower. She had felt naked. It was a reaction to his humanness, she knew. But now when Oz looked at her, she felt a kinship between them, creature to creature, monster to monster. They were more alike than they were different. It was something she had realized long ago, but she had the sudden feeling that Oz now understood it as well.

"Thanks."

He started to rise again, shaky but still swift.

Jinan laid a hand upon his shoulder, her eyes smoldering, so that she saw him in flickering shades of red and orange.

"What can you do?" she asked. "Like this, I mean? If you can't change."

Anger rippled across his face, there a moment and then gone, but it was one of the first genuine and open emotions she had ever seen him give in to. When it was gone, he stared at her a few seconds longer, and Jinan thought he looked lost.

"I don't know," he said at last. "Maybe nothing." His fingers curled as if they were claws, and he hunched over slightly, the way he walked as the wolf. "But maybe something."

Then he started down the mountain again, and Jinan leaped after him. They moved as quickly as they could, but as they drew closer, sliding and stumbling in the snow, two figures slithered from the darkness beneath the walls of the monastery. They ran across the ledge, moving like scythes cutting the shadows of the night. Thin creatures, pale and severe, their hair black and their faces ridged and hideous, mouths open to reveal gleaming fangs.

Vampires, Jinan thought. She froze. Though she had come across them now and again, the vampires Jinan had seen had been starving scavengers like carrion birds, coming to the back door of the butcher shop to beg for fresh kills or the blood drippings from a carcass her father had cut into chops.

Not like this. Not predators.

"Oz?" Jinan said, voice quivering.

He did not even slow.

• • •

Oz recognized the Pierrault brothers immediately. A hundred thoughts went through his head. If the Pierraults were here, that meant Cain was here. If they were here *now,* it meant Cain had thrown in with Muztag. He had no idea why the demon of the eastern mountain would let a human keep breathing, no matter how many kills were on his résumé, but he didn't care that much, either.

Cain, he thought.

The hairs on the back of his neck prickled. His back and chest both felt exposed. There was a kind of arrogance that being nearly unkillable gave him but that dissipated instantly at the thought of a silver bullet ripping through him. Oz felt a sudden urge to drop and roll, to hide his face.

But Cain had picked the best possible time to have a go at him, because there was no way Oz was going to turn away from the monastery while Master Shantou needed him. Even now he could hear roars from inside, could hear the crackle of magical energy. On the wind he caught a scent that smelled like burning fur.

The Pierraults raced at him, so light on their feet, it was as though they walked on air, never touched the ground. This was a different breed of vampire from what he was used to. More practiced, deadlier . . . older. The Pierraults weren't some recently resurrected high school boys or insurance salesmen. In his darkest dreams, in his primitive subconscious, in the mind of the wolf . . . *these* were vampires. Swift and savage and hungry.

"*Oz,*" Jinan called to him as she leaped again, trying to catch up.

"Don't let them slow us down!" he replied. "Master Shantou needs us."

Then they were only yards away, and Oz and Jinan raced straight at the vampires. The Pierraults were like elegant animals, hissing as they slowed their pace and began to dance in close, taking his measure.

"Not your fight, demon," one of them snapped at Jinan.

She raised her tail up, ready to strike out with it. Fire licked around her fingers, sending up wisps of smoke. "Yeah it is. Master Shantou is my teacher."

The vampire let out a wild, hyena laugh. "We are not here for the monk."

Jinan cast a quick, sidelong glance of astonishment at Oz. He ignored her, trying to figure out Cain's game. Why not hunt him during the full moon, when he'd have a pelt? Unless he had just arrived, why wait until now? It didn't make sense, unless it was to tie in with the attack on Master Shantou.

And where the hell is *Cain*? he thought.

"You killed our brother, wolf-boy," the other vampire snarled at Oz in his French accent. "I can't wait to taste your blood. Werewolves always give me a rush."

As though a bell had sounded, all of them paused. Oz and Jinan were side by side. He could feel the heat of her skull-fire as it flickered in the dark beside him. The sound of a clock ticking was in his head, though he knew it was only his imagination. One of the vampires stood directly in front of Oz, but the other seemed to be studying Jinan carefully.

"Guess I could say it was self-defense," Oz said, staring into the glowing red eyes of the one in front of him. "Especially 'cause it was. But, gotta say, vamps are for dusting."

With a loud hiss the two vampires attacked. Out of the corner of his eye, Oz saw Jinan swing her tail hard and crack the one that lunged at her on the side of the head. Then the other was on Oz and he couldn't worry about Jinan anymore, or about where Cain was in all this or why he'd waited.

The vampire was too fast. Oz grabbed one of his wrists, but with the other hand the creature reached up and clutched Oz's throat. His air cut off, Oz stumbled back, and the vampire started to force him down. Fury rose up inside Oz, and again he caught the scent of burning fur inside the monastery, heard things shattering in there.

He got his feet under him.

The moon was no longer full, the wolf gone for another month. But it was not really gone. Just submerged beneath the calm surface of his flesh. Oz felt the wolf down inside him, waiting, and he woke it up. Touched its savagery and its hunger.

The edges of his vision went black as the vampire choked him. The slick, black-haired leech lowered his head toward Oz's throat, fangs bared.

"I can't kill you, not yet. But Cain did not say we could not have a taste," it hissed.

A low growl rumbled in Oz's chest. He got his footing and surged forward, cracked his skull against the vampire's in a vicious head butt. The vampire lost his grip, and then Oz was driving him back farther. He had not changed yet, not on the outside, but he was no longer holding back the wolf. Oz grabbed a handful of the vampire's hair, lunged, and snapped his teeth shut on the vamp's own throat, slicing skin and drawing blood.

The vampire roared in pain.

Oz let him go, then kicked him in the chest so that the vampire fell to the ground, reeling.

He turned to look for Jinan just in time to see her standing over the other Pierrault brother, who was completely engulfed in flames. Fire roared up in a blazing pyre from her skull, poured off her fingers as though each were its own flame-thrower, and consumed her attacker.

Oz didn't know the Pierrault brothers' first names. Whichever one had attacked Jinan, he exploded in a fiery shower of cinder and ash. Then she turned her attention to his brother. The one who had attacked Oz sat on his butt on the snow-covered rocky ledge and stared in wide-eyed astonishment, one hand clapped to the wound in his side where Oz had bit him.

One eyebrow arched wickedly, Oz spit the vampire's blood onto the snow and then wiped it off his lips. "Wonder what would happen if we let you live," he said. "A vampire bitten by a werewolf."

But then Jinan reached for the vampire, and fire arced from her hands and he, too, was consumed by the flames.

"Thanks," Oz said.

Jinan stared at him. "They knew you."

He nodded. "And if they're here, they didn't come alone."

But even as he said it, Oz stared into Jinan's eyes, at the reflection of the fire that gleamed there. At the distant figure mirrored in her gaze. She tensed at the same moment, for of course she saw him as well.

Oz caught his scent. Even amidst the stink of all the demons and trolls and the fire, he knew that scent.

"Down!" he shouted, grabbing Jinan.

But she was already moving. She wrapped her arms around him, and the two of them dove to the ground just as a rifle barked twice, whipcracks on the air. Oz felt a sting on his shoulder and Jinan cried out, her breath hot on his face, voice close to his ear.

Oz gritted his teeth as he lay on the snow and clapped a hand to his shoulder where the bullet had grazed him. Cain had winged him on purpose, a warning shot. The hunter didn't want him dead unless he was all wolfed out.

"You all right?" he rasped to Jinan.

As if in response, she stood up. Though the way her tail unfurled it was more as if she had uncoiled herself from the ground. Just below her left breast there was a hole in her oily blue-black skin. Liquid fire spilled from it and dripped down her belly like molten lava.

"No," she said, glaring across the ledge.

At Cain.

The hunter stood not far from the entrance to the monastery. A couple of *Draco Volans* flew idly above him, and a huge troll was visible just outside the door now as though it were standing guard.

Jinan began to stalk across the snowy ledge, tail swinging dangerously behind her. Cain raised his rifle to his shoulder again. Oz cried out Jinan's name, but even as he did so he felt a wave of heat washing off of her that he could feel even ten feet away. It seared his skin.

Cain fired twice more.

The bullets never reached Jinan. They melted in the air three feet from her body. Oz swore in amazement, both eyebrows raised.

"You're the luckiest son of a bitch I've ever seen, Osbourne!" Cain shouted up to him. "But I'll see you skinned before too much longer."

"Not if you don't ever get off this mountain," Jinan muttered.

Oz nodded in agreement but said nothing. He got up, hand clapped to the wound on his shoulder, grateful it had only been a superficial wound. He'd gotten lucky. Jinan started toward Cain.

In that moment, the front of the monastery erupted with an exodus of demons and lumbering trolls. Two followed them out. Oz blinked, trying to see through the sudden monstrous stampede, but Cain was gone, swept away with the horde.

A flurry of wings beat the air above the monastery's courtyard and flashed through the rising smoke from the chimney fire. *Draco Volans* filled the night sky, followed by a trio of winged demons. One of them, a chittering thing that made Oz think of scorpions and praying mantises, flew out over the ledge and the valley below with Master Shantou limp in its arms.

Oz ran, Jinan beside him, her fire subsiding. But they slowed moments later, perhaps fifty yards from the monastery. He stared after the flying things, their shapes in sharp relief against the moon and then melting into the darkness.

Cain was gone. The demons were gone. All was silence now save for the distant crash and whisper of the descent of that fiendish throng on the mountainside below.

Jinan whispered the old monk's name.

Together, numbly, the two of them walked into the monastery. It was a shambles far worse than the way they had first discovered it. The corpse of a sorcerer lay sprawled beneath crumbled stone, his head nowhere to be found. Burnt, charred things that Oz thought must have been *Draco Volans* were scattered about the halls. In a long corridor they found a seven- or eight-hundred-pound troll that had been cut in two, its viscera still steaming in the cold air.

In the courtyard, they discovered two demons whose bodies seemed to have melted together. Master Shantou's sorcery was more powerful than Oz had imagined.

But not powerful enough.

Oz stared up into the sky, empty now save for the stars and the moon, and Jinan reached out to take his hand. For once he did not pull away. Instead, he slipped an arm around her, trusting that in this moment she would not make more of it than it was. They were in this together.

"What do we do now?" she asked.

Oz gazed at the moon.

"We go get him."

• • •

Alone in Master Shantou's sanctuary, Oz let his fingers trail over bottles on the shelves. He brought several of them to the table, working quickly, glancing several times at the parchment paper with Jinan's scrawl upon it. She spoke English better than she wrote it, but he could decipher it well enough.

Careful and meticulous, unwilling to allow even the slightest possibility of error, he recreated the compound he had ingested each of the previous three afternoons. It was the first time he had done so without Jinan looking over his shoulder, but he had it now.

Whether it would do any good, he did not know.

All he knew was that it *had* to.

Jinan rapped on the door as Oz was pouring the bilious green liquid into a water skin.

"Ready?" she asked.

He capped the water skin and slung it over his shoulder on its leather strap, then he wiped his hands on his jeans and looked up at her.

"Maybe."

Oz had been reluctant at first to go to the village. It was a slight detour from their path, and he wanted to get to Muztag's fortress as fast as possible. Also, he remembered the people there as fearful and suspicious and doubted they would be willing to help. They expected Master Shantou to protect them, to come to their aid in times of tribulation. Chances were, the idea of going into the lair of the demon to rescue him was not going to sit very well.

But Jinan was right. They needed all the help they could get. And without Master Shantou, the people of Lingka were going to have to fight or flee.

Or, at least, those were Oz's thoughts as he and Jinan trekked tirelessly across the brittle grass and frozen ground of the valley floor. There was no accumulated snow here yet, and Oz wondered how these people survived the winter under normal circumstances. The question was moot, of course, for these were not normal circumstances. They would not survive this winter without fighting for their lives.

When they came within sight of the village, all such ruminations left his mind. Buildings he had seen only weeks ago were in ruins. The bridge that crossed the narrow river was shattered. The surface of the river, already dotted with places where calmer waters had frozen over, was clogged with bones, stripped clean. A clutch of uneaten corpses had dammed the river where it bent slightly south and the water spilled over the banks and ran around the twisted limbs of the dead.

Oz felt nausea burn in his gut, but somehow he kept himself from being sick. He averted his eyes as they walked farther into the ruined village, and he noticed that Jinan did the same. A plume of black smoke began to rise ahead, just around the other side of one of the few dwellings that still seemed relatively untouched. Then Oz took a closer look at the house and realized that darkness had hidden the truth. In the moonlight the awful, five-eyed face on the side of the structure seemed to have been painted in black.

But Oz had caught the scent now, and he knew that it was neither black nor paint. It was blood.

"That face," Jinan said.

"It must be," Oz told her.

Neither of them said his name.

They walked around the marked dwelling and came in view of a pyre of burning corpses. Oz was both startled and profoundly relieved to see that some of the villagers still lived. There were perhaps eight people standing around watching the flames, some with hollow eyes and others weeping copiously. A tall, formidable old man carried a corpse over his shoulder and tossed it into the flames, then stood back to watch it burn, his face immobile.

A gunshot split the night.

Oz and Jinan froze in place as the people turned toward the sound—toward them. A wide-eyed boy of perhaps twelve stared at them, rifle shaking in his hands. He took aim as shouts of alarm rose from those around the pyre.

"I don't think we're going to find much help here," Jinan whispered.

Oz said nothing, only stared down the barrel of a rifle held by a boy not much older than Jordy.

The broad-shouldered old man came toward them, snapping at the boy. Oz had no idea what he was saying, but the kid lowered the rifle, so that was good. Only then did he study the man's face and realize that he recognized him. His features were haunted now, and the side of his face was covered in bloody bandages, but Oz knew him. His name was Tsochen.

"Remember this guy?" Oz asked Jinan. "He speaks Chinese."

"You want me to ask him what happened?"

"Pretty obvious, I'm thinking."

"It's the polite thing," she chided him.

Oz didn't think they had much time to be polite, but these people had lost a great deal—their village, most of their friends and loved ones—so he didn't balk as Jinan began speaking to Tsochen in Chinese.

A teenaged girl rushed from the home behind them and ran up to the old man. From the way she held him, Oz figured Tsochen was her father. She snapped something at Jinan.

"She speaks Chinese, too?" he asked.

Jinan glanced back at him. "She doesn't want her

father to talk about what happened. She's afraid the demons will hear and come back."

Tsochen grew angry then. He raised his fist to the sky, shook it at the mountain that loomed to the east, and shouted so that his words echoed through the village. When he stopped, the surviving villagers stared at him in horror. Several of them stepped back as though they feared lightning might strike him.

"He says he wants them to hear," Jinan quickly translated. "That some in the village said the demon of the eastern mountain was only a legend, but he knew it was true. Now his wife is dead. He wants them to come back so he can spill their blood as he dies."

Oz gazed at the man. He had no idea how to respond to that and was glad he could not speak Tibetan. Tsochen's daughter struck her father on the chest with an open palm, and her lip quivered as she stared at him. Then she turned and waved at Oz and Jinan as if ushering them out of the village. The girl gestured to the ruins.

Again Jinan turned to Oz. "She said—"

"I think I got the gist." He ran both hands through his hair and looked around at the carnage. The village had suffered enough. It seemed to him somehow unfair to ask for their help, but then when he thought about it, Oz realized that nobody needed Muztag dead and Shantou home safe more than these people.

"Tell them we've seen the demons and we're looking for volunteers to join a posse to go after them."

Jinan frowned. "Posse?"

"You don't watch Westerns. Just tell them we'd like help."

She nodded and turned to explain to the survivors what they planned. As Jinan spoke, people stared at her in horror, eyes widening. Some even waved at the air as though they might erase her words. One by one they began to turn their backs on her.

Only Tsochen and his daughter did not ignore them.

The older man touched his bandaged face and then muttered something to his daughter. She shook her head firmly, and the Tsochen gave them an apologetic look.

"It's all right," Oz told the injured man. "Can't blame her."

A deep voice rumbled behind him in Chinese, and Oz turned quickly to find before him one of the oddest sights he had ever confronted. There were three men standing at the edges of the light thrown by the fire. One was small and seemed almost to crackle with energy. The man next to him was of average height and had long white hair, though he did not look old. But the other, the one who had spoken, was so huge, he seemed barely human himself.

From their headgear and the thick wool and fur jackets they wore, he knew they were nomads. Packs and canteens were slung over their shoulders, but that was not unusual. What were new and different were the weapons they carried, which looked to Oz's only vaguely educated eye to be assault rifles. He knew the nomads had given old carbines to the villagers. Clearly they had kept the best weapons for themselves.

"He said the villagers are afraid because the demons are myths to them."

"Another guy who speaks Chinese. You'd think there'd be more of them, given that this is part of China."

"Just be glad we've found a few," Jinan noted.

Then she rattled off something in Chinese to the huge nomad, who began a long-winded answer. Since Master Shantou and Jinan both spoke English, Oz had gotten away fairly easily in the language department since he had been here. Now he wished he had spent part of the last month studying Tibetan, or even Chinese.

"His name is Ganjin. They call him the son of the mountain because of his enormous size. The little one is Ritsu, and the other is Tang."

"Tang," Oz repeated.

Jinan glanced at him. "What?"

Oz shook his head. "Nothing. Go on."

"They say that as nomads they see everything that goes on in the mountains. The demons have always preyed upon the valley, but lately they've grown more bold. They say they know the trail up the mountain to Muztag's fortress. Ganjin has offered their help."

One eyebrow raised, Oz appraised the three nomads. They looked carved of stone these men, though he knew it was the wind and the terrain that had sculpted them. Anyone who came with them was going to be in terrible danger, but somehow Oz had a feeling that Ganjin, Ritsu, and Tang understood that in a way other people might not. They knew what was at stake for them, and for anyone else in the valley.

Oz strode over to Ganjin and had to crane his head back to look up, so huge was the man. He stuck out his hand and Ganjin took it. They shook.

"Let's saddle up."

Chapter Fourteen

Twenty-nine Nights Until the Full Moon

In the weeks he had spent in Muztag's fortress, Gib Cain had learned what it was like to be nothing more than a cog in the machine. From all he had gleaned, the demon lord had taken what had been a little barony of sorts and quietly transformed it into a thriving center for occult activity that rivaled any other on the Asian continent. Muztag's reputation alone had been enough to draw visitors and ambassadors from all over Asia and Europe, and from as far away as the States. More than a few of the demons and magicians Cain had talked to had compared Muztag with an ancient Chinese warlord, and the hunter thought maybe the demon lord perpetuated that image quite consciously.

Though Muztag rarely took Cain into his confidence, it was clear to the hunter now that the demon lord intended to continue to extend his influence. Quietly, but as quickly as he could manage, the demon was building a core of power from which he might spread tendrils of influence and one day have most of those born of or dabbling in the supernatural at his disposal.

As far as Cain could tell, none of the organizations that played at international sorcery and espionage were taking Muztag seriously yet, not the Council of Watchers, not the Order of Sages, not any of those other legions of pompous windbags. The five-eyed s.o.b. was going to be very dangerous, very soon. Cain had his priorities—mainly his own wealth and personal safety—but he was well aware that Muztag presented a threat. Maybe when he was safely in Europe or back Stateside, he'd drop a dime to one of his contacts at the Order of Sages.

But not now.

Now, he had a werewolf to skin.

Just the thought of it made him tremble with anger and frustration. He'd spent the better part of the night climbing mountains—down from Muztag's fortress, up to the monastery, and now back up to the fortress—and what had he gotten from it? Not a damn thing.

Muztag had forbidden him to hunt Oz until Master Shantou had been captured, and then declared that they would not attempt to take the monastery again and capture Shantou until *after* the full moon. The whole thing was ludicrous. Granted, the first time Muztag's horde had attacked the monastery, just after the full moon the previous month, they had been fewer in number. But still, how much trouble could one old monk be, magic or no magic? Cain was surprised Muztag hadn't executed every last one of them for screwing up that badly the first time. There *had* been executions, of course, or so Cain had been told. But only a few.

For weeks he had been forced to cool his heels and wait for the moment when Muztag would give him permission to do what he had come to do. Granted, the demon lord made him feel welcome. He had a comfortable doss and plenty to eat and the company of several Sashuall demons, which was pleasant enough. But the Pierrault brothers had done nothing but whine to Cain for weeks, as though he could have changed anything about their circumstances. Then, when the time finally came to make their move—after the full moon had come and gone, meaning even with Oz his prisoner it would take Cain another month to get the pelt—the Pierraults had screwed up completely and gotten themselves killed.

Torched, actually.

How the hell was Cain supposed to know Oz was hanging out with Kaohsiung demon? Muztag had either not known it or not bothered to mention it. All Cain had managed to do was wing the werewolf with an ordinary bullet.

Damn it, he fumed. It was always much easier to kill something than to capture it.

Cain angrily shoved a troll aside as he reached the massive front doors of the fortress. A couple of demons were moving slowly ahead of him. One of them was a slug-like thing that was leaving a trail of slime on the stone floor. Torchlight flickered in the corridor and gleamed sickly yellow off the slime, making Cain wonder if the stuff was radioactive or poisonous. Revulsion churned in his gut, and he pushed past the demon, making certain only to touch its robes, not the sticky, boiling flesh of the thing. The other demon was a spiny thing like a humanoid sea urchin. He steered well clear of that one, certain that its spines must have poison tips.

What the hell am I still doing here? he wondered. He should never have approached Muztag, just taken his chances that first night he'd arrived. It occurred to Cain that he might be getting too old for this kind of thing, but he would not give voice to the thought. That would be too much like surrender.

A winged Faw-Ch'ak demon blocked his way now. The corridors were too narrow, Cain realized. Narrow entrances were an asset in defending a stronghold, but one ought never assume their fortress impregnable. The way this place was designed, if someone lay siege and actually got inside the fortress, the width of the corridors meant they'd be able to take on a few defenders at a time. The same principle that would work in favor of the demon if the place was attacked would work against him if someone ever got in—or if he was attacked by someone *already* inside the fortress.

Maybe Muztag wasn't the warlord everyone made him out to be.

Cain slapped the Faw-Ch'ak's wings aside.

A hand clamped on his shoulder. When Cain turned, he was eye to eye with the sorceress he'd met on that first day. She had not spoken a word to him since, and now her eyes and hands seemed to leak with a magical mist charged with electricity.

"Maybe you shouldn't be so impatient," the sorceress told him, her tone ominous.

Cain glared at her. "And maybe you should mind your own business. Not overstep your bounds. Muztag's had me on a leash since I got here, and I haven't tried to break it. So back off."

She looked like she had more to say, but Cain tore his arm away and stormed off along the corridor away from her, and took a flight of stone steps at the first junction in the warren of tunnels. He needed to be off by himself a bit, figure out what to do next. He was free to hunt Oz now that Muztag had the old monk. Whatever Muztag's hesitation had been, certainly that had to be done with.

But Cain was alone now. The Pierraults were dead.

Tomorrow he would make his way around the western mountain, scale it from the rear, away from the monastery, try to get above the place. Then he'd make his way around it until he had a clear view down at the building. With a scope on his rifle, he could put a bullet through the Kaohsiung's fire-skull from a vast distance.

After that, capturing Oz would be child's play.

They would be on a mountain, with nothing but the valley below. Cain knew his skills as a hunter were unequaled. But he had no plans to transport Oz while he was still alive. No, Cain would track the werewolf and he would capture him, and then he would cage him up in that monastery until the next full moon, so that all he had to carry home with him was the monster's pelt.

The stone stairwell was dark, with the glow of torches back down below him, and a flicker from above. Cain made his way through the unfamiliar passage carefully, feet searching for each next step, fingers gliding along the walls. His rifle thumped against his lower back with every stair he took.

The light above grew brighter, and at the top of the steps he emerged in a part of the fortress he had never seen before. For a full minute he stared around him in open astonishment. Demons snarled at one another. Small booths had been set up to sell herbs and potions. Animals chortled and purred and growled as they tested the limits of their chains. Carts and wagons were laden with goods. Mediums and necromancers offered their services.

It was an occult marketplace, right here in the heart of the mountain . . . here in the middle of nowhere. Cain shook his head and actually laughed softly to himself. He had underestimated Muztag. The demon lord was not merely going to take control of the supernatural underground by force and fear, he was going to use commerce as well.

Off to Cain's right, a reptilian demon who had a sort of spiny fin on his head and wore the uniform of a Chinese soldier spoke to a pair of Black Forest Woodsmen—their skin like bark, their limbs sprouting leaves—in butchered German.

" . . . really are a full-service facility, from research and consulting to custom sorcery, weaponsmiths, and Hellhound breeding," the reptilian soldier was saying. "Lord Muztag can provide it all."

Amazed and intrigued, Cain stepped out into the busy marketplace-under-the-mountain, with its barkers hawking wares and its menagerie of customers wandering the booths. No one so much as glanced twice at him. He passed a booth where a homunculus nattered on about "discount talismans and charms" and the offer to translate runes, and the hunter merely shook his head and kept on.

Out of the marketplace. Around a corner. He came to a broad set of stairs that led upward still. Yet another area of the fortress he had not explored. Torches lined the walls, and it was far brighter here than in most areas of Muztag's complex.

At the top of the stairs he found himself in a corridor whose ceiling was higher than any he had seen elsewhere in the fortress. He heard shuffling feet off to his right and glanced over to see something that made him stiffen and then press himself back against the stone wall in the shadows just outside the reach of the torchlight. The massive troll he thought of as Union Jack, with his cigar and soiled British flag T-shirt, was walking with a blue-skinned demon with a clicking, grasping thing on the back of his head that looked like nothing so much as a huge spider made of bone.

The two monsters were escorting Master Shantou—bound in chains—toward a huge set of double doors. Given the trolls guarding the doors and the wrought-metal symbols bolted to the wood, Cain realized that this must be Muztag's quarters, or at least an audience chamber of some kind.

The guards pulled open the doors. Union Jack and Bone-spider ushered the chained monk into the chamber beyond. Cain's curiosity got the better of him. He slipped through a patch of torchlight until he came to another shadowy place in the hall. From that vantage point he could see between the heads of the troll guards, who had not closed the doors but now stood within, waiting for instructions.

The doors were open perhaps a third of the way, but that was enough. Through them, and past the guards, Cain saw Muztag atop a throne that had been ornately carved out of solid rock. Atop that platform upon which sat the throne, the massive demon with his five eyes and quivering, furred antennae was flanked by a pair of his sorcerers. A handful of other demons—*courtiers,* Cain thought—were arrayed about the room, including the three Sashuall females he himself had been keeping company with, and a leather-clad warrior with bone spurs in his chin and pate, and an array of feathers that grew in a spray out of his forehead.

Master Shantou was silent. From this angle, Cain could just make out a streak of blood on the side of his face. Bone-spider gave him a wicked shove that sent the old monk staggering toward Muztag's throne, but Shantou did not go down.

"Well, well, Shantou," Muztag said in Chinese. "To think that all this time I could have been marauding the valley if I had not been so worried about opposition from you."

Observing from the shadows between torches out in the hall, Cain flinched when he heard Master Shantou spit on the ground.

"You were worried, pit-born worm," the old monk sneered, "because I nearly killed you once."

Muztag's huge, central, Cyclopean eye seemed to grow even larger. His antennae twitched as he reached and grabbed hold of Master Shantou's face with one enormous taloned hand. He raised the old monk so that his feet dangled below him.

"I thought monks were supposed to be silent," Muztag growled. "No matter. You and your students provided precious little opposition in the end. I ought to have done this a very long time ago. And now that I have you at my mercy, it appears I won't be needing the hunter after all."

In the hall, Cain stiffened.

He did not like the sound of that at all.

By the light cast by the pyre of burning corpses, Oz watched Jinan mix a small tincture of herbs and chalk and dyes into a damp paste. Somewhere, walled off from his conscious mind, a thousand ideas and possibilities spun in upon themselves as he looked at her petite form, at the meticulous gravity with which she approached even this small magic, at the perfect flower of her lips and the way her hair fell across her face while she was bent at her task.

But whatever those thoughts were, whatever possibilities another man might have considered, Oz did not allow them to enter his conscious mind. *Master Shantou must be saved. Muztag must be destroyed.* And his own curse must somehow be lifted. Jinan was beautiful and good, and he cared for her, but there was no connection between his own plans and goals and his fondness for his traveling companion. Oz was here to find peace so that he might go home.

Nothing else was allowed into his mind. His thoughts were already far ahead of this moment, up on the mountain, inside Muztag's fortress, trying to figure out how to keep them all alive.

Still, when Jinan rose and daubed a bit of the paste on the cheeks of the three nomads who had volunteered to accompany them, and then moved over to do the same to Oz, he felt a kind of sadness for what could never be.

"If I made it right, this ought to make us invisible to any mystical wards Muztag might have in place around the fortress that would alert him to intruders," she said, lingering a moment as she painted the paste in stripes on either side of his nose.

Oz gazed at her. "That's handy."

After a moment he took a breath and turned away. He reached for the water skin that was slung over his shoulder, shook it vigorously, and then uncapped it. Trying not to breathe in the terrible odor of the herbal compound, he tilted his head and gulped it down, not stopping for a single breath until it was gone. He wiped his hand across his lips and dropped the water skin on the ground. It had never occurred to him that the vile-tasting concoction might be used to free that within him that he had worked so hard to cage. The compound was meant to separate his lycanthropic nature from the lunar cycle, give him control over the beast within. But Oz had never imagined needing to use that control to summon the wolf.

He heard the rustle of clothing as Jinan approached from behind.

"Do you think you're going to be able to . . . you know?"

"We'll see," he replied. "They ready?"

Jinan gestured to the Ganjin, Ritsu, and Tang. They were all armed with assault rifles. The enormous bear of a man, Ganjin, had several grenades clipped to a strap across his bulky jacket. All three of them had hats pulled low on their heads.

"They look ready," Jinan said.

But Oz hesitated. He looked from the nomads to Jinan and took a steadying breath. "I'm thinking they're going to see you change, and you don't want to distract them at the wrong time. You should show them now."

"What, tell them Muztag's not the only monster in the mountains? That not all demons are evil?" Jinan said, staring at him, her concern obvious.

"Pretty much."

Jinan closed her eyes. Several seconds passed before she opened them again and nodded. She turned to the nomads and spoke to them quickly in Chinese. With her hands propped on her hips, her black hair loose this night, falling around her face, she looked beautiful . . . normal . . . human.

Then she changed.

Oz hadn't ever asked Jinan about the *physics* of the change, where the clothes went—if they were absorbed or shunted to another dimension or something—and he did not know if he ever would. What he did know was that there was grace and wonder to the Kaohsiung shape-shifting, instead of the pain and ugliness of lycanthropy. Her skin flowed into blue-black, oiled silk, and her tail undulated like a serpent as it stretched out from her tailbone. The blaze of fire from her open skull above those long, tapered ears was extraordinary. In this form she looked more like some ancient goddess than a demon.

The nomads stared at her, eyes wide. For a long moment, none of them moved or even seemed to breathe.

Then the wiry little one, Ritsu, smiled and whistled in appreciation.

Ganjin nodded, said something to Jinan, and stepped forward to offer Oz an assault rifle.

"He says it will help in battle, me being . . . what I

am," Jinan told Oz as she shifted back to human form. "But he thinks you should take a gun."

"Tell him thanks, but I wouldn't have the first clue how to use it."

Jinan repeated his words in Chinese, and Ganjin shrugged, then turned and began picking up the rest of his gear. The survivors in the village stayed far away from them save for Tsochen and his daughter. Oz and Jinan waved to them as the nomads said their good-byes. Then the five of them started off into the darkness toward the mountain that loomed black against the night sky to the east.

Oz felt a tap on his shoulder. The third nomad, Tang, who had been mostly silent, held out a huge hunting knife to him.

"You . . . take . . . ," Tang managed in English.

Oz nodded gratefully and took the knife. "This, on the other hand . . . pretty simple to use."

Twenty-eight Nights Until the Full Moon

It was long after midnight when Cain found his way to the marketplace again. He had returned briefly to his room to change his clothes and pick up a rucksack with his essentials. The heavy jacket and army-issue pants he wore now were perfect for concealing weapons, and there was not a single blade or gun in his possession that was not now secreted on his person and easily accessible. The rifle slung across his shoulder was certain to draw attention this late at night, despite the freedom Muztag had given him during his stay, but Cain stuck mostly to narrow back stairwells and corridors less traveled.

The lateness of the hour did not aid his efforts at stealth, unfortunately. These were demons and monsters and workers of dark magic, and they were more comfortable milling about at night, even in the bowels of that mountain, than they would have been during the sunlight hours.

His skin tingled, and his heart pumped loud in his chest. He ground his teeth together as he slipped from a darkened stairwell into the still thriving marketplace. If anything, it was busier than before. Yellow torchlight flickered across the carts and stands, across monstrous fortune-tellers rolling bones on blankets spread out on the stone, across twisted nightmare things from dimensions even demons spoke of in whispers, now prostituting themselves. Cain kept his head down and he went among them. The scent of a human passing cast a ripple of curiosity over the throng, but when the guards paid him no mind, the merchants and their customers lost interest.

On his third pass through the marketplace, Cain found what he was looking for: A hideously gnarled goblin faced a wall beyond a stall where a demon with two faces was hawking potions. The goblin had stepped away from the bustle of the marketplace and held a cellular phone clapped to one ear, a stubby, grimy finger jammed in the other to block out the noise from the hucksters around him.

Cain raised his gaze cautiously and glanced around. As surreptitiously as possible he backtracked around the potions stall and slipped up beside the goblin. In his hand was a jagged-edged hunting knife with which he could eviscerate the goblin in just shy of six seconds. With his body blocking the blade from the view of the rest of the marketplace, he punched the tip of the knife into the goblin's side, just deep enough to draw blood and a little chirp from the creature, who fell silent the moment he glanced up and saw Cain's furious eyes.

"Hang up."

The goblin offered a pained smile and clicked the

phone off. His gaze began to drift, searching for aid, and Cain prodded him again with the tip of the knife.

"Over there," the hunter said. "The stairs. Like we're old friends."

In a low voice, calm as could be, the goblin began speaking to him in Gaelic. Cain frowned dangerously. He had learned a lot of languages over the years, hunted all over the world. But he couldn't speak Gaelic. "You were speaking English on the phone."

The goblin's smile faltered. He glanced over at the side corridor Cain had indicated. "Over there, huh?"

"Now."

"Am I coming back out of there?"

"If you shut up and move."

The goblin moved. Cain followed him into the corridor, away from the marketplace, with an amiable expression on his face. He had no idea if they were being observed but hoped that anyone who might spot them would assume they knew each other.

Once in the darkened corridor—its width barely enough to accommodate them both, its wall sconces empty of torches—Cain grabbed the little creature around the throat with a huge, scarred hand and pressed him to the stone wall.

"We're inside a mountain in the middle of Tibet," Cain rasped. "How is it you have a cell phone that works?"

The goblin's eyes were wide, and he swallowed nervously. "It's not a big deal. A simple spell. You can buy them like this, already with the enchantment on them. There's a Xihal demon out there selling them—all different colors, too. You could call for pizza from the bottom of a coal mine. It's just a kind of a magical booster, I guess."

Cain shifted his rucksack and rifle so they sat more comfortably on his back. Then he moved the knife to his left hand and held out his right for the phone. The goblin hesitated.

"I'll give it right back. One call."

"And if I say no?"

The hunter rolled his eyes and cut the goblin's throat, peeling the phone out of his gnarled hand as the creature slid to the ground, green blood already pooling quickly beneath him.

Cain sheathed his knife, glanced once back into the marketplace to make sure no one had witnessed the murder, then disappeared down the darkened corridor with the phone clutched in his hand.

He had a call to make.

Oz could not feel his feet. Inside the thick gloves he had gotten from the nomads, his fingers still had some feeling in them, but considering that they were so cold it felt like someone had hammered nails into them, this was hardly a blessing. In his time at the monastery—where the stone walls and the single large fireplace were hardly sufficient at keeping the chill at bay—he had grown used to being cold. But this was different. With the numbness of his feet and the pain in his hands, as well as the sting of each gust of wind on his cheeks, it felt to him a little bit like he had been drinking too much and gotten into a bar brawl. On top of all of that, the cold was making him tired.

Still, he climbed in silence, without complaint or hesitation.

He had not yet accomplished what he had set out to do here in Tibet, but that was no fault of Master Shantou's. The old monk had lived for centuries, and now the ambitions of one persistent and patient demon might cost him his life, on top of all of those lives down in the valley that had been snuffed out by the hungers of Muztag's lackeys.

Oz had seen the burning corpses. The hollow-eyed expressions on the survivors. The devastation of the monastery.

Even if he did not feel as though he owed Master Shantou, even if he didn't want to settle things with Cain once and for all, Oz would have climbed this mountain. A practical part of him thought this was a spectacularly stupid idea, but the truth of the matter is that even before he had discovered that monsters were real, even before he had thrown in with the Slayer and done a little light sidekick work in the battle against the forces of darkness, he had never been the kind of guy to walk away from a fight.

He wouldn't pick one, of course. But if the schoolyard bully was tearing up the recess yard with the new kid, Oz had never been the type to cheer or even just keep quiet.

A pained smile crossed his features at that thought. *Never been the type to keep quiet.* That was a good one. And the smile brought a little bit of warmth to his features.

No, there wasn't going to be any walking away from this fight.

Freezing, Oz pulled his wool and leather hat down tighter over his ears and continued to climb behind Ritsu. The charismatic little man had become grim the moment the terrain had grown difficult, and now he was as quiet as Oz was. It would have been far easier to scale the face of the mountain that led up beneath the fortress. According to Ganjin, amazingly enough, there were actually stairs once one reached a certain point in the ascension. But the sentries guarding the doors would have seen them long ago had they followed that most direct of routes.

His fingers began to grow numb, and Oz made a fist inside his glove and punched the snow-covered stone several times to bring the blood rushing through his hand.

The pain of the cold returned, but that was all right. He needed to be able to feel his fingers in order to get a proper handhold. And it appeared that their path became less torturous just a short way above.

Oz was grateful when the slope of the cliff face became less severe, but when, several minutes later, they actually came to a ledge upon which all five of them could stand together, he was as close to ecstatic as he had been since his journey began. He stamped his feet, and spikes of pain shot through them as the motion got his blood circulating again. The nomads were also cold. They flexed their hands and jumped quietly in place.

Jinan, on the other hand, only looked impatient with their antics. She had explained to him weeks ago that while she felt the cold, it did not really bother her, as Kaohsiung demons obviously had their own internal heat. Now she glanced at him, and her gaze narrowed. Whispering apologies in Chinese as she pushed past the nomads, she made her way to Oz and her brown eyes searched his.

"Let me hold you a minute," Jinan said.

Her lips were pursed, and her jaw set defiantly, as if daring him to argue. Oz knew that this was not a flirtation on her part, that she meant to warm him, but even so he felt awkward as he slipped his arms around her. Jinan unbuttoned his heavy coat and slid her hands inside, moved in tight against him and pressed her body to him, laying her head on his chest with the intimacy of a lover.

Nothing could happen between them. She knew that. And perhaps because he knew that she realized that, Oz felt a certain guilt at the comfort he took from her embrace, at the warmth that seeped into him, emanating from the fiery inner core of her being. Even when she wore a human face, that heat came from inside her. "Thank you," he whispered.

Jinan did not look up at his eyes again.

"You'll be all right now," she said. "Ganjin says we're nearly there."

And that much was true. Fifteen minutes of moderately difficult climbing later, and then the huge nomad whose people called him son of the mountain, Ganjin, led them to an outcropping of stone that looked down upon the massive double doors of Muztag's fortress. A pair of hideous trolls and a dark-skinned man in the robes of one of Muztag's sorcerers stood guard below them. Oz was stunned that they had been able to get so close without detection, and he remembered the tincture Jinan had painted on their faces and wondered if it had been her magic or sheer luck that had allowed them to escape notice.

Almost at the same moment he thought it, he crouched down with the others and his left foot slipped, the boot kicking loose a small stone and a light cascade of snow that spilled over the edge of the outcropping and fell before the doors. Oz tensed and held his breath, but the wind that whistled across the face of the mountain stole away the sounds as they did the voices of the guards below, who continued to talk and laugh darkly together, not noticing the presence of the intruders above them.

Jinan touched Oz's shoulder. She put her lips to his ear, and when she whispered to him, her voice was warm and moist. "Stay put."

He nodded and signaled to the nomads, who seemed not to need his instruction. Jinan altered her physical form again, fire blossoming from her skull. Tail curled up behind her, she slipped forward with almost insectoid agility. She perched at the edge of the outcropping, squatted there, and her tail slid over the edge. Silently, she slipped it down behind one of the trolls, who chuffed with laughter as if at some filthy joke. With a swift motion and a single, upward jerk, Jinan snapped the monster's neck.

The sorcerer was the first to notice. His right hand glowed with sickly orange energy as he looked up, alarmed by the snapping of bone and the troll's strangled gurgling. But then the huge Ganjin dropped down off the outcropping onto the robed man and punched a knife into his neck. The nomad leader cut the sorcerer's carotid and dark arterial blood sprayed the snow all around, steaming where it touched the ground. The orange magick sparked around the dead man's hand for a moment before it was extinguished.

The only surviving guard, a troll with huge golden hoops in his ears and thick matted hair and beard, was under attack by Tang and Ritsu. Oz hesitated. These men knew what they were doing and he had only a single knife, and no training in how to handle it. The truth was, he knew why he had come, knew that there was only one thing he could really offer this group if it came down to it, and save for a tiny sliver of wonder inside him, did not believe he could even provide that.

Tang hacked at the troll with an ax. Ritsu slipped a dagger between the monster's ribs. Then Jinan leaped at the troll, and Oz watched in horror as the beast snatched her tail in midair and swung her out and over the edge of the mountain.

The nomads forced the troll down, stabbing at it again and again. But Oz paid no attention to the creature's death.

"Jinan!" he shouted as he leaped off the outcropping, dropping down in front of the doors to the fortress. But even as he ran toward the edge he saw her black talons, burning with flame, clutch at the ledge. Oz ran closer, reaching down to help her up, and realized that she had landed on the wide stone steps that led down the mountain, carved out of the cliff face.

"I'm glad you care," Jinan whispered. "But do you think you could keep it down?"

"Right," he said, relieved. "Us, stealthy."

When Ganjin pushed open the doors, Oz was amazed to see that the entrance corridor was deserted. Torches guttered on the stone walls. They moved inside, and though Oz was very much looking forward to the time when they could go back down the mountain, he pushed the doors closed behind him. Immediately he felt warmer. Whatever horrors awaited them within, he was pleased to know that he would at least have feeling in his extremities.

On second thought, it occurred to him that numbness might be an asset. But it was too late for that.

Twenty feet inside the doors, Jinan and the nomads waited, watching him expectantly. It took Oz a moment to realize they wanted him to take the lead, and another few seconds to understand why.

Why else, after all?

I'm their bloodhound.

With Jinan at his side and the nomads arrayed behind him, Oz sniffed the dank air inside the fortress. He closed his eyes, trying to separate one smell from another, and his stomach churned in revulsion at many of the stenches that rose up from the tunnels. Then, in amongst the odors of offal and sweat, he found one that was familiar to him. Eyes still closed, he nodded in satisfaction and took several steps forward. Master Shantou was here, and the tunnel off to their right would lead to him.

But then Oz caught a second odor and his eyes opened. As he had expected, Cain was here as well. And the hunter's scent came from the same direction as the monk's.

For what seemed an interminable length of time but was probably no more than twenty minutes, Oz led them through a warren of tunnels and winding stone staircases. Several times they had to make their way through darkness with only Jinan's skull-fire to light the way, and other times she was forced to extinguish it while they slipped past rooms that were occupied. Twice they encountered demons in the corridor who seemed to be residents or visitors rather than guards, and whom they let pass without incident. With Jinan there, the demons did not seem alarmed at the presence of the others.

Three times they retraced their steps to avoid trolls and sorcerers whose robes or insignias revealed them to be guards or prominent members of Muztag's "court." Once Ganjin walked straight up to a Vauxhall demon that challenged his presence immediately, and then died on the end of the nomad's knife.

Then, at the bottom of a set of winding stone steps that had seemed to go down and down forever, Oz stopped and sniffed at the two passages that led away from the stairs.

"This one," he whispered, and then he focused on Jinan. "I think we're close."

Oz had his knife in hand when he stepped into the corridor. His knuckles whitened when he heard shouting down the hall. He did not need to know the language to know that they had been discovered. Jinan raised her hands, and arcs of fire lanced from her fingers as Oz spun around to see what she was attacking.

He cussed under his breath.

There were no trolls this time, only goblins and demons. A goat-headed thing and a winged demon with a body like a preying mantis led a charge toward them, followed by four or five hideous little goblins and a trio of other demons unlike any Oz had ever seen. A stray thought went through Oz's mind, completely out of place, that Giles would have been overjoyed to have the chance to catalog all the vile things Muztag had working for him.

The mantis was screaming in a high-pitched staccato voice.

Automatic weapons fire cut it in half. The gunfire was too loud in the enclosed place, echoing off the stone, hurting Oz's ears. But he wasn't about to complain. When all three of the nomads opened fire and the demons and goblins began to jitter with the impact of the bullets, blood and gore spattering the stone walls, he was more grateful than anything else.

Again, though, he stood useless, the knife like dead weight in his hand. His mind raced. They would have to hurry now. Master Shantou was near, but the weapons fire had given away their presence and their location. Oz sniffed the air, but now his enhanced sense of smell was baffled; the air was filled with the stink of cordite and blood.

"Oz," Jinan urged.

He nodded. A moment later he caught the scent again, just ahead. He was about to announce his discovery when the sound of leathery wings filled the stone corridor along with loud, piercing screeches. Then the hallway turned dark, sputtering torchlight blown out or simply occluded by the huge mass of winged beasts that flew at them from both directions. Like a cross between bats and mythical dragons, they descended in a vicious throng upon the intruders. The nomads began to fire again, and some of the creatures were hit, falling with a dry flutter of wings to the stone floor. Oz was attacked, and he slashed at them with the knife, killed two, then a third. His thick jacket protected his back and arms, but their talons slicked easily through his gloves and cut his hands deeply. One of them lashed at his face. He killed another. Gunfire took several more.

But there were too many.

The nomad Tang was the first to die. The *Draco Volans* tore him apart with their tiny talons, like winged piranha. His weapon fell, smoking, to the ground, the echo of gunfire still filling the hall. Ganjin raised his arms, shouting, trying to draw the creatures' attention to himself. It worked. The *Draco Volans* swarmed the huge nomad, the son of the mountain. They flocked to him and lashed out with their talons and their fangs.

Ritsu cried out at the death of his comrade and the sight of his friend and leader being driven down beneath a flurry of the savage, winged creatures. But Ganjin was shouting something in Chinese as the things buried him and he thrashed around, drawing more and more of them to him.

Oz gripped the knife and started toward him.

"No!" Ritsu snapped, and hauled him back.

Stunned, Oz spun on him. "They're killing him."

The wiry little nomad worked his assault rifle frantically, but it was jammed or empty and he threw it down in a rage. He nodded and turned to Jinan, shouting at her.

Jinan shook her head, lips pressed together, eyes wide with horror. Already the *Draco Volans* on top of Ganjin were restless, wings fluttering. They were spattered with his blood, and Ganjin twitched helplessly beneath them, arms moving slowly now. Oz knew that it was too late to save the son of the mountain.

Ritsu screamed at Jinan, spittle flying from his mouth, desperation in his eyes. And suddenly Oz understood: Ganjin had drawn the creatures to him on purpose. They were here to destroy Muztag, to avenge the deaths of so many innocents in the valley. The *Draco Volans* would kill them all if someone did not stop them, and their mission would go forever unfinished. Ganjin had given his life.

"*Jinan.* Do it," Oz told her.

Her eyes raged with liquid flame that licked up her face toward her ears. Her skull-fire rose higher, black smoke searing the stone ceiling. Jinan opened her hands and motioned them back, and then she incinerated everything before her. Dozens of *Draco Volans* burned, shrieking, and fluttered limply before falling to the ground to char and blacken. The body of Ganjin burned as well.

Oz dropped the knife. It was useless. He stared at the two dead nomads, at the terror and shock in Jinan's eyes, and then he turned to Ritsu, who seemed almost made of stone.

"I'm sorry," he said, though he doubted the nomad understood his words. "We should never have come. If I could have changed, those guys might still be alive. Turns out . . ." He looked at Jinan, the words coming hard from his lips. "This was a bad idea."

Torchlight flickered behind him. Heavy footsteps and soft, running steps and the sound of something dragging suddenly came to him. In the stink of the fire and the dead he had missed it all, his ears resounding with the echo of gunfire, he had not heard them until now.

But he heard the low, rumbling laughter. Oz turned to see another clutch of demons approaching. This time, though, there were only a few of them and a trio of sorcerers, and a troll wearing a Union Jack T-shirt who dragged a bruised and bloodied Master Shantou in chains along the ground. Behind them were half a dozen others in robes not unlike Shantou's own; a demon, four men, and a woman, and it took Oz a moment to realize that these hollow-eyed, mindless-looking people were the old monk's students.

The demon in the forefront of this slow, grotesque parade was a towering thing with strangely twitching antennae jutting from the sides of his face. His leather garb reminded Oz of Vikings somehow. The demon had five glowing eyes, two pair and a much larger fifth on top of the others.

The laughter had been his.

Muztag, Oz thought. It had to be him.

And Muztag laughed again.

"Bad idea?" the demon lord said. "Now I wouldn't say that."

Chapter Fifteen

Twenty-eight Nights Until the Full Moon

It was over. They were done.

Oz was furious with himself for even attempting something so idiotic. He had no idea how he could have been so foolish as to think he could lead a rescue attempt into a mountain fortress riddled with demons when he could not even rein in the monster that lived inside him. The weight of his regrets in that moment was almost more than he could bear. He had led these three brave nomads to this place, and two of them were already dead. Master Shantou and his students were doomed. He would never return to Willow, never help Jordy to deal with his own lycanthropy.

But worst of all in that moment was the expression on Jinan's face as she gazed at him. Beneath the fire that licked out from her eyes he could see her staring at him expectantly. She believed in him. In that moment Oz knew that his biggest mistake, his greatest sin, was that he had never been able to have that kind of faith in himself.

It was in his head to surrender, then, to try to convince Muztag to let Jinan and Ritsu go. He wasn't stupid enough to think the Vastaghri demon lord was going to set Shantou free. But then he saw his knife on the ground, the knife Tang had given him. Tang, whose two comrades had died getting them this far, and who would die himself if no one intervened. Then Oz—who would not look into Jinan's eyes again—settled his gaze instead upon his teacher, the wise old monk who had been so patient with him.

The torchlight flickered across the stone walls in that wider segment of corridor, casting deep shadows on the nightmarish faces of Muztag and his trolls and the veils of his sorcerers. Even Shantou's former students, now mesmerized somehow, had haunting splashes of torchlight casting their features in grim detail.

But Oz could not see Master Shantou's face. He looked half dead, beaten and smeared with dried blood. On his knees in chains, the old monk hung his head as if in shame and would not look up.

Muztag laughed.

"What a pitiful little collective you are," the demon lord said. "I had not imagined anyone was left to come to Shantou's aid. Imagine my surprise when I received word that there were intruders sneaking about, killing guards and my pets. But now that I have seen you . . . well, it's magnificent that you survived your visit as long as you did."

Oz gritted his teeth, bristling at the Vastaghri's supercilious attitude. His thoughts were at war with themselves. He had to do what he could to get Jinan and Ritsu out of there. But he also wanted to tear the smug smile right off Muztag's face. As if sensing his thoughts, the demon lord gazed directly at him, those five eyes glowing, antennae twitching as his eyes narrowed.

They faced one another in that stone corridor—Oz and his two companions against Muztag and his lackeys, who clustered around and behind the demon lord. One of the sorcerers pushed past a demon with a kind of ridged bone cage around his skull. A dark purple light glowed and sparked around the sorcerer's hands, and he took another step toward Oz.

"Not yet," Muztag grunted. "I want the monk to relish this moment a little longer. Anything that will add to his pain and humiliation is worth spending a few extra minutes on."

The demon lord smiled at Oz almost politely. He rested his left hand on the hilt of the huge sword that hung at his hip. When he spoke again, it felt to Oz like Muztag was talking directly to him.

"I have taken his students from him and twisted their souls. I have made him my captive, driven him to his knees. And now I shall destroy his last hope. Those who would rescue Shantou will die at the hands of his former students. I let the hunter skin those two werewolves, but the others are mine, body and soul."

Muztag raised a hand. "Hauck. Miyu. The rest of you. Come here."

A demon in monk's robes—Oz figured this to be Hauck—stepped out first. Then the Japanese woman, Miyu, followed him along with the rest of those who had once been Master Shantou's students. Oz cursed inwardly. *What are they supposed to do now?* To defend themselves, they would have to kill Shantou's other students.

Ritsu stood to Oz's left, wielding a blade that looked like an old bayonet, his useless assault rifle on the floor of the corridor somewhere behind them.

To Oz's right, Jinan crouched with her tail swaying, skull-fire burning high, flames leaping from her fingers. Her scent had changed, and Oz knew she was terrified, could smell the fear rolling off her in waves and figured Muztag could probably smell it, too. But what the demon lord might not understand was that beneath that terror was a grim and unwavering determination. Jinan was afraid, but she was ready to fight. And it was her resolution that finally made Oz realize that there was no way to alter the circumstances here. They had not started this, nor decided how it would come together. Muztag had done that, and he was not about to let any of them walk away.

Miyu and Hauck and the others came forward, and Oz thought of Shen and Ferric, the two werewolves Muztag had given over to Cain. They'd surely been killed and skinned by now. That's what his own future held—which made him wonder where Cain had gotten off to.

The students had stepped up around Muztag, pushing the sorcerers, demons, and the troll in the Union Jack T-shirt aside, the demon lord's lackeys all jostling for position in the corridor, which here was perhaps a dozen feet across and no more than fifteen. Wide compared with many of the halls in that fortress, but still offering them very little room to move.

"Kill them," Muztag said. They started forward, and he shouted again. "Wait!" The demon lord grabbed Master Shantou by his long braid and yanked his head back so that he was forced to watch the proceedings. "Now you may continue."

Master Shantou's eyes were narrowed, his expression grim. But Oz could see that he did not look defeated.

In silence, the mesmerized students rushed at them. There were only three of them against many, but in this case Oz knew their lesser number helped them. They had more room to move.

Jinan sketched her fingers in the air, and a wall of flame erupted between her and her attackers. She did not want to kill them. Oz did not blame her, for he felt the same. But Ritsu had no such hesitation. The first student to lay a hand on him was a Nordic-looking man with a stringy beard, and Ritsu stepped in close to the man and head butted him, their skulls whacking together with a sound like wood cracking. Then the wiry nomad punched his bayonet through the student's heart, and the man fell to the stone floor, dead.

"Perfect!" Muztag howled gleefully.

A thin man with black hair and a goatee lunged at Oz, who slashed at his arms with the knife, drawing blood. Then Miyu, the Japanese woman, was there as well. An aura of bruise-yellow light glowed around her hands, but it was weak, as though whatever force was controlling her made her unable to focus her mind enough to wield sorcery with any accuracy.

"Oz!" Jinan shouted to him, panic in her voice. "You've got to do it! You've got to let the wolf out!"

He slashed at the goateed man, then kicked Miyu hard in the back of the leg, driving her to the ground before he danced away, knife at the ready. With a cry of anguish, Jinan set two of Master Shantou's former students on fire. Their robes went up in a curtain of black smoke and orange flame, and they cried out in pain and confusion as they regained their senses. Then they ran off down into the tunnel and fell to the ground, rolling, trying to put out the flames.

"Oz!"

"Not . . . that . . . simple," he replied as the goateed man gripped him by the throat and grabbed his wrist, trying to wrest the knife from him. They went down in a tangle of limbs, and the man struck his head on the ground, his grip weakening. Oz glanced up and saw Miyu spring to her feet and start toward him. He shot an elbow into the goateed man's face and started to rise.

No more regrets.

No more fear.

It was all or nothing.

Then he heard Master Shantou shout his name. Oz was startled—his teacher had been silent until now. He shot a glance over at where the monk still kneeled at Muztag's feet in chains.

"My friend, it *is* that simple," Master Shantou said. But his voice was a growl. "This is what I have been trying to teach you. There is no beast. There is only *you.*"

Then Master Shantou *changed.*

The old monk had never sprouted so much as an extra hair during the nights of the full moon Oz had spent with him, but he was a werewolf, nevertheless. He was huge, his fur completely white. The wolf Shantou snapped his chains as if they were twine and lunged upward, ripping out the throat of a sorcerer who stood nearby.

"Hunh," Oz said. "Didn't see that coming."

Lord Muztag shouted in some strange demon tongue and staggered back. He spoke again, this time in English.

"But the moon is down . . . ," the demon lord muttered as he faced off against Shantou.

Something dark moved at the edge of Oz's vision and he turned just in time to see Miyu leap at him. She struck him in the side of the head, and he went down hard.

Skull-fire roared up to char the stone above Jinan's head. Flames simmered in her eyes, and the blaze from her fingers roared in a kind of fiery cyclone around her, shielding her from her attackers, who cowered at the fury of the inferno that roared in her heart. Her fire held back a pair of trolls, a demon student of Shantou's, and one of

Muztag's sorcerers. But in that moment a troll whose shirt bore a picture of the British flag let out a bellow of surprise.

"Bloody hell!"

Jinan turned to see what had caught the troll's attention, and her eyes went wide as she saw Master Shantou shape-shift into a huge, slavering wolf with fur as white as a polar bear's.

"He never said a word," she whispered in amazement.

Which is when the troll with the British accent leaped over the wall of flame she had erected. Jinan reacted instantly, whipping her heavy tail around to try to knock his feet out from under him. The troll was huge and angry, and Jinan was small and tired. The big creature stomped on her tail, and she cried out in pain and her fire wavered enough so that Shantou's demon student and the sorcerer leaped over the dying embers and then they were all over her. The other troll tried to attack as well, but Jinan lashed out with her right hand, and flame spurted from her fingers and engulfed him instantly.

The first troll swore again in that accent and cuffed her on the side of the head. Then he grabbed her by the back of the neck with one huge hand and the other clamped on her arm, pinioning it behind her. Jinan cried out in pain as her arm was nearly torn from the socket, the beast's fingers digging into her slick, blue-black flesh.

The troll spun her around and she could see Muztag and Shantou then. They were head to head, the Vastaghri demon lord and the wizened, white-furred werewolf. Other demons came in around them. She saw a Hrastgur slash razor wings down at Master Shantou, but the wolf ripped its head off with one swipe of a huge clawed hand. Then Shantou and Muztag were slashing at each other again. Apparently the demon lord had not known that the old monk could shape-shift at will, no longer ruled by the waxing and waning of the moon. And yet Muztag had been afraid of Master Shantou even when he was not a wolf; afraid of the man, of his magic, of his indomitable will.

Shantou drove Muztag backward, slammed the demon lord against a stone wall, and his claws raked the hard shell-like carapace that covered Muztag's body. The demon slammed a huge fist into the side of the white wolf's muzzle and Shantou staggered back, giving Muztag time to draw his long sword. The blade rose, flashed down, and the werewolf cried out as its crimson blood stained white fur.

"You have certainly made this more interesting," Muztag told Shantou in Chinese.

Then he lifted the blade again.

Jinan had been so caught up in these few seconds of battle between the demon lord and the monk that her own plight had seemed unimportant. Now the British troll shook her hard enough that she thought her neck would snap.

"Pay attention, girl," the troll rumbled. "I'm killing you, here."

A surge of rage went through her, and though the troll held one arm and Shantou's demon student held the other, Jinan let her inner fire begin to blossom around her fists again, where they were held behind her back.

"Ah, ah, none o' that now," the troll snarled, and he gave her arm a hard tug.

The bone snapped, and Jinan screamed.

Then the sorcerer was in front of her, his dark eyes peering over the black veil that covered his nose and mouth. His voice was deep and menacing as he intoned a verse in Latin; he lifted both hands in front of her and mimed pulling something toward him. Jinan felt more exhausted than ever, as if he were sucking the life out of her. Her focus, her concentration, fell apart completely, and her skull-fire began to dim. Tiny tendrils of flame licked at her fingers, but she could not control it, could not direct it.

Her fire was dying.

"Jinan!" Oz shouted.

All his doubts had long since been washed away by the adrenaline that surged through him as he fought for his life and the lives of his friends. Now he saw the sorcerer casting a spell on Jinan and her fires beginning to dim. Her legs weakened, and she fell into the arms of a demon in monk's robes. The huge troll in the Union Jack T-shirt let her go, and his dull, dumb eyes ticked toward Oz, who swore under his breath.

Deep within him, the Wolf snarled and gnashed its teeth. Ever since they had entered Muztag's lair, it had been stirring. Now it bared its claws, and Oz felt its savagery rising up within him. In the back of his mind he reached out to find the moon, though he knew that it was on the wane. But this had nothing to do with the moon. The bestial part of his nature was primal, yes, but it was intimate and came from inside of him. The moon might pull at it, might draw it out the way it controlled the tides. But right now, the moon was not in control.

Oz was.

His breathing quickened, and he darted his head about, trying to find a way to save Jinan. The nomad Ritsu was still alive but bloodied and limping as he lashed out at a demon with his bayonet. The white-furred werewolf that was Master Shantou slashed his claws at Muztag again, only to have the demon lord's blade whisk through the air and hack into his shoulder, separating flesh and fur and cracking bone.

"No," Oz whispered.

Master Shantou was going to lose. He was going to die. Jinan's flame dimmed, her skull still open, but only the barest flicker within. Ritsu went down beneath the onslaught of his demon attacker.

"No," Oz said again.

Miyu, Master Shantou's student, kicked him in the side of the head. Oz hauled off and cracked her across the face with a strength that seemed to well up from that primitive place within him. He felt her cheek give way, and she flew through the air and struck the rock wall, then fell unconscious to the floor. On the ground, the student with the goatee tried to rise, and Oz kicked him in the head with such force that the man rolled across the ground, unconscious.

But the troll with the Union Jack T-shirt was racing at him now. Oz had its scent, and the stink of the thing was repulsive. Something flashed in his grasp, and as the troll lifted his hand, the torchlight revealed that somewhere the troll had gotten his hands on a crescent-bladed ax.

Oz did not flee.

He crouched, his hands curled into makeshift claws, and he growled deep in his chest. The wolf lent him strength and ferocity.

Which was when Gib Cain stepped up beside him, raised a rifle to his shoulder, and shot the troll through the eye, blowing out the back of his skull. The troll fell backward and landed in the mess of his own blood and brains, red and blue Union Jack T-shirt now all orange and purple in the light of the torches.

Oz snapped his head around and gaped at Cain.

"Do something, wolf-boy."

Shantou roared in agony, and Oz tore his gaze away from Cain to see the white-furred werewolf fall to the floor at Lord Muztag's feet. The Vastaghri demon raised his sword again, unmindful of the cracks in his carapace and his own blood streaming down his body.

When Oz looked at Jinan, he found he could not breathe. Her skull-fire was little more than a candle flame now, and the glow from the sorcerer's hands engulfed her.

He could taste blood on his lips and was not sure whose it was. A savage awareness rose in him, then, a sentience that had hunted the forests of the world since ancient times. Oz felt frightened and small, like a tiny child again. The source of his fear was not the horror surrounding him, however. It was the thing within him. It was the truth.

In his mind he sees Willow, that time on the lawn in front of Sunnydale High, after his first bout with the full moon is over . . . three rounds in that fight and the best he can say is he's still standing. What scares him is he's gonna have to go another three rounds next time the moon comes round, and he doesn't know if he's going to have anyone in his corner. He's never felt so alone.

Then Willow smiles. "You're nice. And you're funny and you don't smoke and, okay, werewolf, but that's not all the time."

And he wants it to be true. He wants it so very much.

But it isn't true. He knows that now.

Master Shantou is right. "There is no beast," he said. "There is only you."

Tiny streaks of liquid fire tears ran down Jinan's face. They were all the flame she could muster as the furnace within her sputtered. Her mind was numb, her body nearly paralyzed. She felt cold. So very cold. On her knees, now, the only thing that kept her from falling to the ground was the grip the demon in monk's robes had on her throat.

Hauck, she managed to think, her brain muddled. *His name is Hauck.*

She had heard the sorcerer call him by name, this demon that had been a student of Master Shantou. Somehow Muztag had gotten control over him and all of the others. Just another affront against the old . . .

Monk. But not only that. Werewolf, she thought.

Her fire began to sputter even more, and for a moment it flickered out. One last ember burned, and her blurred vision cleared briefly. Above her she saw the face of Hauck the demon. She had thought his eyes were hollow, devoid of conscience. But now as she gazed into him she thought she saw some spark there, and a more horrible possibility occurred to her: Hauck was not out of his mind, not insane, his persona not erased. Rather, he was a prisoner within his own self, and Jinan thought that she could see deep in his eyes Hauck's own horror at what he was doing.

Even as his hands closed on her throat and he strangled her.

"Kill her, Hauck," the remaining sorcerer commanded. "Show your old master how well Lord Muztag has corrupted you."

Jinan's vision dimmed again.

A gunshot tore through the cavern, echoing loudly. The pressure on her neck lessened, and again she could see Hauck above her. The demon hesitated, and Jinan thought he was trying to fight the control over him. He grimaced as though in horrible pain, but his hands remained about her neck, tight enough so that she still could not breathe, and the sorcerer's spell had all but doused her fire.

There came another gunshot, and a bullet punched through Hauck's chest and spun him backward and away from her, where he flopped to the floor with a wet thump. Dead.

Weak, amazed, Jinan swayed on her knees and put a hand out to steady herself. She glanced at the sorcerer, but his attention was no longer on her. Stunned, still befuddled, she turned to see what had drawn his gaze and saw Cain standing not far away with his rifle in his hands. The hunter had shot and killed a troll nearby. But despite the impossibility of Cain's presence as an ally, the hunter only kept Jinan's attention a moment. For a few feet away from him stood Oz.

The wolf.

Its fangs gleamed a savage white, and its black lips curled upward as it sniffed the air. Thick cables of muscle rippled beneath the fur of the huge beast, and its ears twitched for just a moment.

It was staring at her with its vicious, yellow eyes.

Then the wolf sprang at her. Jinan did not have the strength to scream as it landed above her. The sorcerer's spell was broken, and she felt her fire flicking up inside her again, but it was not going to restore itself quickly enough to save her life. Oz was going to kill her.

The sorcerer had time to mutter a prayer before Oz lashed out with lightning speed. One huge paw swept around and with a snap and a tearing sound tore off the sorcerer's head so that the body staggered headless a few pages before falling.

The dead man's head thumped and rolled across the stone floor and came to a rest not far from where Muztag was about to bring his sword down to decapitate Master Shantou. The demon lord frowned, all four antennae twitching at his temples, and looked down in shock.

Muztag grunted in surprise.

The sound that erupted from within Oz at that moment was some horrible combination of howl and scream and snarl, some trace of his human voice buried in the roar of the wolf.

Oz leaped upon Muztag, claws slashing down. The demon lord reacted instinctively, put an arm up to try to ward the werewolf away, and Oz's razor teeth clamped down hard and ripped the demon's hand off. The wolf tossed back its head and swallowed the hand in a single, choking gulp, Muztag's blood soaking his muzzle.

Jinan's fire stoked up within her again, the furnace roaring, and flames danced upon her fingers. The sorcerer and Hauck had nearly killed her, but her skull-fire blazed again. Oz was dealing with Muztag but there were more of them. She turned to see the nomad, Ritsu, backed into a corner, trying to fend off a pair of demons with his bayonet. Weak but determined, Jinan let her broken arm hang at her side as she went to Ritsu and incinerated the demons that were attacking him. He shot her a grateful glance and then looked around from another enemy. There were a few more students yet alive, one remaining sorcerer, and a few demons. But even as Jinan looked around, more trolls and demons were coming down the corridor.

Out of the corner of her eye she saw Gib Cain. He leveled his rifle again and shot the last sorcerer through the chest, then fired twice more and dropped two trolls as they entered the wider area of the cavern.

Jinan wrapped her powerful tail around him and pulled Cain to her, the end of her tail tightening around his neck. The hunter held on to his gun but did not try to fight her.

"You!" she snapped. "Why are you doing this?"

Cain choked and gurgled laughter. "I've already sent two pelts home to my clients, girl. Muztag thought he might need my help with Shantou 'cause the old man's a werewolf. When he caught him on his own, he was gonna punch my ticket. I figured my best chance was throwing in with you folks. Plus, I made a couple of calls. You have any idea what the shell of a Vastaghri demon is worth?"

A skittering, darting goblin raced at Jinan. She

glanced at it, and fire lanced from her eyes. It screamed and ran away, beating at the flames on its head.

"Fine!" Jinan snapped at Cain, releasing him. Then she pointed at Muztag. "But if you want to help, shoot *him*!"

Even missing a hand, the demon lord was extremely powerful. As Jinan watched, Muztag drove a knee up into Oz's abdomen, and the wolf staggered back far enough that Muztag lifted his sword and drove the blade through Oz's chest.

The wolf howled in agony but remained focused. Its right hand swung around, and its claws tore off the two antennae on the left side of Muztag's face. The demon lord staggered back now, pulling his blade with him, spinning as though suddenly unable to judge his location or the distance of the wall.

He stopped spinning, regained his balance. Though shaky, he advanced upon Oz again.

Cain lifted the rifle. "Hey, Your Lordship!" the hunter shouted.

Muztag turned at the sound of his voice.

Cain shot him through the bulbous fifth eye at the center of his forehead. Viscous pink fluid spurted from the exploding eye and sprayed the ground. The shriek of the demon lord was like a swarm of locusts as he dropped his sword and clapped his remaining hand over his face, stumbling backward to crash into a sconce on the wall, knocking a torch loose. It went out, casting that section of the wall into shadows and silhouettes.

But Muztag was not dead. Still, he lumbered there in the near dark.

Horribly wounded, however, the demon lord was no longer a threat to the wolf. No, to Oz, Muztag was only prey.

Oz leaped upon him, this demon of the eastern mountain, this legendary evil, and though Muztag tried to fight him, the wolf drove him down into the fluttering shadows. Jaws snapped, claws descended, and tore, and in only a few moments, the demon lord's body stopped flailing, twitching now only when the wolf tore into it.

Jinan stared at him, emotions churning in turmoil within her. At last Oz had met the wolf on his own terms, embraced it for what it was: himself. But to see him like this, behaving so savagely, as though the animal had taken over completely . . . a chill ran through her, and she was afraid for him suddenly. This was an accomplishment, but it was incomplete. She knew that by instinct.

For it was one thing to accept the beast, and another to control it.

Her broken arm dangled at her side, but she moved toward the wolf in the shadows. Muztag was only a corpse now. All around the cavern the few trolls and demons that remained fled along the corridors and into darkened stairwells. Their master was dead, so they no longer had anything to fight for. The few of Master Shantou's students who still lived shook their heads as though waking up from a very long dream and seemed to wander the cavern almost aimlessly. In a far corner, Gib Cain slung his rifle over his shoulder, lit himself a cigar, and waited for them all to clear out so he could claim what remained of Muztag's carapace.

Ritsu came up beside Jinan, limping and bloody, but alive. "Your friend had a surprise for us," the wiry little man said to her in Chinese.

"A surprise for himself, I think," she said. "To learn at last what it means to be what he is, for better or worse."

"Yes," a voice rasped behind her.

Jinan glanced back to see Master Shantou shifting his form again, the white wolf disappearing beneath the skin of the wise old monk. His robes were torn and bloody, and Jinan could see horrible slashes on his flesh, but thanks to his magic and the nature of the werewolf, they were already partially healed.

"Now we will see if he can control it," Shantou said.

She turned again to peer into the shadows. Oz emerged, slavering and bloody, leaving the dead demon lord behind. His ears twitched as he rose from all fours to stand on two feet, yellow eyes gleaming and feral. The wolf bared his fangs and growled dangerously at them. Then it crouched slightly, as though it might spring.

Jinan stared at him. "Oz," she said, her voice barely above a whisper. She was frightened, but more for him than for herself. "You did it, Oz. Muztag is dead. Master Shantou is alive. It's over. You can change back, now."

Master Shantou appeared beside her and leaned on her, one hand clutched over a wound on his shoulder. Though Jinan was not yet recovered herself, she helped to support him.

"Even a normal man must struggle to find the balance between human and beast in his soul," the old monk said as they both watched the wolf. It seemed to hesitate, to study them, sniffing the air. "How much greater, then, for one such as Oz? He cannot force a change. It must happen as simply and as naturally as the coming of the dawn."

Jinan turned to look at the monk, fearful for Oz and hoping for more comforting words than these. None were forthcoming. When she glanced back at Oz, he was human again, crouched on the stone floor, naked and cold and staring at them, with his eyebrows raised, the ghost of a smile on his face.

"Easy for you to say, old man."

Epilogue

One Month Later

Oz had grown used to the cold. Winter at the roof of the world was an unpredictable season marked by sudden blizzards, deepening snows, deathly frigid nights and days when the mountains seemed so close to the blue sky and the warmth of the sun that the snow melted and the process began all over again. The silence up there was unearthly, and yet the landscape was breathtakingly beautiful. In the past few months Oz had been halfway around the world, had visited Hawaii and Fiji, and yet in these last weeks he had realized that in so many ways, *this* was paradise.

At peace, he sat crosslegged in that same place where he had spent so many days and nights meditating. His eyes were closed. Though he had on his thick jacket and beneath that a sweater woven from yak's wool, and thick mittens and a hat pulled down over his ears, his teeth still chattered and he wondered why he did not simply go inside.

On the bitterly cold wind he could smell the smoke from the fire that burned inside the monastery. A sudden burst of laughter erupted from the huge wood and stone building, but Oz did not open his eyes. Laughter was still rare, but not as uncommon as it had been before Muztag had been destroyed and his demons driven out of the fortress in the eastern mountain.

Down in the monastery, hammers rang out. Once upon a time that would have broken his concentration, but the sound of the work in progress only merged with his peaceful mindset now and gave him an added measure of comfort. While the collapsed wing of the monastery remained closed, it was being rebuilt at last. The first few weeks after Muztag's defeat had been spent healing and repairing the damage from the attack that night when Master Shantou had been abducted. And they had plenty of hands to do the work.

Four of Master Shantou's students had survived and returned to the monastery with Oz, Jinan, and their teacher. In addition, however, some of the survivors from the village, including Tsochen and his daughter, had climbed the mountain to help and to live within those walls. Ritsu had left for a time, but returned with half a dozen herders from his nomadic tribe, who offered their aid until such time as Shantou no longer needed them. The old monk insisted they remain until spring, at which time the survivors from the village could stay, join the nomads' tribe, or try to rebuild their village.

So, after all the horror and death and grief, there was new light and life in that monastery. The shadow cast by the demon of the eastern mountain had been lifted.

Oz and Jinan had continued their studies under Master Shantou, along with the rest of his students. In addition to his meditation and efforts at centering himself, Oz had learned a bit of herbology and begun a daily martial arts kata that did more to help him focus his mind and find a peace within himself than any amount of hiking or meditation ever had. His control was still tenuous at best, but he was learning. Though it was a long way off, he could believe that there might come a day when he could shift back and forth between human and wolf with barely a thought. For now it was enough that he could stave off the change under the light of the full moon, could be around people without endangering them.

What had become of Cain, none of them could say. By the time they had tended to the injured after the battle inside Muztag's fortress, the hunter had fled and taken the corpse of the demon lord with him. Oz was in no rush to catch up to him, but he knew Cain was still out there. In time, Cain would set his sights on other prey—some of whom would be werewolves. Oz knew that someday soon he would have to try to track the hunter, to turn the tables, to stop Cain from killing anyone else.

But not yet. For now, Oz had promises to keep.

He shivered now, there on the mountainside. Soon he would go in. Soon. But for now he listened to the wind in the trees and he breathed in the crisp winter air and the scent of the fire from below, and he thought of all the people who had helped get him to this place, all of the people to whom he owed the greatest debt he could imagine.

Giles, of course. Caesar and Desiree. Mr. Ostergaard. Sarah Atwill. Qing and his family. Wuxi. Jinan. The nomads who had given their lives. Master Shantou, who had taught him best—as all real teachers do—by example.

A smile played at his lips, and he opened his eyes.

Oz looked up into the night sky and for a long moment he only stared at the moon.

The full moon.

He would need the herbal compound and he would

continue with his meditation and his kata. It would not always be a simple thing to keep his focus enough to control the savagery within him, but there was something he had already achieved that could not be taken away from him: understanding. That was half the battle. There was no wolf deep inside him, no beast to cage within his flesh and bones. There were only aspects of himself, the faces of his dual nature, and it was up to him to choose which face to show the world.

Oz gazed at the full moon, a kind of aura shimmering around it. For the first time in a very long time, he found it beautiful.

His cheeks had gone from stinging to numb, and he shivered again, then rose to his feet and started down the mountain toward the monastery, a place he had begun to think of as home. Sometimes he felt that he did not want to leave, even though he knew that his cousin, Jordy, needed to learn what Oz had learned, and that Willow would be wondering what had become of him.

All the more reason he ought to go soon.

Before he decided to stay.

Twenty-eight Nights Until the Full Moon

Jinan's lips were soft and warm when he kissed her. It might have been that he lingered with his mouth on hers just a little too long. But that was all right. They had been through a great deal together, and what harm was one kiss?

Especially when it was a kiss good-bye.

Oz gazed at her a long moment. Jinan smiled, but it was bittersweet. When he pulled away from her, she lingered with her hands on his arms for several seconds, and then she let them drop to her sides.

"You'll give the letter to my father?"

"Got it."

He buttoned his coat up a little higher. Though the sky was clear and blue and the sun bright above them, it was early morning yet and still very cold. Oz pulled his hat down over his ears.

Jinan stepped in close to him again and gazed sternly into his eyes. When she spoke, it was in a whisper. "I wish you weren't leaving, but I really am happy for you. Just don't forget me, okay?"

Oz touched her cheek with his fingertips. Despite the temperature, her skin was warm as always.

"Deal," he said.

Then he turned away from Jinan and faced Master Shantou. Oz had already said his good-byes to Ritsu and Miyu and all the others inside the monastery. Only these two had come out to see him off, his friend and his teacher.

He bowed low to the old monk, his mentor, the only other werewolf he had ever known who had not tried to kill him. Master Shantou bowed low in return.

"Thank you, Master Shantou."

"You are gracious, my friend, but never forget. All I have done is show you the path. The journey will be long and difficult, and you must make it alone."

Oz knew that the words ought to have troubled him, but somehow they did not. Instead, there was a spark of excitement inside him, a wonder at what the journey would bring. He thought of Jordy, and of the comfort his return would bring to Aunt Maureen and Uncle Ken.

And he thought of Willow.

"I'll be all right," he said. "I've never minded traveling alone. Especially when I'm headed home."

ABOUT THE AUTHOR

Christopher Golden is the award-winning, *L.A. Times* best-selling author of such novels as *The Ferryman, Strangewood, Of Saints and Shadows, Prowlers,* and the Body of Evidence series of teen thrillers, which was honored with an award from the American Library Association as one of its Best Books for Young Readers.

Golden has also written or cowritten a great many books and comic books related to the TV series *Buffy the Vampire Slayer* and *Angel,* as well as the script for the *Buffy the Vampire Slayer* video game for Microsoft Xbox. His other comic book work includes stories featuring such characters as Batman, Wolverine, Spider-Man, The Crow, and Hellboy, among many others.

As a pop culture journalist, he was the editor of the Bram Stoker Award–winning book of criticism, *CUT!: Horror Writers on Horror Film,* and coauthor of both *Buffy the Vampire Slayer: The Watcher's Guide* and *The Stephen King Universe.*

Golden was born and raised in Massachusetts, where he still lives with his family. He graduated from Tufts University. There are more than six million copies of his books in print. Please visit him at www.christophergolden.com